CHIPS AND GRAVY

Chips and Gravy

NJ MILLER

Copyright © 2025 by NJ Miller
All rights reserved.

No part of this publication may be reproduced, stored or transmitted in any form or by any means, electronic, mechanical, photocopying, recording, scanning, or otherwise without written permission from the publisher. It is illegal to copy this book, post it to a website, or distribute it by any other means without permission.

ISBN (print): 978-1-9191843-0-2
ISBN (ebook): 978-1-9191843-1-9

Dedicated to my family and friends

You've been my safety net, my hecklers, my tea-makers,
and the people who never stopped believing
I could write a book without a drink in my hand.
This one's for you.

Plan B

Jake peeled his cheek from the plastic pillow and groaned. His temples throbbed, and the familiar kidney ache that had become a regular visitor to his lower back reminded him to stock up on Panadol.

'Come on then, fella, you know the score.'

'Can I get a late checkout?' Jake asked cheekily, pulling the itchy blanket over his face.

The officer in charge that day was in no mood for jokes; he had seven more to process that morning, and at least two of them were soaked in vomit.

'Move it, sunshine, I've got an hour left on shift and I don't want it dragging on.' Jake hauled himself up and rubbed his eyes. The officer took Jake to the front of the station, where belongings were returned and charges were made.

'It's just drunk and disorderly today; you're lucky because you were this close to an assault charge.' The desk sergeant used his finger and thumb to show just how close Jake was to appearing in court.

Jake bowed his head; the shame started kicking in as the alcohol wore off. The officer handed him a plastic bag containing his belt, wallet and watch.

'There's a lovely woman waiting for you outside, she's been here half the night.'

Jake shut his eyes; he hated this bit. The officer had seen it all before, but he lowered his voice and leaned towards him. 'You need to get a hold of this before it ruins you. You can't keep doing this, Mr Peterson.'

Jake nodded and turned to leave.

'See you next week,' the officer said wearily.

'Probably,' Jake replied without turning around.

Jake Peterson was one of those people who should never ever drink again. Not after what he did at Christmas, or what he did at Easter or at his cousin's birthday – in fact, his general behaviour at every single family occasion in the last five years was reason enough for him not to dabble full stop.

Jake was not the kind of guy who could moderate anything; he was all in or all out, so although there were periods when he was on the rampage and couldn't be tamed, he had completely sober periods, leaving him to experience the hideous flashbacks of the dire things he had done with torturous clarity.

This latest arrest came after he made an inappropriate comment about a bus driver's chest whilst travelling over London Bridge; she wasn't at all amused, even though he had meant it in jest. He had then made a honking noise before trying to wedge his can of Strongbow between her bosoms whilst he looked for his bus pass. Jake had received a well-deserved throat punch from Valerie, the driver of the number 32, but she hadn't pressed charges for assault. She really couldn't be arsed with the paperwork and hoped that a night in the cells would be enough to sort this particular wino out.

'I missed my mum's birthday brunch because of this,' Nicky had said sadly as she drove Jake home from the police station. Jake put his head out of the car window, hoping the city air would reduce the swelling of his eyelids.

'Don't make me feel even worse than I already do, Nicky. She'll have loads more birthdays, hopefully.'

Nicky made Jake a bed up on the sofa that day, and then made fresh scones so the house smelt nice.

This was just one of Jake's recent 'ale tales', and they were progressively getting worse.

The next month, Jake swiped a hot dog from a stand on Clapham Common and casually walked off without paying – well, he had to soak up the seven pints with something. Unfortunately, he had left his wallet in his trousers and his trousers were on the floor in Wetherspoons. He involuntarily sobered up overnight on the floor of a holding cell and was released the following morning, having got away with just a caution.

That particular incident was filmed by some nosy picnickers, and thanks to them, Jake went instantly famous on Facebook Live in just his undies whilst consuming the stolen hot dog like a Scooby Snack. The title of his debut viral video was 'Broken Britain'. With technology the way that it was, some things just couldn't be erased.

The breakup of his relationship was what they call 'a sore one', although thoroughly deserved, Jake always thought that Nicky would stick around no matter what. But she wasn't blood and she wasn't his wife yet – therefore, Jake had to accept that Nicky had a choice as to whether she would stay or leave. On this occasion, as tough as she found it, her choice was the latter. And although he didn't actually cheat on her, he definitely gave it a damn good go. Bringing a Russian prostitute back to the house whilst Nicky was on a yoga retreat in The New Forest ended up being the final nail in the coffin; Nicky had endured an awful lot, too much actually, and she really did deserve better. Jake tried to make amends; he knew this was possibly 'the big one' in terms of relationship-ending behaviour, so he splashed out and bought Nicky a horse.

The racehorse, Firefly, was sixty-seven grand and had lots of potential, but Nicky had told him that not even fucking Red Rum himself would get him out of this one. In hindsight, with neither of them knowing a thing about racing, Nicky was more of a dressage girl (think Katie Price meets Zara Tindall), so it was probably a rash decision. And so after the booze had worn off, Jake had realised that this grand gesture was most likely fuelled by fear and guilt rather than remorse. Shortly after, he had no choice but to call the stable and plead his case for a refund; he lost money on the resale as the horse had developed a cough that wouldn't go away.

The Russian, who was incredibly striking but completely soulless, strategically left her card by the bed, hoping for another twenty-four hours on the clock. The most pathetic thing was, he couldn't even perform, so he actually paid the woman to watch him sleep. Nicky had stuffed the black velvet calling card into his open mouth after she found it the following morning, propped up next to a warm glass of red. It took a whole week for her to pack her things and leave the man she thought would be her lifelong partner. She had told Jake before she walked out on their relationship that he was a 'beautiful mess' and that she would always have so much love for him, but she had nothing left in the tank. He watched her drive away whilst he stood in the bay window in his dressing gown, swigging Bells straight from the bottle. He didn't try to stop her from leaving; he allowed her to carry a 43-inch television down the path with no offer to assist. He was drunk at the time, so didn't actually care. 'She'll be back,' he yelled through the glass to one of his nosy neighbours. 'She knows what side her bread's buttered.' Nosey neighbour shook his head before heading into Jake's to make him a strong coffee and to put him in the shower. The neighbours were all used to these embarrassing displays, plus he was not the only pisshead on the street.

The six months that Jake lived as a single man in the house were nothing short of a disaster. He somehow thought that if he worked hard until two p.m. every day, and then drank until eleven-ish, this would suffice as a good work/play balance. But two p.m. became lunchtime, and nobody knew what time he went to bed because he was so completely smashed. Nicky's presence had somehow kept him functioning; she had been an arse-wiper, not an enabler. She was pure, good and accepted most of his flaws. She had been the one who threw his soiled trousers into next door's bin so he didn't feel shame, she had swapped the vodka in the bottle for water, and she had made numerous elaborate excuses each time he ruined dinner parties, weddings and in one case… a pantomime. Nicky had gently suggested activities that didn't involve alcohol – things like escape rooms, theatre trips and Highland hikes. She really tried. But Jake would always sniff out a substance to spice things up, which inevitably fucked things up. She fought a losing battle for many years, but high-class escorts getting into her side of the bed was the end of the road.

Jake was initially unable to accept Nicky's decision – when mistakes are made whilst drunk, could he really be held responsible? It wasn't the real Jake who hurt his beautiful fiancée; it was the illness, AKA the devil on his shoulder. So, he started to pester Nicky, hoping that she would come back and give him one last chance; he just wasn't quite over the fact that she was moving on without him. One evening, he booked the table right next to her and her Tinder date in a local Chinese restaurant after he had managed to infiltrate her iMessage from an old handset she'd left at the house. This led him right to the spot she had planned for a second date with Ian, a green-eyed brunette with a GSOH who loved to travel. The staff of the New King were unsympathetic, particularly when he used a soft-shell crab as a missile to stop 'Wanker Ian' from holding Nicky's hand. He was ejected quite quickly, and two waiters roughed him up in the car park for upsetting a pretty lady and disrespecting a very popular starter.

Once Jake's life revolved around the first drink with no supervision from his significant other, his superiors at the office staged an intervention and sent him off to a swanky rehab in Somerset. Maxwell and Lucas, the big bosses at Morris, Webb & Butler, were familiar with this sort of thing; they had both done stints in rehab, and many of the workforce had addiction issues of some sort. It was the nature of the beast – the beast being investment banking, the nature being any substance that blocked out life. They didn't do this for everyone, but Jake was really very good at his job, and had a natural talent when it came to making money. The last thing they wanted was to lose him to another firm, so they showed their gratitude, and he was sent to dry out at the expense of the company.

Jake endured the whole three weeks and, quite honestly, he had a bloody lovely time. Yes, it was tough going with the sweats, the shaking and the horrible visions that made his skin crawl but, after all that had passed, aerial yoga, group therapy and professionally cooked meals were just what the doctor specifically ordered.

On week three, Jake had so much clarity that he sent a completely compos mentis email to Nicky thanking her for the ten happy years she had kindly given to him, and ended it with a heartfelt apology for being a grade-A bellend for the majority. She replied almost immediately with a smiley face and a kiss, so he naturally presumed he was completely forgiven. He left The Meadows with a spring in his step; the realisation that he could control his addiction was big news. It almost seemed ridiculous that people went back to their old ways after a few weeks in rehab – these people were weak, silly, pathetic even. What an absolute waste of thousands of pounds it would be to throw it all away.

The train back up to London was initially very tranquil – a stale tuna sandwich and an Earl Grey tea was the only refreshment needed. He chatted to a gay couple for the first hour and was sort of interested in their love story at the start, but it soon got quite tedious. He was irritated about how proud they were to have both left their 'bastard husbands' high and dry and grew underarm hair because 'why shouldn't we, eh, why?'

The empty seat next to him was then occupied by a soldier in uniform, a man with a crew cut and nut-cracking fists, not quite the lesbians' cup of tea. They all then became embroiled in a rather heated discussion about war, the women aggressively insisted that it was unnecessary and barbaric, and the soldier calmly told them that without it there would be pure anarchy. Jake got quite excited; it was fun meeting new people with strong opinions. And that was all it took for Jake to stop the drinks trolley.

He started light with a gin and tonic – well, two – then he had a couple of lagers, wanting something manly so the soldier wouldn't think he was a pussy. After that, he bought a bottle of champagne for the table to share, and he toasted his new friends loudly.

'To shooting people and muff-diving!' They all clinked glasses.

He arrived at Paddington with red wine on his t-shirt and blue teeth. He didn't bother going home to change but took the soldier – whose name he cannot remember – on a pub crawl and ended the night with a call to Vika, the Russian prozzy who watched him sleep again for £400.

Two days later, he headed back to Somerset, this time with a driver who was instructed by Maxwell and Lucas not to stop at any service station en route. He did another ten days; however it wasn't as pleasant, the novelty had worn off, and the disappointment from the staff made him feel weird, almost like a child. It didn't help that there was a 'soap star' in the room next door who thought she was the dogs' bollocks and kept pacing up and down the corridor outside his room, screaming down the phone to her agent, 'David Platt's dressing room has a shower, and I get a packet of wet wipes?'

Things got a bit heated in group therapy on the first afternoon when one of his fellow drunkards told the soap star that her top knot reminded him of E. Honda, the Sumo wrestler from *Street Fighter*. She had flounced off in tears and had all her meals in her room after that. It was for the best; she rubbed everybody up the wrong way. 'She ain't no Helen Mirren,' said one of the cokeheads to her empty chair.

It was Julie, Jake's very pretty therapist, who suggested that he move closer to family and make a fresh start. She was the one who had made the connection between London, the drinking and the bad behaviour. She really felt he needed to break free from his current situation – a rebirth, if you like. According to Julie, it was a lifesaving decision, and if he ever wanted the chance to have a family, then he had to stop drinking and change his scenery. She'd seen it all before – city bankers with shrivelled-up livers and missing noses – but Jake wasn't too bad in comparison, and there was still hope for him. She laid it on thick and said he was wasting his life, his looks and his brain. She said that with her hand on his shoulder, and she smelt strongly of peonies.

Jake was actually a good-looking man; he had been described by others as a 'silver fox'. His eyes, although frequently red, were actually a pale blue, and when his face wasn't swollen, his jawline was sharp enough to attract attention from good-quality women. He was tall and slim, although his gut had started the middle-aged protrusion process, but he carried it well because of his height. Add his healthy bank balance and rather spectacular eye for interiors and, quite honestly, Jake was a catch. He really liked Julie – he respected her, she was an English rose who oozed class. She was quite intelligent too, which he needed in a partner – looks were great at first, but they didn't last. His own mother had looked like a cabbage for the last ten years, but his father still adored her. At the end of the session, Jake asked Julie if she would like to go to Amsterdam for the weekend once he was out. She laughed very loudly and then said, 'Don't be bloody ridiculous!'

That very afternoon, Jake instructed an estate agent to put his house on the market for offers in excess of three million. He was told it would sell very quickly as it was a gem of a property a stone's throw from the King's Road. He then sat in a sunny spot in the gardens of The Meadows with some turmeric tea, and he found the house that would eventually change his life. Initially he started the search for renovated homes, ones that had been modernised and were ready for him and his Louis Vuitton luggage. It was a little difficult because, unless he wanted to live in a mock-Tudor mansion and look like a lottery winner, his other options were big and old and needed love; he wondered if he would have the patience. There was a former pub for sale. The Inn on the Hill had tons of potential, its location stunning and character plentiful. But even the faint whiff of stale lager could be enough for him to jump off the back of the wagon and start licking the carpets.

There was a lovely Georgian house with acres of land about three miles from civilisation, but he would be isolated; he may get up to his tricks with no supervision, so he ruled this out as a potential hazard. There was a penthouse that had 360-degree views overlooking Pendle Hill, it was almost all glass and very modern, but it felt a bit *Wolf of Wall Street,* and that would surely end up in tears – reminding him of the endless sessions he had overlooking the Thames in Lucas's gaff. Nights like these would always end with Jake's jaw swinging and his eyes bulging – not a good look for a middle-aged man who wanted to settle down.

It was a property called The Coach House that piqued his

interest on Rightmove that day; it felt strangely like home from just the pictures. There were peonies in the front garden – they were his favourite – while the front door was dark green, and the window frames were black. It was very pleasing on the eye, and somehow Jake felt in his gut that this house could be the making of him. The Coach House was essentially a farmhouse, quite cottagey in style. The ceilings were low and cosy, the stone was pretty, and the position was fabulous – high on a hill looking down across the village in one direction and over the valley in the other. He would like it up there; he would still feel successful. The virtual tour was unfortunately a little depressing. It was clear somebody with very poor taste in decor was selling up, but all that could be dealt with – it was cosmetic. He looked past the battered pine kitchen and the dated gas fire; he winced when he spotted office blinds at the bedroom window. He was mostly unhappy with the bannisters; they were a major feature in the centre of the hallway but were painted with a mint-green gloss. An awful lot needed to be done, but Jake needed something to do.

He showed Julie the house that he intended to buy during their next session; she was quite taken aback by such an extreme decision. She hadn't realised that when he said 'the North', he hadn't meant Watford or perhaps even Cambridge. She said The Coach House reminded her of a period drama, and asked if they could get Sky television up there. He went off her a bit after that; that made her sound completely stupid, and stupidity was a turn-off.

On leaving rehab, Jake left half a packet of cigarettes and a Snickers outside of the soap star's room. His final session had been about kindness and, by the sounds of the latest phone call, her character was to drown in the bath as soon as she was well enough to film. Although he found her extremely irritating, her demise was being plotted and she could not control it – she would be nothing without *Corrie*.

Within four months, Jake put the keys to the Chelsea house into an influencer's hand and left London to repair the damage. He was cash-rich but poor in the way of friends. There weren't many people he could, or should, associate with on his path to sobriety. He would need to get comfortable with his own company and find out who he was without a crutch.

After living in London for over twenty years, Jake knew in his gut that his environment was a big part of his demise. Blaming a location for your addictions is possibly a cop-out, but with temptation on the doorstep, it was hard for an addict to break free. You wouldn't find a sex addict working on reception at a strip club, nor find a food addict flipping burgers in McDonald's. Working in the city was the equivalent, and 24/7 access to very bad things had become quite tricky. Eventually, he imploded, and it was time for plan B.

Jake had originated from Lancashire; his parents still lived there, as did his sister and niece. They lived quite happily without being addicted to anything. Yes, they had their habits – his dad had a thing for bulk-buying meat, filling up various chest freezers in the garage with tons of cheap cuts for a rainy day. But 200 Iceland sausages didn't cost you your relationship or your career, as far as he knew. Going home felt like the right decision, where he had a supportive family, far away from the arty-farty types, the coke dealers and the city bankers. They had to be the reason that Jake was forty-two, childless and a chronic drinker – or at least that's what he hoped. He'd tried every which way to get clean and to straighten up, but as long as he stayed in the city, he fell off the wagon over and over again.

So, heading up the M6 twenty years later without a job or a family was a very sobering experience indeed. It wasn't all bad, though – a three-bed townhouse in Chelsea could be swapped for something quite grand in the North, and he wasn't skint, not by any means. He could have been had he stayed in London any longer; his drunken decision-making was starting to affect his finances, and being a numbers man, that had frightened him.

Although moving back home did have the stigma of failure, anybody from the North knew that leaving the grimness of a hometown and heading down to the big smoke had once meant you were cool, daring and that you were following your dreams instead of settling for familiarity. A chippy tea on Friday night was no young go-getter's idea of fun – even if they did do gravy.

Soggy Yorkies

The first Sunday lunch was a tough one. Normally, a heavy red would be the drink of choice with a slice of roasted sirloin, rare, but today it was a warm glass of whole milk.

'Right, Jake, me and your dad want to see that plate clean – no excuses, let's get your strength up, son.'

Jake looked at his mum with pity; she really was going back to basics using tactics from his school days – starve a cold and feed a drunk.

'And don't you dare leave them sprouts, they are little balls of goodness, so cover 'em in gravy and get 'em down.'

Jake crushed a sprout with his fork; it took no force whatsoever to turn it to mush.

Diane Peterson was a proper Northern mum who wore an apron almost every day. She had been the type of mum who would lick her thumb and wipe food from her kid's chins. The sort of wife who made corned beef sandwiches for her husband every day of his working life. She was a little plump these days, and had arthritis in her hips, so she waddled like a duck. She had a neat grey bob, a style she hadn't changed for as long as Jake could remember, although it had been blonde when she was younger.

'Mum, I hate sprouts, I always have, and that will never change.' Jake looked down at the pile with exhaustion; it would take all afternoon to get this lot down.

Alf Peterson leaned over the table and pointed at the sprouts with his own fork. 'Do as you're told or go to your room.' His face broke into a smile; he was trying to make light of what was a very uncomfortable position for Jake to be in. He understood that coming back from 'sin city' with your tail between your legs and being told to eat your dinner by your mam was quite demeaning.

Alf was not a man to be messed with; he was firm but fair, and he had never been able to understand Jake's need to be different. They had never really clashed because Alf didn't do too many words; he believed people should work things out for themselves. But he had made it clear that he thought London was full of weirdos, and that Jake would eventually see sense and get back to reality. It had taken twenty years, but it's never too late, he had thought to himself, when Jake had sent a text to say he was 'coming back' for good. Alf had practically shit himself initially as he presumed Jake meant he was moving back into the family home. He relaxed when a screenshot came through of a fancy house twenty minutes' drive away. He loved his boy, but a grown man in the spare room on a permanent basis was a recipe for disaster.

The three of them sat with their roast dinners and glasses of milk embarking on what would be a strange new journey.

'Can we come up to the house tomorrow, Jake? I'll bring the cleaning caddy and give the place a once-over.'

'Yes, Mum, come at eleven so it gives me the chance to do my exercise.'

Alf screwed up his face. 'What exercise? What are you into this time?'

'I'm not into anything, Dad, it's just a morning walk and some Pilates.'

Alf raised his eyebrows to Diane, and she shook her head to try and stop him from pushing it.

'Yes, me love, eleven is fine. We're really looking forward to seeing the inside of the house, aren't we, Alf?' She widened her eyes, trying all she could to ensure the road to getting her son back was smooth. Alf nodded, but he was clearly concerned this Pilates shite was a euphemism for lager-swigging.

Jake waded through the roast dinner as best he could; the Yorkshire pudding was stodgy and soggy at the bottom, whereas he preferred his crispy and light. He also preferred to be drunk on Sundays, and to wear that comfortable, cosy glow it normally gave him. He liked the thought of a cheeseboard with a vintage port, followed by a wander down the King's Road with Nicky, stopping at various pubs along the way. Not this shit show – not a Yorkshire pudding with the same consistency as a wet sleeping bag washed down with warm milk. He put down his knife and fork as he stood.

'I have to go, I'm sorry. I need to get some fresh air.'

His dad glared at him. 'Go where? Your mother has cooked your dinner, son – sit down and finish it.'

Jake zipped up his jacket. 'No, Dad, this is sending me under. It's just too soon.'

'Too soon for what, a roast dinner? What's he on about? Sending you under... under what?'

Diane dabbed her mouth with a paper towel, and put her cutlery down. She calmly got up and took Jake's plate into the kitchen. 'I'll cling-film it for you, my love, and you can have it tomorrow.'

He didn't think it was possible for the Yorkshire to get any wetter, but an overnight soaking in the back of Di's fridge would certainly give it a good chance. Jake put on his sunglasses and patted his dad on the back. 'Sorry, Dad, the demons are coming. See you in the morning.'

Alf shook his head in disbelief, and then said under his breath, 'It's not even bloody sunny.'

As Jake went into the hallway to put on his trainers, he heard his parents talking.

'Don't worry, Alf, they won't serve him in the shop, and they won't serve him in the pub.'

'Are you sure, Di? Shall we follow him?'

'No, I gave them a photograph of him, and they said they would call me if he even tried to get his hands on any booze – there's nowhere else round here on a Sunday.'

'You did right, love. The lad's a fiend for the stuff. Bloody London, bloody demons!'

Jake smiled to himself; his parents were adorable. They were completely oblivious to the fact that if Jake actually wanted a drink, he could get one. He'd actually planned his route back to alcohol meticulously, and it certainly wouldn't be via The Lamb and Packet or the badly stocked and very backwards village store. He would get a taxi to a wine bar in Manchester, one that was dark and had wine glasses without lip gloss on the edges. He would have one bottle of very expensive red wine – a Chianti or perhaps a Rioja – and he would sip it whilst reading a hardback book about Churchill. It would be a classy affair, this 'falling off the wagon', and then afterwards he would return to sobriety quietly, unfazed by his little bump in the road.

So, on account of this, he sniggered at his parents' well-meaning plan to stop him drinking WKD in a damp doorway. He was an adult now, and he owned a house with history. If he was going down, he would go down with style. Although it was a plan, it was just a backup plan – something that Jake had thought about when he'd had weak moments. He normally managed to walk the feeling off, or to distract himself with his new project.

It hadn't been easy, but as he had been told by Julie, it was one day at a time.

Late Monday morning, Jake watched his parents climb the driveway of his new gaff as if it were Kilimanjaro. Diane was red-faced as she carried her plastic cleaning caddy up to the house, and she was wearing her trusty turquoise tabard. Alf huffed and puffed behind her with a very sturdy old hoover under his arm, the plug trailing on the gravel. Alf was a big man, unusually tall and, unusually, he still had a full head of thick hair at the age of seventy-five. Alf always had brown arms – the sun damage from years of working outdoors had left an indelible tan. It was funny, really – Alf's arms could have belonged to Barry White, and the rest of his body to Ed Sheeran.

Jake had only been in the house a week since moving from his parents where he endured a single bed and a shared bathroom. It was nice to spend some time with his family, but he found their house a bit depressing. It was a reminder that he had achieved nothing of substance since he left twenty years ago.

'Right, son, let's get a look at the place.' Alf dumped the hoover in the hallway and folded his arms. 'Well, blow me down, this is something else, eh?'

Jake had no idea if this was a good or bad thing; his parents were very unpredictable with their opinions.

'Do you like it then?'

Diane reached for a hanky in the tabard pocket and dabbed her eyes. 'This is what twenty years in London gets you, Alf – a bloody palace. I can't get me breath.'

They were both in absolute awe of The Coach House, even though the interior was shambolic.

'Well, once we get everything ripped out and do a complete refurb, it should be beautiful.' Jake sighed, running his hand over the shiny bannisters.

Alf and Diane looked at each other in confusion.

'What do you mean, son? Rip what out?' Di's brow rose as she tried to comprehend this comment.

'Everything,' Jake shrugged.

'Sorry, come again, son?'

Jake tried to explain that he had a vision and, in its current state, this was certainly not it. 'You must understand that this is very dated. I want to put my own stamp on it, modernise it. I'll respect the original features, but there's so much to do beyond that.'

'Why would you want to change a thing? It's absolutely spot on son, just like it is now,' Di sighed. She'd have killed to have owned a property of this quality.

That day, Alf tinkered in the garden of The Coach House, digging over the beds and trimming the edges of the lush lawn. Jake had been used to astroturf in Chelsea, so he was glad of a green-fingered family member to help out with this part of his new life. Di gutted the house; she hoovered the shit out of the stinky old carpets, and she got down on her hands and knees and scrubbed all the skirting boards, showing Jake each cloth she had filled with dirt. 'Look at that, disgusting,' she'd say every time she'd done another swipe.

Jake was grateful – he didn't like dirt, but soon the carpets would be gone, and the skirting would be sanded down and repainted. This was okay for now, but 'polishing a turd' was all he could think of. Di and Alf spent the day complimenting every nook and cranny.

Di then made at least six calls to friends and family, and she repeated the same spiel to all of them. 'It's gorgeous, absolutely perfect. It's almost a mansion. Yes, plenty of room for some grand-kiddies; he'll need to get a move on. Eh, you could fit my whole house in the kitchen. Hahaha. He's going to change a few things, but not much needs doing. Closest pub is two miles away, so we'll all need to keep an eye. Tata.'

Jake listened to these calls with gratitude – at least he still had both parents, lots didn't after forty. At least they cared, even if their archaic opinions irritated him. Jake loved his mum and dad, and they literally only gave a shit about their kids and nothing else. When Jake had thumped a boy in the nose at school for laughing at his market-bought trainers, Diane had been beside herself about the graze on Jake's fist. Couldn't give a monkey's about the busted nose – in fact she said, 'It needed breaking as it was bulbous anyway.'

When his sister Leanne was put in the family way at fifteen, the whole village took to referring to her as 'the Lancashire bike', but Alf took the stance that she was destined for motherhood, and he loved it when a plan came together – Hannibal Smith and his philosophy had worked a treat for dirty Lil Leanne.

Up until Jake revealed himself as a hapless wino, his parents would have defended him to the death, but the second they knew the dreaded drink had got a hold of him, they questioned his every choice. When he told his parents that he was an addict in recovery, they immediately blamed themselves and decided they would try to 'bring him up' again under their watchful eye. During a visit to TK Maxx Oldham the weekend before, Di Peterson had sent the trolley hurtling into a wall just as they were about to hit the tills. She then strong-armed Jake out of the fire exit whilst holding him under the arm tightly. It was a strange incident, and Jake was only made aware of the reasons for it on the way home.

'Who pays £18.99 for a candle? A drunk, that's who! I mean, for ten pence we can boil up a bar of soap and have the whole chuffing village smelling of lilies. It's crazy that is, it's actually nuts.' And just when he thought it was over... 'And what the buggery bollocks was that wafer-thin coat you had picked out? Absolutely pointless. A coat is for keeping warm, it's not a fashion accessory, Jake. £120 for a coat made from baking paper – you've absolutely lost it, son.'

Jake sat in the passenger seat of his mum's van with absolutely nothing to show from their trip to Oldham. Nobody goes to Oldham for no reason, he thought, whilst imagining smothering Di with the Helly Hanson cagoule.

'And another thing. You might think that casserole dish was a "fashion statement" but up here in reality, we don't need Le Creuset written on the side of the pot to make our stews taste better.' She said this whilst sucking on a Murray Mint and spitting the juice onto the steering wheel.

She meant no harm, just that Jake needed retraining like a middle-aged dog who had been spoiled by its clueless owners. In her mind, Jake had been putting fifty-pound notes into furnaces for the last couple of decades in a wicked and demented manner. Her imagination didn't allow her to realise he had maintained an expensive home, held down an extremely important job, and had actually been in a very serious relationship. Jake's mum could only see the negatives, and she intended to rectify them. Somehow, she felt responsible for his addiction, and when they first had confirmation that Jake was in trouble, during a conversation with Alf, she tried to pinpoint what she had done to cause it.

'Maybe it's because whilst I was carrying him, I had that half a stout on Christmas Eve. Do you remember? I was right lightheaded the next day.'

Jake's dad reassured her that nothing she had done in the seventies had turned her beautiful Jake to the bottle. 'If that were true, Di – that your actions whilst "with child" created their personalities – then what made our Leanne so promiscuous?'

Di gazed out of the window whilst searching for the answers, before suddenly remembering, 'Oh my god. Oh my lord. I think I might have watched *Barbarella* the day before me waters broke – it's absolute filth.'

Alf took a deep breath; it had been a long marriage.

Jake rolled three cigarettes on the journey home from TK Maxx; he would smoke them one after the other the minute he got into the house. When all you want is a good drink – well, lots of lovely drinks – buying a bit of nonsense from TK could have really taken the edge off.

Our Leanne, Jake's little sister, was a liability; she had literally dropped her pants for pretty much anyone who'd asked since her early teens. Yes, okay, she was a laugh, and she was actually quite a thoughtful person, but she was man-mad and any attention thrown her way was gobbled up without thought. Jake had cringed many a time when his friends from London had made the trip up to Lancashire, mainly just to get out of Dodge. On many occasions, whilst sitting in the front room of Jake's parents' house, Leanne would appear in an outfit that showed off her 'bits and pieces' in the hope that one of them would take the bait. Some of them did, and it was usually Jake who had to steer his wanky London mates out of her bedroom and away from his nightmare of a sister, who really should have been doing her homework or feeding her baby.

Alf ignored it as best as he could; he had little time for Leanne, although her daughter, the one that hadn't asked to be born, was his absolute favourite. There were two reasons for this – the first was that Alf had pretty much been Marnie's dad and grandad, since she had lived with them for most of her life, and all the school runs had been done by Granny and Grandad as Leanne was normally at work or in bed. The second was that Marnie was a tomboy – she had been the one person who actually wanted to learn how to grow award-winning courgettes or build a shed so, for that reason, her and Alf were thick as thieves.

Marnie's dad was apparently 'a piece of shit' – he was an Asian guy from Burnley, and that's all anyone knew apart from the fact he had a family who would not accept Leanne or Marnie, and that he owned a takeaway. So, at fifteen, a very blonde and fair Leanne gave birth to a very dark baby, with black silky hair, huge almond-shaped eyes and lashes as long as a camel in a very judgmental village in deepest, darkest Lancashire. As for Alf, he never went to Burnley again – even though his brother lived there.

There had been a little racism after Marnie was born, the sort that was mild and excusable, hidden behind the ruse that 'people just weren't expecting it' when they looked into the pram because the baby looked a 'bit foreign'. There were many awkward moments when the locals would visibly wobble, having realised that not only was Leanne a little tramp, but she'd been outside of the village to commit the act. The people in this area were so stuck in their ways that they would have preferred the father of the child to be a local – and an English local, if you don't mind. Even the parish priest would have been better than this.

The rumour mill was very active after the birth of Marnie. The locals had said that Marnie's dad was a taxi driver, and that Leanne had done it with him instead of paying the fare. It wasn't true, according to Leanne; she said the guy owned a takeaway, and even if she did get a large doner and chips without putting her hand in her pocket, none of that was Marnie's fault. Marnie had developed a thick skin and a blokey personality; she was still absolutely beautiful and had a look of Cleopatra, but you could tell she had grown up against it, and that always having to justify her existence was a heavy cross to bear.

Jake liked her; he was a little afraid of her bluntness, but he liked her all the same. There was talk of her being on the spectrum in her early teens. 'Aren't we all,' Alf said, whilst writing a cheque to a therapist. 'Tell us something we don't know!' He stormed out of the office with his arm around a confused Marnie.

'Is that why I don't like my mum then, Grandad? 'Cause I'm on this spectrum?'

Alf told her with absolute clarity, 'Nope, we don't like her because she's bloody useless. We love her, but we don't like her.' And after that, Marnie and Alf went up to the allotment and sacked school off for the day.

Leanne worked in The Lamb and Packet, a shitty local for shitty locals. She was actually the manager, and had worked her way through the brewery staff until they gave her the title. She didn't have much ambition, but in her very small world, she had hit the jackpot with this position – it meant she could be on view day and night, and she enjoyed the power. Her leggings-and-baggy-shirt combo, teamed with high boots, had all the locals thinking she was a fashion icon.

'Where does she get these ideas from?'

'I mean it's crazy stuff, but it somehow works.'

This was the sort of reception she got from the punters when all she'd done was add a belt. At the quiz night, she had tied a silk scarf she'd found on the bus around the top of her head and nipped into Claire's Accessories for some gold hoops. Apparently, this was 'pure class' and a 'bold move'.

'She looks like a bleeding pirate is what she looks like. Daft cow.' Alf had shared his thoughts with Marnie as Leanne left for work.

'Leave her, Grandad, it makes her happy.'

It was a strange dynamic – almost as though Leanne was the child, and Marnie was the grown-up, and it angered Alf. He felt that Marnie should have been the priority – not putting together outfits from a dressing-up box for a poxy pub job.

Alf and Diane had come to blows over Marnie since she was very little. Leanne was Di's baby, always would be, so she was very soft with her and didn't pull her up on any of her silly mistakes. Alf was determined that Marnie would have a good life even if her mother was a very silly girl, and now a very silly woman. Leanne was sort of pretty, very blonde and blue-eyed, but plain and certainly not striking. She could have bagged herself a decent bloke and perhaps worked on a reception somewhere; she wasn't going to blow any doors off, but she could have done better. Working day and night in a pub was not what a single mother should be doing.

Di's relationship with Marnie was very straight; she was her nan and that was it. Nan would make sure Marnie had a hot meal inside her, and clean clothes to wear, and would whack anyone who called Marnie names around the head with a rolled-up newspaper and wouldn't hear a bad word said about her outside the house. But there was a niggle, a sort of blockage, between them. Di had Leanne when she was in her forties; she'd waited her entire life for a daughter. It had been a difficult pregnancy, and once she had her bundle of joy that she could finally dress in frilly pink, her life was complete.

But not long after – well, fifteen years exactly – Marnie was born. And then Leanne was no longer a child, and all of Di's hopes and dreams for her only daughter melted away as the result of a bunk-up in Burnley.

Trigger

It was a Friday evening in early October, and Jake had been dry for six months. He had mainly managed it using an avoidance technique whereby he never went out, never went near a pub, and never ever answered calls from the London lot.

When he had handed in his resignation to Maxwell and Lucas, his parting shot was, 'It's been a ride, gentleman, but if I want to continue living, I must insist you never call me again.' They had pleaded with him to reconsider, but Jake had emotionally checked out of this three-way, and he dumped them both sitting at a window table of a Starbucks in Tower Hill. They hadn't been what people would call genuine friends; they had simultaneously destroyed one another over the years, and Jake had learned in group therapy that you have to kill the roots to become free of the weed. They were the root of the problem; they had provided the funds to pay for the toxic lifestyle, and the mere fact he saw them more than anybody else from one day to the next meant that this was a breakup that needed to happen. All three had been guilty of turning their Friday afternoon coffees Irish, and they had all been involved in creating elaborate lies to tell wives and partners that the other was working late. Jake was just as guilty, but one of them had to be the breaker of chains.

He hadn't found sobriety too much of a struggle until this particular Friday night. It may have been the fact that when the dark nights came in early, immediately a nice cold pint made an appearance in the forefront of his mind. It could have been that they had found some damp in one of the walls, and his days were being spent with a 'damp-proof course expert' whose conversation was about as riveting as watching the actual plaster dry. Or perhaps it could have been that Di had sprained her ankle and the medication she was on played havoc with her stomach, and she wouldn't stop droning on about it and going outside to pass wind.

But the most likely reason was that Jake had heard and seen on Instagram that Nicky had started dating a biohacker from Slough. Whatever the trigger, Jake felt on edge and a little bit too close to slipping. No amount of Wim Hof cold water exposure or affirmations were keeping the visions away; the very thought of a spicy whisky slithering elegantly into his bloodstream like a warm hug was becoming more appealing by the minute. He needed to change things up; sitting in the house alone, looking at interiors on Pinterest had become repetitive. Perhaps he needed an evening out and some company – it was worth a shot, so he made the call.

'Do you fancy a meal out on Saturday evening, Mum, all the family?'

Di gasped. It was as though he had offered her a meeting with the pope. 'Saturday night out? Crikey! What will I wear? What's the occasion? Blimey, you've not given me any warning. I'll need to get down to Marks and Sparks and pick up a new coat.'

'No occasion, just fancied getting out. Why do you need a new coat anyway? We'll be eating inside.'

There was a silence as Di tried to get her head around things. Jake had not taken them to a restaurant since his return, and they hadn't been anywhere as a family for a while. She was suspicious, and hoped to God that Jake didn't have any 'bad' news.

'I need a new coat because it's heading for winter, and the one with the big hood that I wore all of last year – well, I've put on a bit of weight, and to be honest the buttons are a bit strained across the chest, so I can't fasten it.' She was rambling, a little nervous about this outing – she had come to expect the worst with Jake, and had wondered if this sobriety stuff was going too well.

'Mum, do you want to go out to eat tomorrow night or not? It's no big shakes, a simple yes or no will suffice.'

'Will you be driving?' she asked.

'Yes, I am driving. I'll pick you all up, and take you all home.'

She relaxed a little – she knew Jake wouldn't drink-drive. At least he hadn't put her through that over the years. Luckily, living in London didn't really warrant a car, so he hadn't had the chance to lose his licence.

'I'll book somewhere – there's an Italian about twenty minutes away, sound good?'

'Well yes, that will be very nice, Jake. See you tomorrow.'

Jake ended the call – God, she was annoying, and so obvious, but considering some of the things the woman had witnessed, perhaps he would cut her a little slack. Christmas 2021 had really shaken Di; it was possibly the first time she had realised that her only son was a proper alcoholic. Di's opinion on people with drink problems was quite clear – if you drank in the morning, you were absolutely fucked! Jake had invited his parents, sister and niece to London for three days to stay at his Chelsea pad, where he would host them with Nicky. Nicky had also invited her parents who, in Jake's defence, were a pair of snotty wankers. Nicky had taken the week before the big day off work to prep everything, and had worked so very hard to make sure everything was perfect.

It was the first year after COVID, and Christmas wasn't a jumpy affair – the days of hand sanitiser and designer face masks in everybody's stockings were a distant memory, so everybody was really looking forward to it. Jake was working on a big merger right up until the twenty-third, and it had all been extremely stressful but also very lucrative, so when the deal was done, Maxwell had cracked open a magnum of Bolly at five p.m. and stated that everybody should celebrate hard. Jake knew that Nicky would be expecting him, so he agreed to stay for a couple, but made everybody aware that he would not be having a 'big one'.

On the twenty-fifth of December at eleven a.m., Jake woke up in the glass apartment overlooking the Thames. Lucas was face-down on the sofa opposite, wearing nothing but a Santa hat and a thick black belt; it was not a pretty sight. Maxwell was on the phone in the bathroom, begging and pleading with his wife not to put his passport into the Nutri bullet – they had a flight to Oman later that day, and she was absolutely fucking raging with him, and so were his three young children. A woman from the office who worked on reception was leaning over the balcony dry-retching whilst still wearing the same pencil skirt and blouse she'd had on two days ago – her boyfriend had apparently reported her missing when she failed to show for Midnight Mass.

Jake looked at his phone; it had one percent of battery left, and there were seventy-eight missed calls angrily listed on his screen. This was not Christmassy at all. There was only one thing for it – a breakfast of champions consisting of a double vodka-tonic and a black coffee. He threw on a tracksuit from Lucas's wardrobe, but due to the fact that he had abnormally small feet, Jake had to wear his own dress shoes with it. He drank a bottle of Chardonnay as he strolled through a rather unseasonably sunny London, and crashed into the dining room looking like he had dressed himself from a skip. Alf and Di were absolutely disgusted; they didn't know what to do or say. There was no excuse for this, and they were completely ashamed of their son.

Jake, in his drunken stupor, thought that if he sang Christmas songs at the top of his lungs, the family would somehow forget that he'd been missing all night. He did jazz hands into Nicky's face whilst belting out an out-of-tune version of 'Frosty the Snowman'. She tried to ignore him, hoping he would forget the words and just stop. However, Jake continued his campaign and embarked on his own version of 'Jingle Bells' using his mum's earrings as props. Di and Alf were mortified.

'Just sit down right now and stop the noise, son.' Alf patted the chair next to him. The sooner they got the meal underway, the sooner they could get Jake into bed where he belonged. It was a tense meal for Alf and Di, and Jake's behaviour wasn't the only problem.

They struggled with the seafood platter – neither of them had the palates to cope with this 'fancy grub'. Alf put the smoked oyster in his trouser pocket as his stomach wouldn't accept a sea-bogey that smelt of fags. Leanne, who had been on the Baileys, found the whole thing rather amusing. She'd received a Bobbi Brown eye palette, and a rather generous gift card from Amazon, so for her, the journey to naughty London had been well worth it. Marnie had no opinion on her stupid uncle. It was her view that people were weird, and we should let them be – she just sat with her new AirPods in, ignoring the nonsense.

It was Nicky's dad who really got a bee in his bonnet, and rightly so. His daughter was living with a bloody moron, as he liked to call him, and this – well, this was just more evidence.

'You look wretched, Jake! You smell revolting and I cannot and will not allow you to eat Christmas lunch wearing a hobo's costume.' The Major, as he liked to be called, thumped his fist onto the table.

Nicky's mum, Linda – a weak woman with a permanent tremble – let out a scream as she pointed to Jake's crotch. The guests all looked down to see a wet patch where Jake had dribbled and not wiped himself. He didn't have any underpants on because, well, he didn't know where they were and, without underpants, stainage naturally occurred.

'Oh my god. He's incontinent too. Nicky, did you know this? Did you know he has no control over his bladder?' the Major barked at Nicky, who just stood quietly wearing an apron with 'Season's Greetings' written across the front.

Nicky – beautiful, tolerant Nicky – placed her hand on Jake's shoulder and created some solidarity. She'd had her glossy auburn hair blow-dried the day before, and had made a real effort to make her make-up festive, but after hours in the kitchen, along with keeping all of her guests happy, it had meant her Christmas look was rapidly draining away – she looked and felt shattered. She'd tied her hair back, and her mascara was running due to the steam from the veg, along with the tears from her eyes.

Nevertheless, she stood strong and said, 'Jake has been working very hard and at least he's here now – let's just enjoy the day.' She kissed him on the head, and continued to host Christmas as if this was totally acceptable.

Jake, having got off the hook, got well stuck into the Christmas cocktails. He ate his starter with his bare hands, then spilt an entire jug of gravy onto Di's new Matalan skirt and, during Charades, he acted out *When Harry Met Sally* by pretending to masturbate.

Di and Alf left early morning on Boxing Day, a day earlier than planned because Jake couldn't get out of bed due to the shakes and a feeling of doom. Nicky's parents decided to do the same, but as they left, Jake heard them on the path outside giving their daughter a real talking to.

'I have never been so disgusted in my life – call that a man? He left you to do everything alone, and where the hell has he been for two days? Has he got another family? He might have a bit of cash and a decent job, but his integrity is non-existent.'

Jake lay in his bed listening to his future father-in-law doing everything to get his precious daughter to see sense. He wasn't worried – he felt secure in this relationship, and nobody is actually perfect, he thought. And he knew for a fact that the Major had cleverly avoided a significant amount of tax that year, so the old clown should really shut his big mouth before HMRC got a call from a whistleblower.

Jake knew that he himself was a good guy – he did not ever mean to hurt anybody, and surely that counted for something. He loved Nicky with all of his heart and, sober, he was the perfect fiancé. Once he became a husband and a father, he would sort his act out and would be the person the Major deemed good enough for his daughter – he was just getting it out of his system now, that was all.

That afternoon, Nicky had cleaned away all of the Christmas things including the tree so, when Jake woke, he was surprised to see that Christmas had been totally erased on Boxing Day. Nicky was very quiet well into the new year – she was lost in thought and although she didn't show any anger, he felt something had shifted. Perhaps her dad had managed to get through to her; perhaps he had made her realise she could do better.

In light of this – the fact that Nicky was a little distant and seemed rather sad – Jake stayed sober until his cousin's fortieth birthday in the February. As time went by, Nicky warmed up enough that she and Jake reached the point where they could talk about wedding plans, and which island would be the best option. Although he felt quite smug with his long period of clarity, two things occurred which were not very helpful to the cause. One: being free of drugs and alcohol meant the guilt of his Christmas performance was a very heavy and horrible feeling that he normally expelled with more drugs and alcohol. And two: his cousin Martin, pronounced 'Mertin' due to accent issues, was having a fortieth, and Jake was expected to attend on fizzy water – he dreaded the evening but promised to do his absolute best not to let Nicky down.

Mertin wore Patrick Cox shoes and flared jeans, was a loudmouth, and his family were backwards with their views on abstaining from alcohol. It didn't take too much to lead Jake down their loutish path – they had him doing Jäger bombs by nine o'clock after they said he was pussy-whipped and that London had turned him into a right big girl.

So, on that crisp Saturday evening in October, Jake drove his old green Land Rover – something he had purchased that made him feel a bit farmy and a bit country – and picked up Di, Alf, Leanne and Marnie, and they drove through the country lanes to an old pub that had been transformed into an authentic Italian, The Black Olive.

'Skirt's a bit short, sis.' Jake looked at Leanne's buttock-belt and shuddered. She was heading towards forty, and this outfit was a zero out of ten.

'With legs like these, you need to show 'em.' She bent down, applied a large amount of frosted pink lipstick in the Land Rover's wing mirror, and wiggled her bum to wind Jake up.

'Pack it in, Leanne, bloody hell, do you ever stop?' Alf had caught her and disapproved.

'Dad, chillax will you? I'm a young woman, not an old maid. Plus, I heard there's some proper fit waiters working here.'

The Black Olive was cosy and quaint, and Jake didn't hate it by any means. The log fire was lit, there was greenery hanging from the ceiling and the tables were decorated with candles in wine bottles. The waiter, who did actually look genuinely Italian, came over to take their coats. Di proudly took hers off before holding it up and saying, 'Do you like my new coat, Jake? I got it this morning just for tonight.'

Jake looked at the coat for about ten seconds before stating, 'It's an aquamarine anorak, and it has a faux-fur hood. I can't think of one good thing to say about it, Mum.'

'Cheeky bugger!' Di smiled; she liked Jake's dry sense of humour, and she wasn't offended. It was a marvellously practical coat, and it would last for years.

Marnie quietly observed Jake's honesty – she was very interested in it. She was a person who said things how she saw them too, perhaps she would get along with her uncle now he had moved close by. In the past, he had just been a guy who had turned up every few months, asked her how school was, and slipped her a twenty-pound note before leaving. They hadn't had a close relationship, and she had been told by her grandparents that Uncle Jake was extremely clever and successful and that he didn't really have time for kids.

'What do you think of the coat, Marnie?' Jake asked, noticing her listening to the conversation.

'It's alright for a nan's coat or a dinner lady maybe,' she said with absolute seriousness.

Jake laughed loudly. 'I like your honesty, kid.'

'How come you've got no kids or a wife?' she replied.

Jake stumbled a little with an answer. The truth was too brutal, so he embellished it. 'Well, I'm a businessman, and businessmen are very busy people, so the simple truth is, I didn't really have the time whilst I was in London.'

Marnie screwed her face up. 'Are you sure about that? I thought it was because you were too busy getting off your rocker. Well, that's what this lot said anyway.' She nodded towards her mother and grandparents.

Alf cleared his throat and stepped in, at least having the decency to look slightly embarrassed. 'She's very literal, Jake, you'll get used to it.'

The waiter came back from the cloakroom and showed the Petersons to their table in the corner of the main dining room.

'Mario, that's a very Italian name.' Leanne smiled provocatively at the name tag on Mario's white blouse – it really was a blouse, rather than a shirt, with its pearl buttons and puff sleeves.

Mario was probably in his mid-twenties; he was a slick waiter who had no doubt been pawed by many a desperate Brit. He handed Leanne her menu with pity; she was just another Northern slapper who hadn't received the memo that waiters had feelings, too. Plus, he was gay, and he was Albanian.

'What can I eat, Grandad?' Marnie didn't even open her menu.

Alf got his readers out of his top pocket, and held the menu up in front of him. 'We'll ask them to do you a bowl of spaghetti and Parmesan, that'll do ya.'

Nobody batted an eyelid – this must have been the norm.

Jake looked at his dad and widened his eyes. This girl was fifteen, and she couldn't read a menu or order her own meal – what was going on?

'She's funny about her food, doesn't like too many colours on the plate.'

Jake shook his head, memories of being force-fed Di's stinking casseroles littered with turnips and other ghastly ingredients came flooding back. How come Marnie didn't have to eat her greens, and why was she allowed to eat plain food? He secretly hoped she wouldn't be allowed dessert – that wouldn't be fair.

The waiter came back to take the order. 'Let's start with drinks, shall we?'

The table ordered soft drinks until Leanne made her choice. 'Vodka and Pepsi with ice,' she said. 'Actually, make it a double.'

Alf did a false cough and then kicked her under the table. She immediately remembered herself, and tried to rectify things. 'Oh Jake, I'm such a dickhead, I completely forgot,' she said, going red.

'Guys, it's okay, it's fine. Order what you want, I like it when other people drink.'

Jake was not going to fall off the wagon with his parents watching – that's not how it worked. This was the reason he had arranged to have dinner with them. There was an awkward silence. 'Honestly, please have what you like, it doesn't affect me at all.'

Alf seemed relieved that his Saturday evening would be a little bit boozy – he found it quite stressful going out socially and this would help with that. 'A pint of bitter please, squire.'

Mario scribbled it down. Di nervously changed her sparkling water to a glass of prosecco, and Leanne stuck to her original order. Mario scuttled off, relieved to be getting away from this weird lot.

'So, have you been an alcoholic for long, Uncle Jake?'

Marnie was a strange girl, but in a good way. She was stunningly beautiful, but she definitely didn't realise it. She wore a tracksuit that was probably from Matalan, her trainers were worn and possibly second-hand, her dark glossy hair was tied in a messy bun with bits sticking out all over the place, but somehow this young girl rocked it. How Leanne was her mother, Jake would never know – they were complete opposites as far as he could tell.

'I'm not sure – I think probably from the day I had my first drink, but you don't know that at first.'

'Marnie, stop asking rude questions – we don't talk about that. Sorry, Jake,' Leanne said.

'It's okay – she can ask me what she likes. Carry on, what do you want to know?' Marnie thought for a while. 'My friend's mum is one, you know, and she wets the bed. Do you wet the bed, Jake?'

Jake replied, 'Not any more, Marnie – I'm better now.'

'I'm pleased for you,' she said, before putting her headphones in for the remainder of the meal.

The Petersons enjoyed pizza, pasta and some mindless chatter that evening. Jake felt a warmth that he really needed at the time. He may not have been in the hub of the city, making thousands and living on the edge, but he had a family who cared enough to spend a Saturday evening with him when he needed some company.

After dropping off the family, Jake drove back to The Coach House feeling calmer. He thought long and hard about buying an Aga for the kitchen – they did matte black modern ones, and it would sit nicely in place of a shabby Welsh dresser the previous owners had left behind. He would also have one of those ceiling pan racks made so he could access his new TK Maxx cookware easily. The outside lights lit the porchway and part of the driveway as Jake ascended towards his home, but as he got closer, he saw a figure of a man huddled next to the front door, rubbing his hands together and blowing into them to keep warm. Had Jake owned a rifle, it would have been at this point that he would have had this possible burglar on his knees begging for mercy, but he only had a golf brolly, so he used that instead.

'Who's that? Show yourself,' he shouted loudly from just outside of his car, keeping the engine running in case he needed to leave quickly. He held the umbrella in a jousting position – if this was a local smackhead, he needed to be ready.

The man walked down the steps, squinting and trying to see Jake through the glare of the headlights.

'Don't shoot!' There was a chuckle. 'It's me you silly prick, it's me, Mertin.'

Jake lowered the umbrella and took the keys from the ignition. What the fuck did Cousin Martin want at this time of the night? The visitor stood to one side, revealing two suitcases and a large Sports Direct holdall.

'The missus has kicked me out, mate, I've got nowhere else to go.'

Masters of the Universe

There was absolutely nothing that Jake could do to deter his house guest from infiltrating his peace.

'There's a damp problem!' he declared as Martin, the twat, opened all of the kitchen cupboards looking for a tinny.

'I've got the lungs of a T-rex,' claimed Martin, before thumping his big, fat, titted chest.

'There may be rats under the floorboards, old property like this.' Jake wondered if Martin would be afraid of vermin – he looked the type to squeal like a little old woman if a mouse scuttled across the floor.

But Martin scoffed, 'I've lived with a big fat rat for a very long time, I'm used to 'em by now.' The big fat rat that Martin referred to was his long-suffering partner, Michelle. She was okay, but she had a sharp tongue and was the type of woman you'd expect to work in customer services in Argos. 'No refunds without a receipt' type of girl. Her and Martin were constantly rowing, and him being kicked out was likely a weekly occurrence – the only difference now was this big five-bedroomed country house with only one resident was round the fucking corner, so all of a sudden, Martin had a place to stay.

'I told her, Jake. I said, "You, love, can stick it up yer arse. My cousin, who was my best mate growing up, has a bachelor pad only fifteen minutes away, so if you carry on mithering, then I'll move in with him".'

Jake cringed. Best mate? In his dreams.

'And then what?' Jake asked, wondering how his cousin ended up on his driveway with his 'luxury' luggage.

'Well, she packed all me stuff and she told me that she was glad I had a place to stay 'cause she's fucking sick of me anyway.'

Jake's shoulders dropped; this did not sound like a temporary break-up. 'You can stay a couple of nights, mate, but I'm starting a rip out next week so you'll need to go to your dad's or something.'

'Rip out? Tell you what, I'll give you a hand, that should cover me bed and board.'

'What about work? Don't you need to be there Monday morning?'

'Ah well, that's been part of the issue between me and Michelle. They sort of temporarily let me go last week.'

'Shit, that's bad, Martin – sorry to hear that. What happened?'

'I've been accused of being "inappropriate" with a colleague.' Martin rolled his eyes and then sniffed up a large amount of phlegm really loudly.

'Inappropriate in what way?'

'I made a comment that... what did they say again?' He looked up at the ceiling before remembering. 'Oh yeah, erm, I said something that made a female colleague feel "uncomfortable and unsafe" in my presence.' He then laughed as this was so ridiculous and unbelievable – in his mind.

'Well, what did you actually say? It can't be that bad...'

'I said if her skirts got any shorter, I'd end up with a chub on.'

Jake deeply sighed – this was the exact reason that he and Martin would not, and never had been, best mates. It wasn't even the comment – it was the fact the fool thought this was not offensive in any way. In fact, Jake suspected that Martin considered this to be a compliment.

'Anyway, once the investigation has been done, I'll be back in. I'm just going to treat this as a paid holiday,' he said confidently.

Jake knew full well that Martin would never set foot in Halfords again.

'Have you got any beers, Jake? Could do with something before bed.'

'No, Martin. I'm an alcoholic, remember? I don't keep beers in the house.'

Martin shook his head. 'That's a right shame, we could have got pissed and reminisced about the old days.'

'We could still do that sober, you know.' Martin looked bemused. 'But I'm knackered, so let's do that another time.'

'You're still smoking though? Tell me you're not completely clean?'

Jake could have very easily blamed his nicotine addiction on Martin, as it happened to be him who gave him his very first cigarette. It was a John Player Special, and he'd puked up in a drain afterwards.

'Yes, that's one habit I haven't shaken off just yet – one thing at a time though, eh?'

He put Martin in the room furthest away from his – there was a bed in there that Di had made up for emergency guests. It took a while for Jake to fall asleep that night. He remembered when he and Martin had grown up together, and how they and a few other lads had named themselves the Masters of the Universe. They spent entire summer holidays with pillowcases attached to their shoulders, running through the streets and genuinely believing they were superheroes – good times. Martin hadn't been such a clown back when they were ten years old – he had actually been somebody Jake had looked up to and, at times, he had envied his cousin. Martin always had the latest clothing and the best bike, and he was allowed to stay up later than most people of his age. His parents never insisted he do any homework, so Martin was free to play whenever he liked.

When they hit their teenage years, Martin was the one who brought the fags and the cans of beer to the park, plus he was the first to get wanked off by Lyndsay Chadwick, the fittest girl in school – and also the easiest. It was when Martin left school without any qualifications that the Masters of the Universe kind of realised he wasn't that cool after all. He ended up on a YTS scheme training to be a panel beater which paid about a quid a week, and you were treated like a dogsbody until you qualified. He recalled meeting Martin in a panic at the bus stop one afternoon – he had been sent to three different places that morning and they'd all run out of tartan paint.

Once Jake left sixth form and secured a place at university, the tables had turned. It was Martin who would ask Jake for advice on women, often showing up at the halls of residence having been dumped by yet another barmaid. They stayed close enough, but once London became Jake's home, there wasn't really a place for Martin in his life. Jake had moved on, and Martin never really developed beyond eighteen, even though they were only a year apart.

The one thing that Jake's cousin – and in fact all of his family – had going for them was loyalty. This was something that was non-negotiable in working-class families – you always had each other's back. They might punch you in the face at a wedding, embarrass you in front of your friends, but if somebody was your family, you could always rely on them in your hour of need. It was for this reason that Jake had allowed Martin to unpack his stuff and stay in the spare room – for now.

Martin too lay awake that night, staring at the Artex, wondering what his next move would be. He was homeless, jobless and now Michelle-less – forty-three years and nowt to show for it. He had two kids who needed him, plus his dad was suffering with dementia. With his mum gone, his dad relied on him to keep him out of a home, and he really needed Michelle for that. It was a dark place to be, but he would continue with his jokes and his jolly demeanour and hope, somehow, that things would work themselves out. Deep down, he knew that his rude comment at work would probably spell the end of his ten-year tenure as manager of Halfords – he hadn't meant for it to slip out, but sometimes his thoughts became words. Still, why did that cow have to go and report him? It was just some shop-floor banter. And why the hell had she told Michelle all about it? She must have had an idea this would cause a kick-off.

Luckily though, now Jake was back, he'd know what to do. He'd always been the clever one, and now he had this massive house – at least he would have a place to stay for as long as he liked. The Masters of the Universe may have been a sleeping cell for a few years, but they had made a pact to be there for each other for eternity, a bond that could never be broken as they'd spat on their hands and shaken on it.

The following morning, Martin didn't surface until late. By the time he appeared, Jake had already had his walk and was just finishing a Pilates session on the rug in the front lounge.

'What's this? A gay dance class?' Martin said inside a yawn.

Jake disliked that massively. 'Listen, if you're staying here, you'll need to re-evaluate this homophobic language.'

Martin plonked himself down on a pink frilly armchair in front of Jake. 'I'm not homophobic – there's a gay on the deli counter at Morrisons, and we always have a laugh.'

Jake shook his head. 'How do you know he's gay?'

'Wears the white hat thing at an angle, and calls me sweetie.'

'Fair enough, that'll do it.' Jake smiled. Martin really was a cock, but a pretty harmless cock, all told.

Martin was massively overweight, and was also bald aside from some gingery bits at the side – he was not what you would describe as a looker, and although Michelle was a shrew with a Karen hairstyle, she was the mother of his children, and Jake doubted Martin could do much better.

Over a coffee, Jake broached Martin's family situation. He didn't want to put too much pressure on him, but he also didn't want his house guest any longer than necessary.

'What you going to do about Michelle and the boys, mate? You can't let this go without a fight.'

Martin was sheepish – a night's sleep had washed some of the cockiness away. He mumbled, 'Just lay low, hopefully she'll see sense.'

'Maybe some flowers, jewellery, an apology – that could help,' Jake suggested.

'She said that she needs space. She's got her sister staying there now, and her nickname's the Doberman. I think I'll leave it for a couple of days, if you don't mind.'

Jake nodded. 'Okay, I hear you – I've been there. Let the dust settle. She'll forgive you; it was only a comment, and she'll realise you didn't mean it, right?'

But Martin did mean it, and it hadn't been the first or second time he had been pulled up for being over-friendly with staff and customers. There were only so many chances he could be given and 'I was only having a laugh' just didn't cut it any more – not in the current moral climate. Jake saw the worry in Martin's eyes, and knew that perhaps he was about to lose everything.

'So, do you fancy ripping off some skirting boards and sanding down the bannisters in exchange for a roast dinner?'

Martin immediately agreed. 'Go on then, I don't mind mucking in. I can barely even butter toast properly, so I'll be glad of the grub.'

That afternoon, whilst Jake pottered around the kitchen, Martin sat on the staircase with some sanding apparatus and made a really good start on the bannisters. He had the radio on and seemed to enjoy having a purpose, which took his mind off things.

Around five o'clock, he showered and then requested the keys to the Land Rover – he and Michelle shared a people-carrier, and she'd kept it for the school run.

'Sure mate, where are you going?' Jake asked whilst basting a small chicken.

'Just down to the shop to get some beers in to have with my tea.'

Jake thought for a short while. Would this be a good idea? Could this be something that might relight a fire? But then he relaxed – Martin was in a bad place and something told him it was going to get worse. For old times' sake, for family and loyalty, he would let Martin sink a few cans on a Sunday night in his home.

Like an old married couple, the cousins sat facing each other at the pine table, enjoying a mini roast whilst watching *The Chase* on the telly. Afterwards, Martin washed and Jake dried before they retired to the sitting room and sat by the gas fire. Martin then got slowly pissed, and made less and less sense as the night went on. Eventually, and not a minute too soon, he fell asleep with a can in his hand.

Later, Di had called to check Jake was getting an early night before the builders arrived the following morning. 'What do you mean you've got Martin staying up there?'

'It's just for a few days, Mum, just until Michelle takes him back.'

'Has he been drinking near you? I bet he has. Great lummox he is.'

'Mum, chill, he's sanded down the bannisters, and now he's asleep.'

'You know he's a pervert, don't you?'

'Is he?'

'Alf, come and tell Jake about Martin and his antics.'

There was a rustle before Alf arrived on the other end of the phone.

'Evening, Jake, did you see the football yesterday? PNE are heading for greatness again.'

'Alf, never mind PNE – tell him about Martin and his demented ways,' Di yelled in the background.

'Er, well, rumour has it that he's been using his position of power at Halfords for unsavoury reasons.'

'Who knew Halfords could open so many doors?' Jake said sarcastically.

'Well, all we know is that Michelle is finished with him for good this time; she's got her sister changing the locks. And after last time, you know, I think she might have a point.'

'What happened last time?' Jake had probably already been told all of this, but because of the drinking and all ...

'He propositioned a customer who was browsing cycling equipment for her husband. Used the word "helmet" in one of his jokes, and it backfired.'

'In what way?'

'She took a photo of the manager and sent it to her husband; our Martin got a right kicking in the car park after work.'

'Oh shit, that's not good.'

Di came back to the phone. 'So, you don't want a sex pest staying in the house, do you? He might be family, but let's keep him at arm's length.'

'People make mistakes, Mum, I've made plenty.'

There was a worried silence.

'Anyway, we'll be up with some butties for you tomorrow lunchtime, corned beef and onion, do you?'

He winced. 'Mum, please don't put what is basically ballbags and lard onto any sandwich for me. And what do you mean tomorrow? We haven't arranged to see each other tomorrow?'

'Night, god bless, Jake, see you in the morning.' The line went dead.

This was something that would take some getting used to – living in such close proximity to family meant there was nothing to stop them from just stopping by. It would seem that Northerners did not make prior arrangements to come to your home; they could just turn up with luggage and horrible picnics, and there was fuck all you could do.

The Tickled Trout

For those of you who don't know, The Tickled Trout is a hotel situated conveniently at a junction near Preston where, during the eighties and nineties, all-important business meetings took place. Ask anybody you know from the northwest of England, and it's almost a guarantee that they were interviewed for a job there, or perhaps went there to score on the way to The Hacienda – probably both, on the same day.

Jake sat waiting in the reception, feeling quite smug actually – it had been a while since he had been shrouded in hungover shame on a daily basis. He'd avoided going to the dark side for a long time, and he was proud of that. Meeting Lucas was a decision that Jake had initially struggled with – this was a guy who had led him down many a shady route, but Lucas had big news that could only be delivered face-to-face, apparently. Somewhere at the back of his mind, Jake had suspicions that it was about Nicky. Had she sent Lucas on a mission to help her win Jake back? This wasn't her usual style, but perhaps she had changed and feared a humiliating rejection, so she was going in through the back door, so to speak. He hadn't been given any advance tidbits in regard to the urgent need for this meet-up, but he knew it must be mega-important if Lucas was prepared to drive all the way to the North for what would be a sober chat before lunchtime.

Lucas was the brains behind Morris, Webb & Butler. He was a social disgrace, but a genius in the workplace. He could broker a massive deal after being up all night – in fact, he may have been more productive mid-bender. Of course, he had come from money – his father was the Webb part of the company and had coached Lucas from a young age to be a ruthless money-maker. He was a tiny man, no bigger than Michael J. Fox, but with a Cuban heel and a three-piece pinstripe suit, you couldn't not take him seriously.

When his car pulled into the car park, Jake was slightly taken aback to see Lucas in his casual clothes – this was not a regular occurrence and it immediately put Jake on edge. He wore aviators and a chunky knit, a far cry from his usual sharp attire. He also limped slightly as he entered the hotel – perhaps one of his Cubans had got stuck in a drain, Jake thought to himself as he rose and shook his ex-colleague's hand.

'Hello, matey. Christ, you look well.'

Jake smiled – he had made a special effort just in case Nicky was hiding in the back of the Tesla. He'd had a haircut and worn his new jeans from TK Maxx; without his beer belly, he pulled them off quite well.

'Lucas, how you doing? What's all this about?'

Lucas took his glasses off, revealing bloodshot pupils and more fine lines than a crumpled fifty. 'Where to start,' he said, rubbing both eyes with exhaustion.

'What's with the limp?'

Lucas rubbed his knee. 'Got a little bit squiffy at a lunch last week, and I actually didn't mind the gap. It's a war wound, though – I sealed the deal so it was well worth it.'

Lucas was super–posh – his family home was in The Cotswolds, and when somebody used the word 'squiffy' or the term 'family home' you know they're proper swanky.

Jake gestured toward the waitress and ordered a large pot of black coffee to be brought to the table. He feared that, without it, Lucas may pass away. They sat, and Lucas put his hands behind his head and began to explain.

'It's Maxwell – he's gone. He's actually relocated to the United Emirates. No warning, no nothing – he sent me a message on a Monday morning to say he needed to get away, and that he couldn't work out any notice as he was already at the airport.'

Jake was disappointed – this was of little interest to him. He'd left a rather dodgy plasterer in the house, and Martin had insisted on making a start on the electrics with wet hair.

'Okay, sorry to hear that, but where do I come into this?'

'Well, we need you back, obviously – even just temporarily. I can't do this on my own.'

Jake rolled his eyes. 'You do know that I'm in recovery? I won't set foot in that office again. I have a new life now and, as boring as it is, it's what I need. I have to put myself first.'

Lucas sat forward, agitated. 'Listen, nobody knows this business like we do, there's so much money to be made. I cannot physically cover everything myself, Jake. Come on man, you owe me. Think of all the times I've got you out of the shit, the times I've picked you up from the cop shop, the rehab. I've been there for you over and over.'

Jake shook his head. 'No, no, I'm out. Why don't you poach somebody from another firm?'

Lucas's voice became softer, but also more desperate. 'That's the plan. But that'll take time – I need help right now. You know I don't trust easily. Couldn't you just work from home? Set up an office in your house, do everything from your farm or wherever you live? Come on man, just for a couple of months whilst I find the right person.'

'I really shouldn't – I was hoping for a completely fresh start, a new life.'

'Yeah, and look at you, all sober and Northern. You left the city, but doesn't mean to say you can't keep your hand in and sniff out a few opportunities. It's what you were trained to do, mate, and you do it really well.'

'But I'm concentrating on rebuilding my life – that has to come first.'

'This is temporary – just you looking after a few accounts until I find a replacement. Keep an eye on them, invest a bit and keep things ticking over. It could top up your bank account – I'm sure the refurb isn't cheap.'

Jake was almost listening whilst he drank his coffee, still sadly staring at the front door, hoping beautiful Nicky would walk in with her bags packed, ready for a new life. He felt bad for Lucas – there was a hell of a lot to do at the office, and they'd just about managed between the three of them. He started to wonder what harm it could do, especially if he was working remotely. In fact, he could maybe make some extra cash for a new roof, or a ride-on mower. This house was certainly going to be a money pit, and his savings wouldn't last forever.

'Okay, okay – send over Maxwell's files, and I'll have a look over them in a week or so. I won't be doing any meetings in person, and my phone goes off at five p.m. I like to have the evenings to myself.'

Lucas slumped back into his chair. 'You fucking lifesaver – I was worried we would lose key clients. I'm turning down business left, right and centre at the moment, spreading myself too thin. Another pair of eyes on things will take the pressure off massively.'

The barmaid came over to offer hot milk, but Lucas flicked his hand. 'Bring me a double scotch, gorgeous, I'm celebrating.'

'Aren't you driving?' Jake asked.

'I think I'll stay over and work from here today – that drive was a killer and I could do with having a bit of night, you know what I mean, fella?' He nudged Jake and winked.

That was Jake's cue to leave immediately; no doubt Lucas had a livener in the glove compartment, and this would end very, very badly.

Before he left, Jake looked back and said, with hope, 'Have you seen or heard anything from Nicky?'

Lucas smiled awkwardly. His partner was friendly with Nicky, and they had shared many a tissue when their other halves had taken the absolute piss.

'She's with someone, mate – a proper tosser, but it's serious. He goes about in Lycra and makes his own cheese... out of nuts apparently.' Lucas tried to be sympathetic, but he was only really interested in Jake's business brain. 'Forget about her, Jake, she was never your person.'

Jake didn't agree – she *was* his person but he had lost his way. If she could just see who he was now, and the things he had achieved, then she would come running back. 'She knows that I'm sober though, right?'

'She does, and she's pleased for you. But Jake, if she can't stick with you at your worst, then why should she have you at your best?' He raised his eyebrows judgmentally and wagged a finger.

'Yeah, but I did some really shitty things to her, Lucas. I mean, I was lucky to keep her as long as I did.'

Jake knew Lucas couldn't comprehend this attitude. He thought his own girlfriend should consider herself privileged to even be able to call herself Lucas's woman, so whatever he did, that was just the way it was.

'Say hi to Nicky from me, will you? And tell her I looked good, okay?'

Lucas nodded as he opened his laptop – he wished Jake would move on from Nicky. She was nothing but a fun sponge, and pretty bloody boring.

As Jake sat in the driver's seat, just before starting the engine, a familiar feeling washed over him. Maybe he should stay at the hotel with Lucas and get on it – he now had firm confirmation that Nicky wasn't considering getting back together with him. Jake hadn't looked at another woman since he and Nicky had parted ways – even the barmaid in The Tickled Trout with the nice bum.

He felt lonely in that moment. Was this it? Was he going to be that guy who lived alone for the rest of his life? The weird spinster uncle who never had a family of his own. A man who wasn't allowed in a pub in case he got off his trolley and made a twat of himself. He didn't fit in anywhere any more. Perhaps a night talking turkey in a hotel with an endless supply of booze was appealing. Maybe he needed that every now and again – decisions, decisions. Nobody would know if he did break this fast. Martin was handling the contractors – in fact he was doing quite a good job – and he had no reason to go home just yet. This would be a business meeting, actually, and also a reunion, as he hadn't seen Lucas for almost a year. Plus, it was a drowning of sorrows – the love of his life was probably going to marry a man who didn't even eat real cheese. If there was ever a time when a drink should be had it was today, in The Tickled Trout, just off the M6.

Jake got back out of his car and locked it up – he would hand the keys to the receptionist, and insist she didn't allow him to have them until the following day. He could see Lucas talking on his mobile at the table. He'd ordered another whisky which he swilled around the glass invitingly. Just as Jake was about to embark on his first session in almost a year, his phone rang.

'Jake, where are you? It's Leanne.'

'Out and about, why?'

'You need to go and get our Marnie from school – she's poorly, she's puked twice and they said she's got a high temp.'

'Sounds disgusting. Why can't you do it?'

'I'm on a brewery training course in Bradford, and it's an overnighter,' she hissed. This was clearly an inconvenience she did not need.

'Well, where's Mum and Dad – surely this is their job?'

'Lytham St Annes, having a cream tea.'

'Fuck's sake, Leanne, is there nobody else?'

'No, and you're her uncle – plus you're unemployed.'

'Erm, actually I'm taking a sabbatical.'

'A what?'

'Nothing, forget it.'

'So how long will you be? The school need to know.'

'Leanne, I'm kind of in the middle of something here.'

'Is it more important than your sick niece?'

Jake looked at Lucas and the whisky, then looked at the arse of the barmaid, before taking a deep breath.

'No, nothing that can't wait. Send me the address.'

That afternoon, Jake made a chicken soup from a recipe he found online. Even as the workmen continued to drill and bang around him, he put everything into making a hearty soup for Marnie who lay in front of the fire, wrapped in a quilt whilst scrolling TikTok on her phone. Martin had got his feet firmly under the table, taking on the role of tea-maker for the lads and becoming a sort of unofficial project manager. It had now been three days since his ejection from the family home, and there were no signs of Michelle changing her mind.

'You feeling any better?' Jake asked Marnie as she sat up to eat her soup. She grinned.

'I feel very good, thank you very much.' She didn't look unwell, and there had been no evidence of vomit since he'd collected her from the local equivalent of Grange Hill. 'Please don't tell Leanne I'm not ill.'

'Leanne? Don't you call her Mum?' Jake asked.

'Not if I can help it.'

'So, what's going on, why the skive-vee-i-tus?' Jake hoped to God this was nothing to do with periods – he would be well out of his comfort zone with that.

'Double science is what's going on.'

Jake remembered what that felt like. Unless it was a practical lesson where you could wear a white coat and goggles whilst hopefully setting a classmate on fire, science was boring as hell.

'Sounds pretty shit. I've been there, kid. Do you skive off often?'

Marnie shook her head. 'No, I'm actually quite good at school, I like learning but...' She stopped mid-sentence wondering if she should say the next bit.

'Go on,' Jake encouraged.

'Well, I just like it here, it gives me a good feeling. I literally just wanted to spend the day here and see what it's like.'

Jake smiled – he couldn't for the life of him understand what was so appealing about a building site, with retirement home furniture and a middle-aged addict at the helm. But if this is what made the girl happy, then so be it.

Marnie drank the remains of the soup straight from the bowl. 'Not bad, Uncle Jake, well done, got any more?'

Jake took the bowl to refill it and realised that giving a kid an afternoon off school, making soup and overseeing the renovation of his house was far superior to handing his liver over to The Tickled Trout.

Custard Creams

On Wednesday morning, Marnie made the decision that she would string out her pretend stomach issues for a couple more days. She figured that once you had convinced the school nurse that you were genuinely unwell, then you should really make the most of it. Jake and Martin heard her on the phone in the garden to Leanne.

'Yeah so, I feel extremely weak, in fact a bit confused. What day is it, Mum? Where am I?'

Martin sniggered. 'She's good, very convincing.' He and Jake watched a master at work as Marnie pretty much bagged the rest of the week off school. The only thing was, since Leanne was working and Alf and Di had gone on some sort of Wowcher voucher thing where they stayed in a seafront hotel for less than a fiver, she would have to stay with Jake.

'What the hell did they do before I moved up here?'

Martin dismissed this. 'She's no trouble – my two are a fucking nightmare in comparison. They can barely tie their own shoelaces.' He dropped his chin, remembering a busy weekday morning with Michelle screaming blue murder, the lads punching each other, and the dog shitting on the sofa just as everybody was about to leave. 'I'm not sure she'll take me back this time, Jake.'

Jake silently agreed. There had been no phone calls from Michelle, no yelling on the driveway, and it was radio silence from the boys. Martin had exhausted all of his chances by the looks of things – not only with his family but also with Halfords, and he was now in the same boat as Jake, but without the money.

Still, Martin was a cheerful chap – he would crack a few more jokes and hope for the best.

Marnie was given the role of searching for matte black Agas on eBay. Jake gave her the measurements, and let her use his account to trawl through and watch items that would be suitable. He could see she enjoyed that and felt useful. She was a creative girl, and screenshotted quite a few stylish kitchens which she put into a file for Jake to access.

'Why an Aga and not just a range? They're very pricey,' she said with a pencil behind her ear, observing the space.

'Old houses like this need an Aga – not just because they look good, but they save on energy. These things generate a shitload of heat.' Jake enjoyed educating her on stuff like this – she was actually interested and she seemed to have vision.

'I like this house; it makes me feel good,' she said, taking her position by the fireplace.

'Good in what way?'

'Just like it's got a personality, even though it's a house. It talks to me.'

Strangely, Jake felt the same way. Even in its current state, The Coach House had a feeling about it that couldn't really be described, only that it was unique and nothing in it was familiar.

'Go on,' he urged.

'I've always lived at Nan and Grandad's and it's boring – the house I mean – the walls are all the same colour and they're straight. This house is all bendy and crooked, but in a good way. Look at that corner.' She pointed to a curved alcove in the corner of the lounge, which had a shelf two-thirds of the way up that was so wonky any ornament would have slid straight off. 'That's really cool, I wonder why somebody did that. That's interesting, don't you think, Uncle Jake?'

Jake nodded – there were plenty of these strange little touches on the house, including tiny cupboards with no purpose, odd-shaped doorways with no doors, and some of the windows were so small that you had to bend down to look through them. He had never really analysed all of the quirks.

Marnie was an observant little thing, and he definitely felt that her life had been sheltered – stunted even. Her mother was very one-dimensional and Marnie's strong relationship with Alf had only allowed her to see most of the world through her grandad's eyes. Bless Alf, he was a great guy but he wasn't one for art galleries or travel. He had gravy on everything and he rarely left his hometown. Marnie needed more – she needed to see what was out there beyond meat pies and allotments.

Over lunch, which consisted of toasties from the Breville maker that Di had picked up from a car boot the previous week, Marnie, Jake and Martin chatted openly about their current situations.

'If Halfords don't take you back after the investigation, then what's the plan?' Jake asked.

Martin bit into his sandwich and boiling hot cheese dropped onto one of his chins. 'Christ on a bike, those wankers at Breville owe me a layer of skin.' Martin pressed his glass of lemonade against his developing blister. Marnie giggled

'Well, I could always go to a competitor, you know, if they decide that's it.'

'Who is Halfords' rival?'

'Perhaps Kwik Fit, but I could always approach B&Q, somebody like that. Retail is retail – I could sell sand to the Arabs, me.' Martin was cocky considering he was no Alan Sugar.

'But won't they ask Halfords for a reference, and won't they then be told that you perved on a staff member?' Marnie said, quite innocently.

Martin put down his toastie and turned to Marnie. 'Where the hell have you heard that, young lady?'

'Nan told me. She said that you were a danger to women – she actually said you needed locking up.'

Martin went red – he didn't really know what to say to that, as Northern men did not slag off other people's mums.

'Aunty Di has a vivid imagination, Marnie love. It wasn't like that, it was just a harmless joke.'

Jake quickly changed the subject. 'So, little lady, back to school tomorrow, I take it?'

Marnie nodded. 'I don't mind Thursdays, so I'll show my face,' she said nonchalantly. 'I appreciated you picking me up by the way, everyone was proper jelly.'

He frowned. 'Jelly?'

Martin stepped in. 'It's short for jealous.'

'Hmm, well I was actually quite busy when your mum called, so don't be making a habit of it.'

'Where were you, anyway? Mum said you were in a meeting – I didn't think you had a job.'

Jake shifted uncomfortably, recalling how yesterday nearly went horribly wrong. 'I met an old colleague about a work-from-home opportunity, I'm going to help him out on a project temporarily.'

'What project? What did you actually do in London apart from being rich and drinking?'

'I was an investment banker. I found opportunities and I invested money for people, so they can make more money and so on.'

Marnie was pensive. 'That sounds wicked. So, say if I gave you a hundred quid, you'd take it away and come back with five hundred?'

'Well, that would be the idea, yes – but there's always a risk you could lose the hundred. It's not as simple as you think.'

'But it's more likely that you would make money, rather than lose it?'

'Yes, because we look for sound investments with low risk, mostly.'

'How long does it normally take to make more money from the investment?'

'That depends – if it's a long-term investment, then it could be years, but there are shorter schemes.'

Marnie slowly nodded – she thought this to be a brilliant job with lots of exhilarating moments, much better than working behind the bar like Leanne or in the bra-fitting section at Debenhams, which had been Di's entire career.

'How do you get into this industry, Uncle Jake?'

'Got good grades at secondary, decent A-levels at sixth form, and then studied Business and Finance at university.'

Marnie's shoulders dropped. 'Oh, Mum said that I can't afford to go to uni – she said she went to the university of life which is much better, and it's free.'

Martin laughed loudly – he had known Leanne her entire life, and he had grown used to the shit she spouted. 'Sounds about right.'

Jake was annoyed. How dare Leanne tell her daughter that an education was unaffordable – there were ways and means to make anything happen if you tried. A few less Rimmel lipsticks and Bacardi Breezers might help the fund.

'Of course you can go to uni – don't listen to your mother, she talks a load of crap.'

Simon, the plumber, interrupted their lunch to let them know that the hot water would be off for the whole night. 'Have your showers and baths now, people, 'cause I'm about to rip the old boiler out. Oh, and you'll probably need hot water bottles tonight, and electric blankets if you've got them.'

Martin immediately stood and headed for the bathroom, not a care in the world that this was Jake's house or that there was a teenage girl who may need to go first. 'Bagsy first, suckers,' he said as he charged upstairs to use all of the hot water.

Marnie rolled her eyes at Jake. 'Bless him, what an absolute mess,' she said without even joking. 'Nan reckons that you're not to hang out with your friends from London any more. She said that they were the ones who got you into trouble.'

Jake froze at the sink as he started washing the plates from lunch. If only they knew just how close the old Jake got to coming out to play the previous day. 'Nan tells you everything, it would seem.'

Marnie smirked. Nan did have a big mouth, but most of what she knew she had heard through the closed kitchen door.

'So, for that reason, I've been doing some research on your problem.'

Jake frowned. 'Research on what?'

Marnie held up her phone, and Jake struggled to read the tiny flyer she had screenshotted that morning. 'Go and get your readers, old-timer, I'll send this to you.'

Struggling with alcohol addiction?
Do you need support?
Help is at Hand.
Don't be afraid, we're all in this together!
Tuesdays at seven p.m. – Glaston Church Hall.
Bring your own biscuits. We're not made of money.

As Jake looked up from his screen, Marnie handed him a packet of custard creams. 'It's tonight and don't worry, I'll keep an eye on Martin.'

'I really don't need to do that, Marnie, I'm fine. I've been totally fine since I moved here.'

She cocked her head. 'Well, according to some stuff I've read online, the only way to stay fine is to share your thoughts with others.'

'I do share my thoughts – we just had a lovely chat over lunch.'

'And during that chat, you told us you met one of your London people, didn't that make you want to... maybe have a drink?'

'Of course not, I'm not that weak.' Jake could actually feel the heat from his cheeks.

'I think you should go. It sounds like fun, and you could make some new friends.'

Jake sneered. He didn't want any new friends, and certainly not from Aldi's version of AA.

'Can you just go for me, Uncle Jake? It would make me feel better.'

After a lukewarm shower, Jake put on a tracksuit and a cap, and said his goodbyes to his house guests. He had decided that going to one of these silly meetings would confirm that he was doing okay, and the rest of the local winos were in a much worse state than he was. Besides, Marnie had gone to some effort to research it, and it was only fair to make the effort – to keep her quiet if nothing else.

The meeting was a twenty-minute walk, and Jake decided that would do him good, relieving some of the stress he felt before meeting new people – sober.

The sky hung low that evening, and the atmosphere was still and quiet as Jake walked down the hill into the village. He suddenly missed the buzz of the tube station after a hard day, the laughter he heard from the doorway of his local in Chelsea often enticing him in for an hour or six. People, even though they rarely made eye contact in the city, were what made a man feel alive. He only saw one dog-walker on his journey, nobody else.

Jake walked up to the entrance of the church hall. There was a small group huddled in the doorway underneath a plume of smoke. He hesitated for a moment. Did he really need to share his thoughts and hear other people's woes? He had quite successfully managed to avoid getting smashed without any help from anyone. Well, a very convenient phone call about a sick child had stopped him in his tracks but still, he hadn't gone there, and he could have.

'Welcome, please don't be nervous. This is a safe space.' A bearded man smoking a long curly pipe beckoned Jake towards the door. He was certainly in his seventies, and wore the kind of clothing Jake would imagine a monk might wear on his day off. Fuck's sake, this is going to be full of religious nutters, he thought to himself.

'I'm Keith, I chair these meetings.' He extended a hand. Jake took it.

'Jake Peterson,' he replied, as he would have done to a teacher in school. He suddenly felt like a young boy on his first day, vulnerable and self-conscious.

Some of the group waved and nodded – they all seemed to know each other and, very oddly, none of them looked like addicts, but regular anorak-wearing Northern folk who could well have been setting up for a jumble sale. He wondered if he had the right group.

Jake walked into the church hall; it was colder inside than out. He pulled his cap down and his collar up – somebody needed to heat this place. There were chairs in a circle in the middle of the room, and a lady with a beehive hairstyle and heavy black eyeliner handed out the teas and coffee from a table at the back.

It was a funny atmosphere – all the sympathetic smiling and weird hugging and back-patting wasn't really Jake's scene. The people seemed so regular and basic. He decided he wouldn't be sharing any of his gory tales with this lot – they'd choke on their custard creams.

Everybody sat down, and Keith kicked things off.

'Although you all know me, we have a newcomer, so I'm just going to ask each and every one of us to say their name and give a brief – and I mean brief – description of what brought them to Help is at Hand.'

And so it began – one of the most eye-opening half-hours of Jake's entire life.

'I'm Keith, ex-headteacher, not retired unfortunately – fired! I drank in the mornings before school, I was drunk during each one of my six children's births, I drank when my wife was dying of cancer, and I was drunk when I hit a lamppost at high speed. Two of my children won't speak to me, while the others barely tolerate me.'

Jake gulped and mouthed 'wow' to the floor. The lady with the golden beehive, who honestly looked like the sweetest person on the planet, then began to talk.

'I'm Peggy, fifty-six, and I'm from California.'

An old man across the circle whooped and clapped.

'Err, Frank, no interrupting, thank you.'

Frank put his hands up in apology, and Peggy continued.

'I came here twenty-five years ago after meeting my husband, who was a pilot. We couldn't have any children, and God knows we tried everything, but sadly it never happened so I started drinking to block out my sadness. While my friends took their kids to school and developed their families, I focused on my career, and when I wasn't working, I kept myself company with vodka. I hid it well, I functioned and I put my happy face on every morning, and nobody was wise to it. But one day, my husband decided to rearrange the garage whilst I was away, and my secret was out. I came home to find eight trash bags containing the magnitude of my addiction – they were all filled with empty bottles. Most of them were duty-free I'd managed to get from my work – I was cabin crew for Emirates.'

Jake couldn't help but gasp; even well-groomed Emirates employees drank their way to destruction.

'Anyway, my husband drove me to rehab the following day. That was three years ago, and I've been dry ever since.'

A younger man, a fellow tracksuit-wearer who squirmed in his seat, was eager to talk.

'I'm Tyler, I am only one week sober. I've tried it loads of times and failed, but I have to keep doing this 'cause my mum will kick me out if I don't. She's outside now, making sure I stay until the end.' There was a silence whilst people waited for more. 'I live at home and I'm twenty-two; I can't live alone because of the stuff I do when I'm not supervised. I don't know why I drink – I had a good upbringing and I'm not thick. Once I went to university, alcohol got a hold of me. After a year, I couldn't go one day without a drink. My whole family hates me, but not enough to let me die. Does anyone mind if I eat these spring rolls in here?' He pulled out a greasy paper bag and shoved one into his mouth.

'I'm Frank, just a smelly old pisshead whose liver has handed in its notice.' The old guy in the corner, who looked the part when it came to being an alchy, began to talk. 'I worked as a head gardener at a big posh house in the country. Forty years I gave to that job. It was a solitary existence, really – plenty of time alone to be with my thoughts. I always liked a drink, but once Val – me wife – passed away, it sort of took over. Quite honestly, I was okay with that – being drunk numbs the pain, we all know that.'

The group nodded as one.

'But see, then my employers felt that they needed somebody younger to run the estate and made me redundant. That's when I really got stuck into the booze. I had a lovely routine – pub at midday, back home for a snooze, and then pub again at six until kicking out. I felt I was coping. But then I got told by the doctor that me days were numbered, and the only way to stay about for a bit longer was to give up the ale. If it wasn't for me daughter and granddaughter, I'd have carried on, but for some reason they want me here. So, I got me self a little dog and called her Stella after me favourite tipple, and we watch telly of an evening and drink herbal tea together.'

Jake was saddened by that story in particular. An old man whose only pleasure was taken from him – be happy or stay alive? What a shit choice. Still, he liked the bit about the dog – that made him feel wholesome. Perhaps a dog was something he could share his troubles with at the end of the day.

A couple more people told their stories, which Jake really did find fascinating, but he was also aware that it would be his turn soon and he felt sick. He resented becoming a member of this club. He wanted to be able to, one day, go for a pint with Alf or to have a glass of champagne when Marnie graduated. He didn't want to be that person who sat in a circle telling strangers about his pathetic decision-making. Just as he had geared himself up to talk, the door opened and a woman rushed in, shaking an umbrella. She was wearing quite masculine clothing, and she stomped over to the spare seat and plonked herself down.

'Sorry I'm late, me fucking sister left me with the kids again,' she said with a thick Lancashire accent.

'Good evening, Janine,' Keith said, rolling his eyes no doubt at her foul language.

'What have I missed?' she said gruffly.

Keith pointed towards Jake with his thumb. 'We have a newbie, he's just about to share.'

Janine folded her arms in anticipation. 'Fire away, comrade.'

'Okay, so hi everyone, I'm Jake. I recently moved to the area, but I was actually brought up here. I lived in London for a long time and, well, like all of you, I leaned on substances – alcohol in particular – to get through a lot of my days. I lost my fiancée – she's not dead, she just left – but anyway, now she's met someone else, and they're getting married.'

People sighed, and some nodded as if this was an inevitable part of an addict's journey.

'I went to rehab twice, and it made me realise that my environment wasn't helping, so I left my job and I came home to Lancashire.' Jake was careful not to say that with a sneer.

'So, here I am doing what I can to stay clean and dry. In fact, it was my niece who insisted I come here – she's only fifteen, but she is the one person in my family that I have a good connection with. Not in a weird way, nothing weird,' he said quickly, realising that may have sounded a bit Josef Fritzl-ish. 'Anyway, I'm renovating am old house right now, so that's taking up my time and keeping me out of mischief.'

He smiled to himself at his use of Di's lingo – Jesus, he was turning into an old woman.

'Anyway, I met an old friend yesterday and I almost fell off the wagon. I didn't, but it would have been so easy just to have a good night like old times, but I know myself well enough to know that would not have been enough – one drink, one night will never ever be enough.'

Jake took a deep breath – he hadn't meant to open up like that, he was only going to say his name and age, but he had told them almost everything.

Keith put his hand on Jake's shoulder. 'Thank you, Jake, well done and welcome.'

Janine hadn't taken her eyes off Jake since he had shared his story. She had screwed her eyes up and folded her arms and then, once he had finished, she nodded slowly. How weird and manly and intimidating this blokey woman was, Jake thought. The others had seemed okay, but she had screwed with his dynamic.

'Well, I'm Janine – handywoman, carpenter, sparky, whatever needs doing. I am a local girl who loved to get smashed five nights a week, with the other two spent recovering. I gave up the drink two years ago after I broke a guy's jaw in a brawl outside the chippy. I don't remember any of it, but I ended up with a criminal record and I had to do community service. Drink makes me aggressive and I can't control it; I always had a bad temper but when you add the loopy juice, I was heading one way and that was prison. I've got no kids, no man and I like it that way. Every day is a struggle, and it has never got easier.'

Jake almost laughed. This was one of the most frightening, negative and bizarre introductions he'd ever experienced. And all this coming from someone who looked like they would definitely reach the final of *Gladiators*.

Keith called half time. This was when the group could take a break, have a fag or just sit and wallow in what they just endured.

As Jake poured himself a cup of tea, Keith patted him on the back. 'You've done the hard bit, now comes the support. Well done, that was a big step.'

Being congratulated for being a complete mess was a bit of a stretch, but Jake nodded and smiled in appreciation. He added a sugar lump to his tea, something to hopefully take the edge off, and as he stirred it in, he was approached by lunatic Janine.

'Jake Peterson, I knew it was you – you don't know who I am, do you?'

Jake racked his brains. He hoped he hadn't given her one in a pub toilet whilst in one of his states. 'I'm afraid not. Have we met?' He stepped back, creating some distance.

'I'm Michelle's sister – I believe you've got her pervert husband staying at your mansion.'

Suddenly, Jake *did* recognise her; he had seen her before. She had been at Martin's fortieth, and was the godmother at one of the boys' christenings. She'd had some make-up on and a dress, probably – the workwear had thrown him off course.

'I'm sorry, I didn't recognise you. How are you?'

Janine was almost as tall as Jake, and she was an eyeballer; somebody who made solid eye contact, and faced you like a man.

'I'm good! Not too happy about having to play daddy to my nephews, though. When is that spineless cousin of yours going to step up and look after his kids?'

Jake shrugged. 'It's nothing to do with me, Janine – the guy had nowhere else to go and because he's blood, I can't see him on the streets, can I?'

Janine relaxed a little. 'Suppose not, but it's all getting a bit of a pain for me. She's got me babysitting whilst she goes out on dates. Their dad should be looking after them.'

Jake tried his best not to show any shock. Michelle was already out dating – what the hell would Martin do when he heard? He'd unpack even more stuff, that's what.

'Maybe I'll have a word and encourage him to go home.'

Janine laughed. 'Now that will never happen. She's done with him, but he's still a dad. Tell him to step the fuck up, will you?'

As in-your-face as this woman was, she did have a point. Martin should be on the school run and at the sports events, not sanding down bannisters and hiding from his responsibilities. Was it any wonder that Michelle had kicked him out, especially after what he'd done?

'I suppose you're right; I'll give him a nudge.'

Janine's face softened when she realised that Jake was not running a bachelor pad for losers. 'Congratulations, by the way. This sobriety thing, it's not easy.'

It was that moment that Jake saw a softer side to Janine – the struggle they both shared was real.

'Janine, do we ever disclose that we've seen each other here?'

'I think we keep it to ourselves, don't you?'

'And it's all confidential, right? There are things I wouldn't want my mum to know, especially if I did slip.'

'Nothing that is said in the group leaves this church hall. Safe space and all that, Jakey boy.' She winked and put her finger on her lip. She was scary and annoying and massive, but he wasn't here to make friends – he was here to save himself from himself.

Jackie Chan

On Sunday morning, Alf and Di had arranged a family breakfast at Jake's house. Some cheek, Jake had thought to himself when Di had called him, and he tried his best to steer this breakfast in another direction.

'How come we're doing it at mine? The heating is still playing up and there are piles of rubble where walls used to be.'

Di gave zero shits about this. 'It's people that make a house a home, so we thought it'd be nice for us all to eat together at your house, me love.'

He was also getting a bit fed up with Di constantly telling him to leave things be in the house and to stop wasting money – she'd done it just two days before, when her and Alf had popped in with a huge tray of what she called 'hotpot'. This was the same brown sludge that had been called beef stew the week before, and steak bake the week before that. Di just made one massive vat of stewed beef and veg, and then she added dumplings one day, a pastry lid the next, and then sneakily gave it a different name each time. She wasn't fooling anyone, but with Alf's chest freezer so full of cheap chuck steak he'd bought from a van on the side of the road, it was the only way to reduce the pile.

'There's nowt up with that toilet, Jake, what's it doing in the skip?'

Jake had watched as his mum, even with her bad ankle, had carried a pink toilet with all manner of stains inside it and put it in the back of her car. 'That will come in handy on a rainy day,' she said as she filled her Ford Fiesta with remnants of shit dating all the way back to the 1980s.

Anyway, Sunday breakfast was to be at Jake's, and the whole family were coming. Marnie had gone home on the Friday afternoon as Alf insisted she get her arse back to the house and do some homework. He wasn't best pleased that the minute he and Di had arrived on the Fylde coast, Marnie had used their absence to skive school. He thought that Jake and Leanne were a right pair of thickos for believing her stomach story, and he didn't want her ending up like her 'bloody mother'. He'd said that in a whisper to Jake as he shoved Marnie into the car next to the pink toilet.

Before the family were due to arrive, Jake made sure to have a quick word with Martin, who was becoming more and more comfortable living in a manor house.

'Look, I know things aren't going well between you and Michelle, but what about the boys?'

Martin shifted uncomfortably and threw a tea towel over his shoulder in an attempt to look busy and cheffy.

'Well, she's poisoned them against me,' he said defensively. 'What can I do about it?' Martin opened the three tins of beans, which would be his contribution to breakfast, and emptied them into a saucepan.

'You can tell them that you fucked up and that you're sorry. You can tell them that what happens between you and their mother is completely separate from you being their dad.'

Martin opened the utensil drawer forcefully, causing a wooden spoon to jam the whole thing.

'Nah, she's got the sister there, she'll be putting the knife in,' he said, shaking the drawer aggressively.

'I'm sure Michelle and the Doberman wouldn't want the boys to lose their dad – come on, mate.' Jake went over and slid his hand into the drawer, calmly dislodging the offender.

Martin took the spoon and plonked it into the pan before putting his hands behind his head. 'Fucking stupid cunting spoon,' he said, welling up.

Jake watched as Martin emotionally broke, but he continued to set the table for breakfast, contemplating the best approach without making things worse. Jake hesitated before walking over to put his arm around his cousin's shoulder.

'I know this is getting to you. Remember, I know you, Martin – stop fighting it. It's okay to be upset – not everything needs a punchline.'

Martin tried to hold it all in; he stuttered and spluttered, but he couldn't get his words out. Eventually he managed to say, 'I just miss them though,' before wiping his eyes with both sleeves and taking a deep breath.

'I know you do, and that's okay. I've got you, yeah?'

Martin nodded and sniffed; he needed that. For as long as he could remember, Martin Peterson had built a barrier around himself made purely of banter. He protected himself behind jokes and, without that protection, he was weak and exposed, so he kept his emotions locked away.

Even at his own mother's funeral, he had been the class clown. Jake barely remembered that day – that was a serious day of drinking – but what he did know is that he and Martin wouldn't be allowed to sit next to one another at any other family event again. To be fair, Martin's mum wasn't so different. In the nicest possible way, Jake's Aunty Pam was a fire-breathing dragon who addressed people 'Oi mush!' She was abrupt, she was not maternal, and she had no qualms explaining to people that 'our Mertin were a mistake.' Yeah, she always winked afterwards, but that had to cut deep.

When she died, quite suddenly as cardiac arrests are notoriously swift, Bert just said, 'Oh well, that's that then.'

Martin suspected that a sense of relief had washed over Bert. Although he had loved this woman as his wife and mother to his son, she had made life very difficult, and could be quite a vindictive old sod. Of course, this was no excuse for the cousins to treat the funeral like a school reunion and, during the mass, the priest had to stop the service to separate 'the two twits' on the second row.

Not long after, the familiar crunch of the gravel indicated the arrival of the family. Jake watched out of the kitchen window as

Alf reversed the car as close to the front door as physically possible. He then opened the boot and kicked the front door as both hands were busy.

He staggered in and plonked a large cool box onto the kitchen worktop before slumping into a chair. Carrying colossal amounts of cheap meat was exhausting. 'Right, fire up the grill, Jake, and let's get this full English on the go.'

Jake lifted the lid and peered into the cool box in dismay. Packet after packet of unlabelled grey animal was layered from top to bottom.

'How the heck are we going to eat all that, Dad? Plus, it's all completely frozen.' This was a far cry from Jake's London Sunday mornings, which consisted of sausages lovingly folded in brown paper from places that employed butchers with knighthoods.

After an irritating ten minutes where people argued about what pork-based products were safe to defrost in the microwave and what could be cooked from frozen, Marnie took to Google and gave out the instructions. Although the place stank of warm blood, and Jake couldn't hear himself think, he took a second to realise that he was lucky to have a full house on a Sunday morning. He could have been nursing a double vodka to quell the shakes, he could have been waiting for 'a friend' to collect him from Walthamstow police station, or he could have been concocting a story to explain his whereabouts since Friday night. But today, he was in his country house with his family cooking an English breakfast. Okay, so it was hardly exhilarating – he wasn't living life on the edge – but he felt safe; an unfamiliar and underrated experience.

The family chattered as they sipped mugs of tea and dipped toast into soft yolks. Di beamed as she had her children and granddaughter under the same roof, although this dissipated when Martin blew his nose on a tea towel at the table.

'How long are you planning on stopping here, Martin? Our Jake is a busy man, you know – he can't babysit you every day.'

'Aunty Di, I think you'll find that I have been very useful, actually. I've been overseeing the renovation – it's a big job.'

'Yes, love, but shouldn't you be getting back to your life now, you know – your children, who need their dad?'

Jake saw Martin blush, and felt sorry for him. His life was in tatters and, when all was said and done, he didn't actually have anywhere else to go.

'Well, Jake needs me at the moment – I don't want to leave him in the lurch. He'd be lost without his big cousin, wouldn't you, pal?'

Jake almost choked on his gristle. Martin looked helplessly in his direction; the words 'Masters of the Universe' somehow appeared in Jake's head, and he felt that strange loyalty creep back in.

'He's actually been brilliant, Mum. I don't know what I would have done without him. He knows stuff that I don't about plumbing and plastering. He's welcome to stay as long as he likes.'

Jake had no idea how those words formulated themselves – this wasn't who Jake was, but maybe a new person was emerging, somebody who recognised when a person needed a break.

Di glared at Alf, looking for backup, but Alf just turned away. As far as he was concerned, these were two grown men, and what they did was nobody's business.

'Uncle Jake went to an addiction meeting last week!' Marnie broke the ice, making Jake's so-called anonymous meeting public knowledge.

'Ooh go on, who was there, anyone we know?'

'Even if there were, Leanne, I obviously wouldn't tell you, would I?'

'I won't say owt – go on, tell us all about it,' she pleaded, thirsty for local gossip that she could share in a hushed, important voice across the bar of The Loser Arms.

'No, and don't ask me again. It's private – it's not a joke you know, I heard some seriously grim stuff.'

The table went quiet as every single one of them prayed that Jake would give them a snippet, but he stayed completely silent, leaving them to speculate over people they knew.

'I bet that mental postman is a member, Alf; do you remember him? Red nose and shaky hands.'

Alf nodded sheepishly – he also wanted to know who was in the secret club, but tried not to show it.

'Is there an ex-postman at the club, Jake?' Alf casually asked.

'Why would you think your postman is in this group, Nan?' Marnie asked, pushing beans around her plate.

Di got comfy in her seat and talked in a low voice. 'Well, we had him for years, and he was alright to start with, but then he started putting all the letters through the wrong doors. Pat Bayley from 73, do you remember her, Jake?'

Jake nodded and sighed.

'So, she challenged him on it one morning. He'd put *her* blood results through *our* door. You can't make mistakes like that, it's scandalous. I mean she didn't have HIV or owt like that but still, it's a private thing.'

'What were they testing for, Aunty Di?' Martin asked, chewing noisily.

'Cholesterol, and it were off the charts by the way. She had to go on Benecol after that, the yoghurt *and* the spread.' Di raised her eyebrows for maximum impact. 'Anyway, when she went out to have a word with him, he threw the post bag at her and said something very rude.'

The whole table, even Jake, was now invested in what happened next.

'Go on, Nan, what did he say?'

Di took a deep breath. 'He said, "You fucking do it then, bitch".' There was a collective gasp. 'Anyway, after that we had a residents' meeting, and slowly but surely people came forward with their observations.'

'A good old-fashioned witch hunt then, eh, Mum?' Jake didn't appreciate being dragged into this Northern tittle-tattle that he'd thought himself above.

'Shaky hands, a red nose, a bad attitude and someone said they saw him urinate into the post bag at the end of his round. We concluded, the residents that is, that he had a big problem with alcohol.' Di's case was open and shut, and she sat back, thrilled with herself for delivering the first contender for Jake's 'little club'.

'Sorry to piss on your chips, people, but there was nobody of that description at the meeting – no postman with a red nose. Sorry.'

They all seemed to deflate at this news, like they had lost a game of something.

'Keep your eye out at the next one, he'll probably be lurking in the doorway.' Di sipped her tea.

Jake put both his thumbs up and wondered how a bottle of gin would slip down that afternoon. That settled it. He would attend the next meeting – the pangs were still there.

'Would now be a good time to discuss my news?' Leanne piped up as people began to gather up empty plates. Di and Alf both looked a little nervous.

'Jake, I have been offered an opportunity, and I am going to need your help.'

Jake put down the *Sunday Times*, his last lifeline to civilisation. 'Go on, Leanne.' He was cautious – if this was money, then she could have some, but Leanne wouldn't ask for it face-to-face, normally sending a message with a smiley face and the dollar sign.

'Go on, get on with it,' Alf said impatiently.

'I've been offered an opportunity in Fuengirola. That's in Spain, Jake, near Marbella.'

Martin snorted. 'Aren't you a bit old for stripping, Leanne? *You'd* have to pay *me*.'

'Eh, that's enough, Martin. Go ring your kids, this doesn't concern you. Go on, out you go.'

Martin picked up his mobile and his Silk Cut, and slinked off to the back door.

Jake spoke levelly. 'What's the opportunity, Leanne?'

'The brewery has acquired an English pub in Spain, and they need someone to set it all up and open it. After that, they'll move a couple in to manage it, but for now they want somebody from the UK to get it up and running in time for Christmas.'

'And you want me to do what? Pay for your flights?'

'No, they pay for everything.'

'Okay, so what do you need from me?'

She looked sheepishly at Marnie. 'It's a six-week project.'

'So?'

'Well, Marnie can't come – she's got school.'

Marnie raised her hand and said, coolly, 'For the record, I don't want to go. I've looked on Google Earth and the whole place is wank.'

Di shook her head. 'Watch your bloody language, Marnie.'

'So can you do it?' Marnie asked, looking shyly over to Jake.

'Do what?'

'Look after me? Take me to school, cook my tea and care for my general well-being for six weeks?'

'Why can't you two?' Jake asked his parents, wide-eyed.

'Your dad's having his cataracts done so he won't be able to drive, plus we're off to Devon in the caravan for two of those weeks on a winter break.'

Jake showed his annoyance by picking up the paper again and pretending to read it – a winter break in a caravan in the UK was a grim idea anyway. 'These people, these bloody people,' he mumbled.

'It's all come at a really tricky time, Jake, but she can't miss a chance like this,' Di pleaded.

Jake crumpled up his face and his newspaper. 'Setting up a pub on the Costa Del Crime is hardly a place at Yale, Mum.'

'Eh, don't you belittle our Leanne's achievements – she's worked hard to get to where she is.'

Alf rubbed his knees – so many jokes, so many sarcastic remarks could fill this space right now, but he would leave it there; a sober Jake was a better parent than Leanne any day of the week.

'Okay, well, I suppose so – I can't really say no, can I? Can't have you missing out, you culture vulture, you.'

Marnie ruffled Jake's hair; it was a strange thing for a child to do to an adult, but he guessed this was her equivalent of a hug.

Jake spent the next couple of hours with Alf, going through Marnie's diary. She had after-school clubs three nights a week, and started early on Fridays. There was a list of people she was allowed to hang around with, and then three who were definite no-gos. She was to be in bed by nine-thirty on a school night, and she had to hand her phone in, otherwise she'd be 'getting groomed' until all hours, according to Di. At weekends, she could have sleepovers on one of the nights, but not Sundays because that was a school night. The whole thing was written out in Leanne's shitty bubble writing, and pinned to Jake's old fridge.

'You're not suggesting that any of her friends stay over here, surely?' The last thing Jake needed was for a gang of teenagers to set about him whilst smashed on cider; he could not yet trust himself not to join in.

'That's up to you – you're in charge, Jake. She's a very clever young lady; you need to have your wits about you,' Alf warned. 'I'll drive her over on Wednesday after school and we can go over anything you haven't quite understood.'

'Wednesday – as in four days away?' Jake thought he may have at least a couple of weeks to get used to the idea.

'Leanne leaves on Thursday morning, so this Wednesday would be best, okay, son? Goodbye now.'

Alf, Di, Marnie and Droopy Drawers reversed down the driveway, all smiling and in high spirits. Perhaps because they had all got their own way, or maybe it was because they felt that Jake needed an eye keeping on him. Jake wandered back into the house, wondering what he had let himself in for – was the house a suitable place for an impressionable teenager? Would Martin be able to keep his swearing to a minimum and not use the term 'chub on' or other stomach-churning phrases? Just as Jake was about to sit him down and inform him they were soon to be three, Martin rushed in, all excited.

'The boys have agreed to go with me to some place in Manchester called Wing Stop after school.'

Jake patted him on the back. 'Nice work, this is a good move.'

'Although she told me not to bring them back before eight p.m.'

Jake remained silent – he couldn't see the problem with that.

'She's got a cheek, don't you think? Chucks me out of my own house and then starts telling me when and what time to bring the kids home?'

Jake thought about it for a couple of seconds. 'No, not really. This is the first time you've had the kids in a while. I think she's being pretty reasonable.'

'Yeah, but she's the one in the house, the one I pay the mortgage on.'

'Yes, but you are the one who has been sacked for sexual harassment.'

'Not sacked – I am under investigation, that's all,' he said meekly.

'Martin, nobody could have fucked up more times than me. You're going to have to own your shit.'

Martin laughed uncomfortably. 'Is that one of your London sayings, fancy pants?'

'Yes, I think it might be. But it's true, be accountable.'

'I'm going for a game of pool. Don't wait up.'

Jake left it there – there was no more that could be done that Sunday evening to get Martin to see sense, but he would soon need to accept that he had mouths to feed, a job to find and some hands to keep to himself.

Most of Monday was spent with Jake ploughing through Lucas's files from Morris, Webb & Butler. There were accounts that were active, some were dormant, but there were some very lucrative leads. A fire restarted inside Jake – he still had it when it came to sniffing out potential. If only he'd behaved nicely in London, then things could have been different.

It was this opening to his old world that sent Jake down a rabbit hole. He started with Instagram, but Nicky had her settings on private. He tried her Facebook page, but there was nothing new on there since 2018. He couldn't seem to get even a glimpse of Nicky as she had everything securely locked down. He then tried Nicky's friends – surely one of them must have posted a day trip or a dinner where Nicky had been invited, but she seemed to be absent in every photograph. Even if she'd moved in with this biohacking bastard, she would still see her friends and colleagues. Jake was stumped. He should have left it because Nicky and her dad and even her Pilates instructor had told Jake in no uncertain terms to leave the girl alone. But Jake had an itch that just had to be scratched.

Nicky's password for everything had always been her childhood ponies' names. There had been three and, by the time her and Jake split, she had only used the first two. It was possible that in the last year, Nicky had moved onto her third and least favourite pony, Jackie Chan. The horse was a kicker; it used all four legs to put the Major in hospital when he bent over to tie his shoelaces. Anyway, as Jake put 'Jackiechan' into Instagram using Nicky's Hotmail address, to his delight and dismay, he was in!

Jake knew he was limited on time – Instagram would have sent Nicky a message saying her account had been logged into from a new device. It was only a matter of time before she knew she had been hacked – she would change her passwords, and there were no more ponies for Jake to go at. It was a sobering experience. Nicky was in a full-blown relationship with this creep with blonde hair and a good body. They'd been to Venice, they'd been to Palma, and Jake put his hands over his face to see them in the Seychelles, the place he and Nicky planned to honeymoon. There was one picture that hurt Jake quite badly – a photograph of a snowy place, maybe Norway or Iceland, where, under the Northern Lights. Biohacking Bastard was down on one knee in front of a beaming Nicky.

Jake inhaled deeply; this was very painful.

Biohacker's name was Beau, and he was a prolific poster. Jake clicked onto his profile, and quickly got the measure of him. He wasn't posh, definitely not from money, so the Major hadn't managed to bag the blue-blood he'd been after. He had a lactose intolerance, and liked to post about his runny shits and itchy throat. His parents lived in Slough, and he appeared to live next door running his business 'telling people what to do' from their annexe. His hobbies were travel, wellness and reading. Apparently, 'happiness comes from within, and there is no good reason to poison the body with chemicals.' This was a caption underneath a photograph of Beau squeezing the juice from an Aloe Vera plant.

Jake sneered – what a show-off. If this guy had found a way to get high on life from that little lot, then he should keep it to himself. The rest of the planet were avoiding substances by shaking, crying and drinking Diet Coke.

There was one post that Jake was afraid to look at. He'd seen pictures like these before, and he just had to hope it was an optical illusion. But, on further inspection, Jake's worst fears came true. Nicky and Beau were going to become parents. The scan picture titled 'Baby Biohacker' pretty much sealed the end of Nicky and Jake. She was engaged and pregnant and living with a man who was perfect, as he wasn't a wino and he didn't sniff gear.

Jake logged out. That was a very difficult pill to swallow. There was no other person that Jake could discuss this with other than somebody who was morally bankrupt and almost in the same boat – someone he trusted and somebody who owed him. But he had to talk to somebody – this was massive. Cousin Martin was that somebody. He called him down from stripping wallpaper in the guest bathroom, and gave him the lowdown as he paced the kitchen.

'Wow, so he doesn't even eat actual cheese then?' This was Martin's first concern.

'Nope, he makes his own milk… out of nuts.'

'What, coconuts?'

'No, cashew nuts, but that's really not the point, Martin.'

'I know, I know. She's knocked up by this ponce – I guess it's done then.'

Jake paced his kitchen smoking yet another cigarette. 'It was done anyway, Martin. I treated her like shit, I didn't deserve her. I just wanted to see what she was doing, whether she was happy.'

'Well, she's having a baby and getting wed, so it seems like she's doing okay to me.'

Jake put both hands on either side of his Belfast sink, and shut his eyes. 'But Martin, this should have been me. If only she'd just waited until I'd got clean, that could have been us.'

'Well, maybe she's just not your person. She's very London.' Martin put his hand on Jake's shoulder, trying to comfort his cousin. 'She must love him, Jake. And even if she doesn't, it's too late now.'

'No!' Jake shouted. 'She loved me, she's got with him because she was struggling for time. She's rushed into it because she wanted to be a wife and a mother, and I wasted her best years.'

'Tell you what,' Martin said seriously, massaging the top of Jake's arm, 'let's throw some glass bottles at a wall – relieve some of that tension.'

Jake couldn't help but smile. Stupid Martin, thinking of stress-busting activities that didn't require a pub.

'No, don't worry, I'll be okay. I've got a meeting soon. Shall I pick up some fish and chips on the way back?'

Martin's eyes lit up. A chippy tea on a Monday night was a treat. Michelle had been doing meat-free Mondays over the last year, and it was always some shit she'd concocted with decaying courgettes from the bowels of the fridge.

'You won't have a drink, will you, pal? This won't push you over the edge?'

Jake shook his head, touched by Martin's concern. 'Don't worry about me – if anything, it's made me determined to stay sober.'

'Phew, 'cause your mum said that if you go back to it whilst I'm staying here, she'll know who to blame. She means me, by the way.'

'I know who she means.'

'Fish, chips, mushy peas and don't forget the gravy,' Martin shouted as Jake got into his car.

The Doberman

Jake wondered why any woman, even one who worked on an oil rig, would think it was okay to wear a boiler suit in a public place. In the grand scheme of things, it wasn't important what people wore to addiction meetings, but it was a bold move, and he was absolutely convinced it was used by the Doberman as an intimidation tool.

Janine plonked herself down on the chair next to Jake and side-whispered into his ear, 'Good work on getting that great lummox to step up.'

'He'll be okay – he just needs to get used to things,' Jake assured her.

'He'll be getting used to things, alright,' Janine belly-laughed. 'She wants maintenance and plenty of it. Best tell him to start thinking about supporting them kids financially – he's not sent a penny and he got paid last week.'

'Listen, I'm not his keeper, or his financial adviser – tell him yourself,' Jake snapped, quite bravely of him. Janine swung her head around so quickly her long ponytail whipped Jake on the cheek. 'And for god's sake, keep your hair to yourself.'

Janine just grinned. 'Well aren't you Miss Snippy Pants tonight. What's up?'

'Oh nothing, just had a shit day, that's all. And what you wearing that for?'

Janine looked herself up and down. 'Not that it's any of your business, but I've been clearing some rats out of a loft space.'

Jake recoiled. 'You what? And you haven't even changed or had a shower?'

Janine shook her head. 'I was in a rush and my sobriety is more important than my appearance.'

'When you put it like that...' Jake suddenly felt embarrassed – who on earth got glammed up for a meeting about recovery?

The meeting kicked off with Keith introducing a newcomer, so Jake didn't feel like the new boy any more, which was nice.

'Hello everyone, I'm Dean. I'm an accountant – well, was an accountant. Now I am between jobs due to my addiction.'

'Welcome, Dean.'

'I just turned fifty and my husband threw a surprise party for me. All my family and friends were there – my eighty-three-year-old mother had a night out of the care home especially. My two kids, a boy and a girl from my marriage before I came out, both travelled up from London. Even my ex-wife and her partner were there.'

The group smiled collectively – this seemed like a very nice story, one where a gay man was winning at life without judgment. But his dark look and swollen eyes told a different story. 'Anyway, as it was a surprise, I had no idea all of these people had gone to so much effort and, on that day, I'd told my husband I was meeting a big client. But I'd actually sat in a pub eight miles from our home and I'd been drinking all day, something I did often. By the time I walked through the door, I was in a pretty bad way. Add two bottles of champagne to what I'd already had, and I completely lost it, and I mean totally lost it.'

Dean looked at the floor, then gathered himself. He looked directly at Keith. 'You asked me what brought me to this meeting and, to be completely honest, I don't know exactly because I cannot remember what happened that night and, bless my family, they haven't the heart to tell me. All I know is that I woke up in hospital. I'd fallen down a flight of stairs, broke my collarbone and three ribs. My family staged an intervention at my hospital bed, and told me it was time to address the problem.'

Keith began a round of applause, and others followed. Jake found that part of the initiation process quite bizarre. Why clap a man who has admitted he's a disaster?

'How long since your last drink, Dean?' Keith asked, with his sympathetic monk's voice.

Dean swallowed. 'I'm a month clean. Still not sleeping and wondering how I am supposed to do life, like this. Any tips welcome.' His smile was the vacant one, the one all recovering addicts seemed to have after parting company with their very best friend.

The meeting that day was about forgiveness – forgiving yourself primarily for past mistakes and accepting forgiveness from loved ones who had also been the victims of addiction. Each member was to put forward one example of where exercising forgiveness could benefit them. Janine spoke up first and, sitting with her elbows on her knees and her head resting in her hands, she revealed quite an interesting part of herself.

'My sister has always been the weak one. She always ended up being the one who did the washing up or took the blame for our childhood mistakes. She was used to being dumped by men for someone better looking. I even got off with a couple of her boyfriends because, well, I could.'

Jake looked at the floor – he didn't want Janine to see what he thought of that. 'Anyway, it was when I was at my worst with the drink, just basically being a fucking nightmare, she was always the one who came to my aid. Not me mum and dad, they were done with me at eighteen, and all my friends or so-called friends thought 'drunk Janine' was a right laugh. But Michelle, she never gave up on me, even when she had her kids or marriage problems. She even went through breast cancer in her thirties. Not once did she ever ignore my call.'

The silence in the circle was necessary – anyone who was lucky enough to have a Michelle in their lives knew how valuable that relationship was. For a moment, everybody thought about that one person who always picked up the phone to them no matter what.

Janine dabbed her eyes with her boiler suit sleeve, her soft side showing temporarily to the group. 'I want to forgive myself for putting my sister through the ringer. I'm trying to make it up to her. I've become the man of the house, she needs me right now, so for once it's me that's looking out for her. Thanks for listening,' Janine signed off, opening the floor to anyone wanting to speak next.

Emboldened by Janine's show of vulnerability, Jake decided to open up and share. 'I want to forgive myself for what I put my ex through. Her name was Nicky.'

'Is she dead?' Dean asked innocently.

'No, her name is still Nicky – it's just that we're not together any more. I loved her, I still love her, but as I'm sure we all know, we do bad shit when we drink, and I did some shit.'

'Did you hit her?' Dean asked, becoming more and more comfortable as the hour went by.

'Christ no, why would you think that?'

'Err Dean, we don't interrupt here,' Keith schooled Dean quickly before he made any more inappropriate comments.

'I just didn't respect her, I took her for granted, I left it too late to get sober, and now she's with someone else. He's not a drinker, so I guess she's traded up, but he's not right for her.' Jake winced and massaged his forehead. 'I know she'll be thinking that he's as good as she can get, and that's my fault. I never ever meant to hurt her, but I did. So, I want to forgive myself for that, and I want her to forgive me, but I can't tell her or speak to her—'

'Why not? Is there a restraining order in place?' Dean blurted out. He then thumped his own leg. 'Sorry, sorry, I can't help it.'

Jake gave him a forgiving nod. 'Because she's moved on, and because she's getting married, and mainly because she's pregnant.'

After the meeting, Jake stood in the doorway of the church hall smoking, as most of the members did. People generally needed five minutes before they got into their cars to decompress or process, or because they didn't want their cars stinking of cigs. Janine saluted Jake as she drove her van out of the car park – it was a friendly gesture, and Jake thought that perhaps she wasn't so bad after all.

Dean made a point of approaching Jake before he left. 'Look, I just wanted to say I'm sorry for butting in, I was a bit nervous really and didn't quite understand how it all worked.'

Jake smiled. 'Don't worry about it, it's only my second time. Well done for coming.' Dean sighed; Jake could feel from his demeanour that he'd had a hell of a time. Hopefully, as it did with Jake, tonight could have made him feel just a little less lonely. Dean thought for a moment, wondering whether it was okay to comment, but he went with it.

'This girl of yours, the pregnant one.' Jake nodded. 'Well, just because she's pregnant or getting married doesn't mean you can't be her friend – on her terms, of course. She may be glad of it, you have a lot of history together.'

'You think that's okay? I'm not sure it's the right thing to do. I could make things worse.'

'Well, not only did I drink my way through my first marriage, but I also then left my wife for a man. You can imagine the fallout.' Dean smiled, and so did Jake. 'I wasn't very popular for a while, but then, as time went by, my ex-wife and I became friends, really good friends. She's over there in the Mini. We're going out for a meal tonight.'

Jake glanced over a little red Mini Cooper – a glamorous lady with an extraordinary amount of jewellery sat patiently nodding her head to what sounded like jazz.

'Just the two of you?'

'No, her partner and my husband are meeting us there – we do this once a month.'

'That won't be easy – the restaurant, I mean. Dinners out sober can be a bit much at first.'

Dean chewed his lower lip. 'You think we'd be better getting a takeaway?'

'This early on in your journey, I think you'd be better getting into bed with some tea and toast.'

'Thanks for the advice, Jake.'

'Ditto.'

Jake watched as Dean's ex-wife got out of the car and almost ran to the passenger side to help her ex-husband into the car. He still wore a neck brace and winced as he lowered himself into the car. She then kissed him on the cheek once he was strapped in and shut the door gently, like you would for a toddler.

Jake pulled up outside Phil's Plaice where, according to the neon sign, 'you can taste the ocean in every bite'. He decided not to point out that the North Sea was littered with Pampers, Tampax and crude oil. Nevertheless, it was a popular venue and Jake waited in the queue for twenty minutes before getting served by a sour-faced young woman.

'Is it true your Leanne is emigrating to Spain?' the chippy girl questioned Jake as he waited for his order.

'Not quite,' Jake said abruptly. Such nosiness was becoming very frequent these days.

'Well, that's what she's been telling folk.' The plump white girl with braids was clearly envious, and quite put-out that somebody was getting out of town.

'She's going to work abroad if that's what you mean.'

'Alright for some – wonder what she did to land that?'

Jake took the two hot parcels from the counter before placing down a twenty-pound note. 'She's always been destined for something beyond this. Sometimes you just outgrow a place.'

Jake smirked as he walked away from the open-mouthed Lancashire Rasta wannabe. He could say what he liked about his own sister, but nobody outside the family could. They were the rules!

Jake's phone rang as he made his way back up the hill to the house – it was a number he didn't recognise. Normally he would have let it go to voicemail, but just in case it was Nicky, he answered.

'Jakey boy.' He immediately recognised the deep voice and thick accent.

'Janine, hi, is everything okay?'

'Don't worry, it's not an emergency or owt. I just wanted to have a talk about the elephant in the room.'

'What elephant?'

'Well, the fact that you're looking after Martin and I'm doing the same for our Michelle.'

Jake rolled his eyes – Janine clearly had no idea what elephant in the room meant, as they had already talked at length about it.

'Go on then, what you thinking?'

Janine paused. 'I think we should meet up. I can't talk for long now because I need to get the boys to bed, and our Michelle is out and about.'

Jake was startled – meet up with the Doberman? Was that even safe?

'Erm okay, well I'm free tomorrow evening – you can come to the house if you want, as Martin's taking the boys out.'

'Okay, see you at seven. Can you cook something? I'll be coming straight from work.'

'Bloody hell, do you want a bath running too?' This woman was very direct. 'Will you be wearing the boiler suit?' Jake asked cheekily.

'Wait and see!' she said with a wink in her voice.

'I'll text you my address.'

'No need! Your mum has given that to me already.'

'Really!'

'Yes, really.'

'Wow.'

'Yes, wow. See you tomorrow.'

Jake thought it best to keep the fact that the rat-catching Doberman was coming to dinner the following evening to himself. Martin was scared to death of her, and he may have spiralled. So that evening they ate fish and chips, and discussed Blackburn Rovers.

Jake popped in at his parents the following morning, mainly to stop them 'popping' into his house. A team of lads had arrived at eight a.m. to remove radiators before getting started on the big job of knocking down the lounge wall to open the entrance hall and merge the two rooms into one. Di would not agree with knocking down anything, and her vision didn't go beyond 'dust'. She would have tried to stop the builders, possibly attempting to rebuild the wall whilst cleaning the surfaces. Di and Alf didn't need to see all of the process – the end result was when they would be happy.

'Oooh, I'm glad you're here, I've got some food for your freezer.'

Di had her hair in a turban after doing her own roots, and she still had her nightie on.

Jake grimaced. 'Oh god, what food?'

'Well, grumpy, I made a big batch of stew and dumplings last night and I've bagged some up just for you.' She waddled over to the freezer and heaved a huge bag from the bottom shelf.

'Don't forget the upside-down cake,' Alf shouted from the conservatory.

'Oh yes and I made a pineapple cake and I put a few portions on one side for your pudding.' She retrieved this from the middle shelf.

How old would Jake be when he had the balls to tell Di he didn't like stew, dumplings or cake, and certainly not in bags from the freezer. Still, he thought, he could palm it off on Marnie – she was used to this muck.

'Thanks, Mum. By the way, I've got something to ask you.' Jake made eye contact with her so he could gauge just exactly what his mum was playing at. 'Mum, why did you give my number *and* my address to Janine?'

Di went a little red and bustled about the kitchen, thinking up a good enough excuse. 'She's a lovely girl, that Janine, very practical, good with her hands. Okay, she had a bit of time of it when she was younger, but she's a strong lass—'

Jake stopped her. 'You're not suggesting that I date this...' he paused, thinking of the right thing to say, 'this handyman slash woman.'

Di got flustered. 'No, no, I just suggested that it could be a good idea if you put your heads together about Martin and Michelle. It's not right him living with you, it's not on.'

'Mum, for fuck's sake, just leave it, will you? Stop interfering.'

Alf put his crossword down and poked his head around the door with a biro behind his ear. 'Oi sunshine, watch your language. Your mother's only trying to help.'

'I don't need help, Dad; Martin is fine with me, thank you very much.'

'He's not fine, Jake, though, is he? He's a wazzock, he's going to take you down with him.' Alf went back to his puzzle; he'd said his bit, and Di would be happy with that. But Jake was not prepared for them to railroad him into anything, and he stayed as loyal as he could.

'He's family – you have both told me that family comes first. I'm helping my cousin, your nephew, you should be glad of that.'

Alf and Di said nothing more on the subject that day – they were contradicting themselves completely, but having Jake around after years of him not being there was a gift, a very special gift. Seeing him well and having him clean was so close to their hearts that nothing, not even family, must take him away again. And yes, Di did think that Janine could be a nice romantic option for Jake – she was a good, no-nonsense Northern lass and she didn't drink alcohol. On a dating app, Janine would have been at the top of the list. Yes, perhaps she was not the delicate little flower that Nicky had been, but middle-aged addicts needed to pick their partners wisely – a straight-talking local girl with childbearing hips was Di's idea of daughter-in-law heaven.

After an hour of *Homes Under the Hammer* that Alf had recorded, insisting it could be a crash-course in renovation, Jake said, 'Dad, this is a joke. There is not one decent result across three episodes.'

Alf frowned at him. 'What about the mid-terrace? It's like a bleeding show home now.'

'No, Dad. A new breadboard and an L-shaped sofa hasn't added any value whatsoever.'

'What about the new downstairs toilet? That will have doubled its market value.' He was referring to an under-the-stairs cubby hole that had been 'transformed' into a state-of-the-art cloakroom.

Jake laughed. 'You can't even stand up in there, you'd have to kneel down to do a wee.' Alf chuckled in agreement – it was very small, and Dion Dublin had smacked his massive forehead on the door surround as he'd tried to look inside.

'That Martin Roberts would never fit in there, size of his arse.' Alf paused the telly on the presenter from behind and pointed. 'He'd need to go to the upstairs one or he'd be wedged in.' Jake and Alf sniggered together like a couple of children.

'Still, it's good for the kiddies and short people,' Alf said.

'Put another one on, Dad, let's look for more mistakes.'

And so, father and son watched daytime telly together, ripping the piss out of builders, sparkies and clueless presenters, and had a thoroughly good laugh. It was a nice morning – quite unexpectedly fun. It had been a long time since Jake had really laughed – not forced fun, not with effort, just being in the moment and being himself.

Once he got back to the house and consumed two large black coffees, he decided to send the email he had been composing in his head.

Hi Nicky,

It's been a while. I wanted to reach out and say hello, and to let you know I have been thinking about you. I saw Lucas last week, and he said you were happy and in a relationship. I'm really pleased to hear that; you deserve somebody to treat you well. We have such a long history together that I think it would be a shame not to keep in touch. I live back in the North now near my parents' – I bought an old house and I'm renovating it.

Sober life is going well, my old ways are well behind me and I think it would be great if we could catch up at some point just for old times' sake. There's no pressure, just me offering the hand of friendship if that's something you would consider.

Hope all is well with you, and I hope to hear from you soon.

Jake x

Jake pressed send. Dean was right – there was nothing wrong with attempting to be friendly, and it didn't have to be anything more than that. It couldn't be anything more as she was having a baby and getting married. But if he wanted forgiveness in any form from the lovely Nicky, then he would need to be the one to make the first move. What's the worst that could happen? She could ignore it, or she could tell him to piss off – either way at least he'd tried.

Jake wasn't sure what he wanted from this approach – had she been single and unpregnant, then perhaps they could have rekindled things in his lovely house away from dirty London. But that couldn't happen, not now. That gave him a strange sense of relief. He had spent a long time imagining their reconciliation and now, knowing that was basically impossible, it allowed him to mentally move on. His head was clearing, and the words 'in recovery' made more and more sense.

Jake had toyed with the idea of serving up the bag of dumplings for Janine that evening, but even though he wasn't out to impress her in any way, he just couldn't bring himself to slop it onto plates and pass it off as his own. For this reason, he bought a gastro fish pie for two from the supermarket and some fresh greens – all that washed down with a bottle of Schloer – and that would do.

Martin was borrowing Jake's car to pick the boys up and take them out. He was quite excited and ironed his shirt for the occasion. 'I'm pretty nervous, why am I nervous?' he asked Jake, tucking the shirt tightly into his dated jeans.

'Well, they're the most important things in your life, mate, they mean everything right?' Martin nodded and smoothed his hair behind his ears in the mirror. 'Well, will I do, squire?'

Jake patted his shoulder. 'It's not a date, it's your sons. Calm down.'

'What if Michelle's turned them against me? I bet that shithead Janine's been in their ear. She's never liked me; she always wanted me out. Have you seen the size of her hands?'

Jake handed him his coat and the car keys to the Land Rover. 'Martin, go take your kids for some spicy wings and talk about footie, tell them you love them and that you'll always be there for them. And then, Martin...' Martin looked at Jake anxiously. 'And then, always be there for them.'

Martin nodded. 'Right, right. I got this. See you later, should be back at ten-ish.'

A strange feeling came over Jake as he set the table. Not jealously, no. Maybe some form of envy that two teenage boys – yes, little tearaways, and from what Jake remembered, had the manners of feral piglets, but still – two little people who probably thought Martin was the main man. He doubted Martin would ever find another soul in his lifetime who would think of him as anything other than just a big tit.

Janine arrived bang on time. Jake watched as she got out of her van and stared in amazement at The Coach House. He often forgot how impressive it was, and only when others took the time to take it all in did he remember just how lovely it was.

Janine cut quite the figure in the distance. She was extremely tall, and Jake wasn't used to leggy women; Nicky had been 'petite' at Karen Millen, and she used a stool when she hung out the washing. Di and Leanne were also classed as short – in fact, one time when she had worn her dark blue anorak with the hood up, a lollipop lady had grabbed Di's hand and said, 'Come on, son, you'll be late for school.'

'Some place,' she said, nodding as she reached the front door. 'I could see myself living up here.'

Jake frowned. 'Okay, erm, not sure what that means.'

Janine bustled passed him and sat down at the kitchen table without being asked. 'I think your mum has planned for us to get together – two dry drunks living on the hill. I have to say, after seeing the house, I'm in – let's do this, tiger.' Janine squeezed Jake's arm in a flirty manner.

Jake spluttered and stepped back.

'I'm sorry about Mum, but I'm not looking for a relationship at all, Janine, not with anyone. I'm very sorry if you've wasted your time coming here, but I'm not in, not at all...'

Janine put her hand up to stop Jake from talking, and she started to laugh.

'You think I'm serious, don't you?'

Jake reddened, realising he'd been a little hasty. 'Err, no. I was joking, actually,' he said, as it dawned on him that he'd just been had.

'You actually believed that I'm up here for a piece of that ass.' Janine was roaring now.

'Oh shut up, Janine – stop it.' Jake was thoroughly embarrassed – he didn't rate himself as all that, but he did consider himself to be at least a bit of a catch.

'London boys with more money than sense do not float my boat, I'm afraid.'

Jake quickly changed the subject. 'Fish pie, do you?'

'I'll eat anything. Not fussy.' Janine put her big boots on the chair across from her and made herself completely at home with her hands behind her head. She wouldn't be doing that when Jake's new furniture arrived – she'd be lucky to get past the porch, Jake thought to himself.

'So, how's Michelle?' Jake was suddenly keen to get this discussion underway, and his dinner guest out of the door as soon as possible.

'She's alright, you know. She's stronger this time, but the boys are getting wilder by the day.'

'Because Martin's not there to keep them in line?' Jake asked, presuming Martin had the same authority as his own father had when he and Leanne were growing up.

'Nah, they're hitting the hormonal phase and pushing boundaries – Martin couldn't control them either. But it's easier when there's two adults.'

'So, what you saying here, that Martin should go home?'

Janine sighed. 'If only it were that easy. Our Michelle seems to have... how can I put it? Gone off the rails a bit.'

'In what way?'

'She joined Tinder and literally went for it.'

'I see.'

'The way things are going, and on account that she is not a good judge of character, my prediction is they'll have a new daddy in months – if not weeks.'

Jake put a spoonful of peas next to the fish pie, and set it down in front of Janine.

'Martin won't like that, not one bit.'

'Yeah well, it's his own doing – he's pushed the girl too far. Years she's put up with his shit, and something's snapped inside her. She's eating men for breakfast, and she's out nearly every night.'

'So, what do we do for the best?' Jake didn't know Michelle well – she was just always in the background rolling her eyes. This was the first time he'd been forced to consider her as an actual person.

'I can't believe I'm saying this, but Martin needs to get his act together, be there for the boys and try, if it's possible, to get her to forgive him. But this time it's going to be different – she's seen what's out there and she's changed.'

'And the kids, how are they responding to this new arrangement?'

Janine snorted. 'Huh, she leaves them with me mostly, but if I'm not there, they're up all night on the PlayStations and doing fuck-all homework. I've been called into school twice this week.'

'Trouble?'

'Farting in carrier bags, putting magic mushrooms into people's sandwiches. Standard stuff, you know.'

Jake gasped; standards were pretty low at 'Degenerate High', it would seem.

'Look, I know I changed the locks when she first kicked him out, but I thought she'd miss him after a week or so. Now, she's talking about getting an eye lift and her downstairs tightened up.'

Jake winced. 'Wow, why?'

'Two natural births, both with heads like pumpkins, I imagine it's pretty roomy down there.' Janine laughed to herself. 'Our Michelle's obliterated vagina has always been a source of amusement for our family.'

'I meant the eyes, to be honest,' Jake said uncomfortably.

'She's absolutely knackered, Jake! She's got a bone idol pervert of a husband, she works in a nursery with toddlers all day every day, they've never really got any money so it's all just a struggle. Her eyelids tell that whole sorry story.'

Jake was suddenly glad that he only had himself to look after – the whole thing sounded exhausting.

Janine dabbed her mouth with the corner of her sleeve. 'Listen,

I owe our Michelle; she's been there for me, and I'm happy to step in for a while, but I can't see this ending well for any of 'em. The grass might seem greener now, but she'll only end up with another dickhead. Sometimes, it's better the dickhead you know.'

Jake played with his fish pie; it was a little dry and not particularly appetising. Janine, on the other hand, wolfed hers down in a matter of minutes.

'You not eating that?' she asked gruffly, looking at his full plate. Jake shook his head. 'Slide it over here – waste not want not.'

Jake watched as she ploughed into a second meal - the woman was a machine.

'I'll encourage Martin to be more present, and maybe we should try to strategically get them together.'

'Good plan!' Janine said with her mouth full, spitting peas and mash onto the table. She slammed down her cutlery once the last lump of mash went in, wiped her mouth with a tea towel and gathered up her stuff.

As she headed for the front door, Janine knelt in the hallway and stroked the old floorboards. 'What's the plan with this?' she asked, dragging her knuckles backwards along the grain.

'I think it needs replacing, to be honest, I don't think it can be saved as some of it is rotting.' Jake had considered trying to restore the original floor, but it was going to be a real 'ball ache' according to a joiner who had reluctantly given his opinion whilst measuring up for another job.

She gazed lovingly at the floorboards. 'Wood is my thing, my guilty pleasure. If this were my place, I'd have that floor back to its original state – well, almost. You just need someone who gives a shit, Jake.'

'I was told I should replace it with a new oak floor – it would still look authentic. Well, that's what the guy told me anyway.'

Janine tutted. 'Why would you want to remove such a huge part of history? Imagine all of the people who have entered this house and walked these boards. If it can be saved, it should be saved.'

Jake agreed – he liked old stuff and, to be fair, the joiner who had given his opinion was eighteen stone, give or take. He was just a lazy lump who only liked the easy jobs.

'Well, can you do it then? Can you take that on, you know, have you got the time?' Jake asked tentatively, hoping he wouldn't regret it. Janine was definitely an acquired taste.

'I'll check my diary, and don't expect mate's rates; I don't care for that,' she said, trying to hide her smile.

Jake patted her on the shoulder to seal the deal. 'Okay, the job's yours – make sure you do it justice.'

Janine looked in the rear-view mirror just before she drove away and watched as Jake politely waited until she was off the drive before shutting the door. She smiled – well, this was a new emotion. Something about Jake made her feel shy and a bit silly; she felt self-conscious about her appearance around him and his sensitivity was something that she had never expected but happened to like.

His cousin, however, was a beer-swilling gobshite, and although he probably had a good heart somewhere behind those man boobs, she much preferred a guy with more depth.

Lucy O

There had been no reply from Nicky after forty-eight hours, and Jake had checked his inbox as many times, if not more. He was a bit deflated, and wondered if she was intentionally ignoring him or whether she was so busy with her new relationship that she simply didn't have the time to respond. Perhaps this tosser named Beau had deleted the email before she could get to it. Jake was tormented by the whole situation.

Martin stormed in for breakfast – he threw a bowl of beans into the microwave and slammed the door with his back to Jake. Jake snapped out of his daze, and sensed that all was not well at Pervert HQ.

'How was it then, mate, seeing the boys?'

Martin took a while to answer, breathing heavily whilst watching the beans spin around for a few seconds.

'How did it go? How did it go?' he said menacingly. 'Well, Jake, it was all going so well until...' Martin buttered his burnt toast aggressively, struggling to get the words out.

'Until what?'

'Until Tommy, my oldest, told me that this was the second time he'd been to this cunting Wing Stop chicken place.'

Jake was taken aback – was this really worth such a dark reaction?

'So what if they've been before? It's just fast food in Manchester, not Disneyland.'

Martin sat down with his toast on beans – he'd placed the toast on top of the beans, a very unusual way to eat this meal.

'They've been before with "Mum's friend Ste" and it would seem this Ste has been taking my kids for chicken wings without my knowledge or permission. *And...* Ste slept over last week, *and* Ste drives a Golf TDI.' Martin shovelled the food into his mouth, leaving orange sauce on his chin and down his white t-shirt. He really did look a pathetic sight.

'Okay, so Michelle's got a "friend" – is it serious? What do you know about this guy?'

'I know he's a wanker,' Martin mumbled. 'Ste this, Ste that. I've only been gone a fortnight, and already she's dropped her knickers. I never thought she'd do this – I thought we would go the distance.'

Jake could somewhat relate; he was going through something similar that was all his own doing, but he didn't have a family, and that surely trumped everything else. 'Right, well, you'll just have to win her back, won't you? Get yourself sorted out and go talk to her, tell her you're sorry and want another chance.'

'He works at the gym, Jake. David fucking Lloyd.'

'What relevance does that have?'

'He's apparently been using the boys as dumbbells, and doing sit-ups with the dog sat on his chest. I can't even take the bins out without coughing up brown stuff.'

'Sounds like a right dick.' Jake offered his support in Martin-speak.

Martin burped loudly before sharing his final thought of the morning. 'A sportscar-driving, dumbbell-lifting, woman-stealing prick.'

'Why don't we pop in later today? It's still your house. You could take some flowers for Michelle, maybe something for the boys?' Jake and Janine's plan might need to be executed swiftly before this Ste got his feet any further under the table, and his Golf any further up the drive.

'But I can't get in – the locks have been changed, remember?'

'Do you have a doorbell?'

'Yeah.'

'Well, let's start with that – we need to go in gently.'

'And Janine? What if she's on the door with her big hands?'

'I'm sure I can get around her, Martin. Go have a bath, and wipe those beans off your chin.'

Martin looked at Jake with gratitude – he needed this, he needed a friend. Normally he'd have just gone and had a few pints and felt up a barmaid, but Jake's advice was what he needed to hear.

> **Jake:** Janine, we're coming over this afternoon. He knows about someone called Ste! Can you make sure she's there?
> **Janine:** Come at 5, we'll all be in. Good work.
> **Jake:** Okay, see you later.
> **Janine:** BTW, I've been up all night. Was that pie in date?
> **Jake:** Yes, it was! The fact you ate mine too is probably the problem. Reduce portion sizes going forward.
> **Janine:** I'll cook for you next time – there's some furry pork I've been saving for a rainy day.

Jake chuckled, but didn't respond to the last message – he needed to concentrate on Martin and Michelle. Besides, Marnie was arriving the following day and he hadn't even sorted her room or done any shopping for her arrival. He remembered that she ate plain food without too many colours, so he would need to do a food shop to accommodate this rather bizarre diet.

He and Martin finally got into the car at four p.m. and were stopping at a supermarket called Booths en route to Martin's old place.

'Eh, it's super-posh, this shop. It's like that other place you like, Waitrose. You'll break the bank in there, you know.'

Martin looked very presentable – his clothes were clean, his shoes polished, and he stank of some sort of Lynx to high heaven.

'I'm only getting a few bits for Marnie, she's arriving tomorrow. You'll need to curb your swearing and wear clothes at all times.'

Martin nodded. Jake had, on more than one occasion, caught sight of a naked Martin wandering the landing looking for towels or his phone, and he'd found it hard to eat after witnessing that.

'Your Leanne's a cheeky cow, eh – buggering off to Spain and leaving her daughter with you.'

'To be honest, Martin, I've not been a good brother or uncle, so maybe it's my time to help out – it's not like I don't have the time, and she's a nice kid.'

'Fair enough. Hey grab me some Silk Cut, two Daim bars and a bunch of flowers, will you?' He handed Jake a twenty from his wallet through the car window.

'You not coming in?'

'Nah, it's full of snobby twats in there, and I definitely don't want to bump into any of the Halfords lot.'

Jake left him in the car and went shopping alone. Booths was a pleasant experience, quite a civilised supermarket with some good quality food and wine. Jake was faced with an offer on a delicate Riesling as he wandered towards the deli. He momentarily imagined a slightly sweet but very crisp German wine being poured into a chilled glass, and wondered which cheese would go well with that – perhaps a smoked cheddar with an onion pickled in balsamic would do this nectar justice. He looked at the elegant bottle with the long neck as if it were Elizabeth Hurley, and then he gave his head a shake and carried on with his shopping.

It was still there, the booze monster – he hadn't killed it yet. Jake did, however, decide to purchase the cheese and the onions, but popped a bottle of sparkling water and a lemon into his trolley – he would at least allow himself to pretend. A small blonde girl wearing a white overcoat and a white hat was restocking cheese whilst bobbing her head to something on her AirPods.

'Got any smoked cheddar?' Jake mouthed to her over the glass counter. She took one of her headphones out and lifted her head.

'You what?'

Jake was taken aback for two reasons – first, her terrible customer service skills, and second, the fact that he knew her – in fact, the whole country knew her.

Lucy O immediately recognised her old rehab neighbour and smiled. Although life for her was at the rockiest of bottoms, she recalled Jake being fairly tolerant of her, and him being kind to her before he left.

'Hey, Jake, isn't it?'

Jake nodded. 'You remembered my name! I'm sorry, I really am, but I can't quite remember—'

'Lucy O.'

'O?'

'It's actually O'Callaghan, but when I got *Corrie*, we decided to shorten it.'

'So, how you been? What are you doing here?'

Lucy O gestured to the counter. 'Currently selling cheese for a living – how the mighty have fallen,' she grinned. 'What brings you here, Jake? The last time I saw you, we were in Somerset.'

Jake leaned onto his trolley. She was better-looking than he remembered her, but she had been mostly crying or shouting at The Meadows.

'I left London, sold my house, bought a house up here to be near my family, and I'm doing everything I can to stay sober. That Riesling display didn't help.'

'I have to walk past that every day, and the flavoured gin – it's a tough gig, this one. The closest I get to happiness is a nibble of Lancashire Crumbly.'

'So, no more acting?' Jake asked. He had gathered she was quite the big deal in the soap world at one point – although that was because she had told him during one of her momentous breakdowns during group therapy.

'I couldn't get any work. I have to let the dust settle according to my agent… my name is mud at the moment.'

'I'm sorry to hear that. Are you living close by?'

'I live with my nan, about ten minutes from here. It's not ideal, but it's my only option 'til they come to their senses and write me back in.'

'Didn't you die? Drowned in the bath, wasn't it?'

Lucy scoffed. 'That was the plan, but they let me off with severe brain damage and put me into a facility, so I could reappear at any time.'

Jake laughed – this was a world he had never even touched on, and it all sounded quite amusing. 'You should come to the addiction meetings in my village – they're surprisingly quite helpful.'

Lucy frowned. 'Yeah, I've avoided stuff like that, what with me being famous. Might meet a super-fan.' Jake was under no illusion that Lucy could indeed meet a fan, but she was no Helen Mirren – something he recalled from rehab.

'Meetings are anonymous, a safe space – give it a try, you never know, it could help. Anyway, it's more likely you'll get recognised by a cheese enthusiast.'

Right on cue, an elderly couple walked by the counter, whispering and nudging each other childishly.

'See, told you,' Jake said. 'They're already in the building.'

Lucy handed Jake a piece of paper and a pen. 'Put your number on there, I'll have a think about it and let you know.'

Jake finished his shopping deep in thought – what a small world it was when you could meet your rehab neighbour at the cheese counter of your local deli, not to mention the fact she was kind of flirty and some sort of celebrity. Perhaps life in the darkest corner of the North wasn't so boring after all. He put his shopping in the boot, and then gave Martin a reason to wish he'd gone in with him after all.

'I just met Lucy O! In the shop serving cheese.'

Martin perked right up. 'No way, the actual Lucy O?'

Jake nodded. 'Yes, I sort of know her, from... London.' He was careful not to let his mouth run away with him as he remembered the code of anonymity.

'You know her? Well, you kept that quiet, Jesus. Wait 'til I tell Michelle. Is she still fit?'

Jake thought for a while. Was she fit? Perhaps she was to most men, but she wore a hell of a lot of make-up, and she was a bit on the false side. 'She's pretty, I guess, and she's got great teeth.'

Martin snorted. 'Who cares about the teeth? God, you can be a freak at times.'

'Why, 'cause I'm not leering at her chest and slobbering all over her? You're the freak actually, Martin.'

The insult was wasted on Martin, as he was already planning a way in.

'I'll go in this week and buy some cheddar, maybe she's looking for a local man.'

Jake groaned. 'Martin, we're going to get Michelle back, remember? This is precisely the type of shit that got you kicked out in the first place.'

'I'm only having a laugh, but Lucy O, mate, she's a celeb off the telly.' He punched Jake's arm in sheer excitement.

Jake was starting to understand why Michelle was exhausted with this man and why Ste from David Lloyd had taken his place. There was zero chance of Lucy being interested in a father of two with a beer belly and a sexual harassment case hanging over his head but, just like Lucy, Martin thought a hell of a lot of himself.

They pulled up bang on time, and Martin did some deep breathing before he got out of the car. Jake handed him a bunch of white roses along with the Daim bars, and they headed towards the front door of the terrace with a conservatory on the back. It looked like a proper family home with bikes leaning up against the wall and muddy trainers outside the front door. Jake rang the bell and Martin hovered behind him as Janine opened the door.

'Oh, it's you – what do you want?'

'I want to speak to Michelle and I want to see my kids,' Martin announced, almost squaring up to her.

'Are you going to be a cock?'

'No, are you?'

Janine stifled a smirk. 'In you come, and no pissing around.'

Martin nodded – this was much easier than he had anticipated. Janine winked at Jake and they followed Martin into the lounge, where two scruffy lads ate waffles covered in chocolate sauce on their laps whilst watching a huge television. The boys could have been twins, only one was much bigger – they both had unruly ginger hair and freckly noses.

They barely looked up from the telly.

'Alright, Dad. Who's your mate?'

'He's not my mate – it's my cousin Jake. You remember Uncle Jake?' The boys looked at one another and shook their heads, quickly getting back to their tea. 'It's Di and Alf's son, Leanne's brother. Jake, this is Tommy and Dylan.'

Jake put his thumbs up – he wasn't really sure what else constituted a hello with teenage boys. They both looked confused – perhaps they didn't remember the drunk from London who only showed up when absolutely necessary.

'Where's your mum?'

Tommy pointed to the ceiling. 'Up there in the bath, getting ready.'

'Ready for what?'

'She's going pictures,' Dylan said quite innocently – neither boy seemed perturbed by this new arrangement.

'Is she going with her new friend?' Martin was getting stressed and uncomfortable; this was his territory, and after just a few weeks, he felt like an outsider.

'Dunno, you'd better ask her,' Dylan said, without taking his eyes off the screen.

Janine leaned against the wall, arms folded, waiting for Martin to make some sort of manly move.

'You're loving this, aren't you?' he said to her nastily, wanting Janine to be the reason his partner was upstairs shaving her legs for a man with a Golf TDI.

'Now listen up, I don't want these lads to come from a broken home, no matter what I think of you, Martin,' she hissed quietly. 'Come into the kitchen – we shouldn't do this here.'

The kitchen was, as you'd imagine, very lived-in. A pair of football boots sat on the dining table, drip-drying on a copy of the *Sun*. Behaviour charts covered the fridge door, and there were more sad face stickers than anything else – although on Monday the fourth of September, somebody had gained a smiley face for getting dressed. Janine flicked the kettle on and opened a steaming dishwasher to retrieve some cups, and then she smelt the milk before making three cups of tea.

'This Ste, is it serious?' Jake initiated.

'He's been the most consistent,' she said without emotion.

'There's more? More Stes?' Martin put his head in his hands. 'Fuck's sake, she's a fast mover.'

'There's been a Mark, a Ben and an Imran, but it's Ste who seems to have taken a real shine to her and the boys.'

Martin looked through the door at his sons, one of whom was licking his plate. 'Fucking hell, it's too late, I've lost them all.'

'Give her the flowers and try and talk to her – maybe she'll go to the cinema with you instead.' Jake pointed to the bunch of quite lovely fresh roses. Martin threw them into the kitchen sink.

'No, I'm done. All I did was flirt – I never took it any further. She's just gone too far.'

Janine pulled herself up to her full height. 'Listen, you plonker, you've pushed her to this. She doesn't think you care, you're actually acting like you don't care, do something!'

'Like what? She's already given herself to some bloke – makes me sick.'

Janine retaliated immediately. 'Hang on, you moved straight into Loser Towers, you didn't even put up a fight.'

Jake's eyebrows shot up. 'Loser Towers? Is that my house you're referring to?'

Janine put her hands up. 'It's just something Michelle calls it. You know, two grown men shacked up together, neither with a job.'

'Charming!' Jake said, mildly embarrassed.

Without even looking at her, Martin stood and zipped up his coat. 'Let's go home, Jake – this was a mistake.' He walked back through to the living room, handed the Daim bars to each of the boys, who didn't even say thank you.

Jake turned quickly to Janine. 'Look, I'll get inside his head – don't worry, this isn't over.'

Janine rolled her eyes. 'Martin is as useless as I've always thought and now, I'm having to hold things together when I really have better things to do – one being to concentrate on my sanity.'

Jake nodded and turned to leave, but she put a hand on his forearm and pulled him back. 'Look,' she said, her tone softer now, 'he needs to fight for her. I know our Michelle, and she doesn't want to be fannying around with all these Tinder twats – she wants to feel wanted. God knows she deserves that.'

Just as they reached the front door, Michelle made an appearance at the top of the stairs. She'd aged significantly since Martin's fortieth; she was always sort of plain and mousy but now she looked a bit deflated, having lost quite a bit of weight and gained rather a lot of wrinkles. However, Michelle was doing her best and wore a halter-neck top with a pair of cropped jeans and high patent heels.

This was date night, alright, Northern style.

'Martin, Jake, ya alright?' Michelle teetered down the steep stairs, clinging to the bannister for balance. She was used to wearing slippers.

'What the frig are you wearing?' Martin's mouth was wide open as his ex-missus applied a dark red lippy in the hallway mirror.

'None of your business what I'm wearing, what are you even doing here?' Her voice was tired; she sounded too exhausted to be going out.

Martin looked her up and down in utter disgust. 'I just came to give the boys some chocolate.'

'Last of the big spenders – why don't you take 'em to Clarks and get them some new shoes, do something useful for a change.'

'How can they need new shoes already? We only just got them a couple of months ago.'

'They stand on the backs and play football in 'em,' Janine said, trying to help.

'Fucking hell, how many times have I told them?' Martin got annoyed. 'You need to get control of them, Michelle, put your foot down.'

Michelle snorted whilst putting on a leather jacket. 'Be great if you "got control" of being a sex pest,' she said. 'See ya boys, bye Janine – don't wait up.' And with that, she tottered down the garden path and got into an electric-blue Golf.

Martin was livid – it was all quite humiliating. His kids ignoring him, their mother putting on her lipstick for another man. She's never been one for make-up when he'd lived there. In fact, getting her out of her brushed cotton pyjamas had been a struggle.

Janine made the 'call me' sign to Jake through the window, and he nodded – their plan had failed, and it was apparent that this would take some grand gestures on Martin's part before Michelle would even consider being civil.

'Mutton dressed as lamb, that's what my old ma would have said. Did you see how tarted up she was?'

Jake stayed silent on the journey home, allowing Martin to sound off the whole way.

'And she's got absolutely no tits; she must have used those chicken fillet things to get her cleavage to look like that. She didn't even bother with a bra with me – she went bare chested like a chubby toddler.'

Jake patted Martin on the back as they went back into the house. It had been sad to witness that nobody at that house seemed to give a shit about Martin's absence.

'Hey, I fancy some cheese and crackers – can I nip down to Booths in your car?'

'No you fucking well can't. There's cheese in the fridge. I know what you're up to.'

Martin smirked. 'I'm only going to introduce myself to Lucy O and let her know if she needs anything, I'm here.'

Jake shook his head, exasperated at Martin's pure stupidity.

'Martin, think of Michelle and Michelle only. Now listen, help me get Marnie's room ready, iron these sheets and bring up six bottles of water.'

Martin reluctantly agreed. He was hurting horribly, and embarrassed that Jake saw first-hand just how unimportant he actually was. Having a chat with a busty soap star would have really cheered him up, but he owed his cousin, and he would do as he was told for now. Still, whilst he completed his chores, he imagined the look on Michelle's face when he was pictured on the front page of the *Sun*, arm in arm with *Corrie*'s fallen angel. He would probably be referred to as 'Lucy's new squeeze', and that would serve Michelle right.

Jake wanted Marnie to feel welcome, so he had purchased some brand-new bedding and some bits and pieces for what would be her home for the next six weeks. He'd bought a little fridge and would fill it with water bottles so she wouldn't have to go downstairs alone in the middle of the night. The Coach House could be a little bit spooky with its windy corridors and creaky old floorboards, and he wanted her to sleep well. The bedding from TK Maxx was no less than Ralph Lauren, and a very reasonable price for the crisp white sheets with satin trim and housewife pillowcases. He also added a heated fleece blanket and some matching cushions to make it cosy.

Jake wasn't sure what a teenage girl used in terms of toiletries, so he'd filled a trolley in Superdrug with all sorts of nonsense – shower foam, deodorant, body spray, and moisturiser. He even bought some little stickers you can put on your spots to reduce inflammation. He left them all on a shelf in the compact en-suite shower room just off the bedroom. Just as he was finishing up, Martin walked in and handed him the badly ironed sheets, and a box of lights covered in cobwebs.

'Stick these around the bed, she'll like it.'

'Christmas lights?'

'Yeah, found them in a cupboard downstairs and they all still work. All the kids have silly lights in their bedrooms these days.'

With that, Jake and Martin Blu-tacked the fairy lights around the bed and set them to pulsate.

> **Lucy**: Hi Jake, Lucy O here. Nice to see you today.
> **Jake**: Hey Lucy, glad you got in touch. The meetings are on a Tuesday, here's the link.
> **Lucy**: I'm going to give it a go – think I need the support and to do something that doesn't involve cheese.
> **Jake**: Ha, I can guarantee there will be no cheese.
> **Lucy**: Was thinking actually, do you want to go for a walk on Sunday? It's my day off cheese. x

(Jake waited for five minutes before replying. He needed to think about this question properly.)

> **Jake**: Actually yes, I think I do. x
> **Lucy**: Okay good. I could meet you outside the post office in your village at ten? (I'll have my nan's dog). x
> **Jake**: I'll see you and your nan's dog on Sunday. x

She wasn't his type – Christ no. She was a heavily made-up, mediocre actress in recovery. His normal type was naturally pretty, low in self-esteem, and willing to take on a 'project'. Lucy O was perhaps a bigger project than even Jake – she seemed far more fragile than he'd ever been, and when it came to prospects, hers were absolute shit.

However, she had something that he liked – not something he could put his finger on, but she was someone he could relate to and, more importantly than anything else, she had just invited him on a date. So yes, there was a stirring in his loins when, for a very long time, he had thought his loins were redundant.

Money Bags

Marnie arrived with both Alf and Di at bang on six p.m. There was no sign of Leanne, who was apparently at the Trafford Centre, looking at maxi dresses. Marnie had her school uniform on – her tie was loose, her shirt wasn't tucked in, and her white socks were splattered with mud and pooled around her ankles.

'You'll need to get this lot washed tomorrow – she's got a clean uniform in her case, but she only has the two sets,' Di sighed as she looked a bedraggled Marnie up and down. 'Look at the state of this little madam.'

'Take your bags up to your room, Marnie, third on the left.'

Marnie smiled at Jake; he could tell she was excited to be breaking free from her grandparents.

'You staying for a brew?'

'Damn right we are, I need a sit down.'

Alf hobbled into the house; he'd had a right day of it with the three high-maintenance women in his life. Driving to Manchester and having to engage in maxi dress discussions was bad enough, but with Di nagging on about her piles every ten minutes, he considered freewheeling into the Thelwall Viaduct. He then had to rush to Degenerate High, where a lollipop lady had tutted at him for revving the engine.

'Most men in their seventies are watching *Tipping Point* with a brandy at this time of the day,' he'd told the woman, who stank of lager and Woodbines.

However, the hardest part of the day was visiting his older

brother, who was riddled with dementia. Alf hated visiting Bert. Firstly, he lived in Burnley – somewhere he avoided if at all possible. Secondly, he just could not forgive his brother for some of the nasty comments he had made about Marnie when she was born. And thirdly – and this was the most selfish reason – seeing his big brother in such a vulnerable state frightened him.

'Oh, I almost forgot, I've got a boot full of bits and bobs for your fridge and freezer, Jake – go out and bring the boxes in will you, love?'

Jake dropped his head – not more food!

'There's a mulligatawny soup that will serve at least ten people.' Di seemed proud of that for some ungodly reason.

'Why would I want soup for ten people, Mum? And mulligatawny of all things...'

'I was just using up all the things in my fridge before we go away and, well, I just got carried away. Before I knew it, I was using three saucepans.'

Alf raised his eyebrows. 'We've already had three bowls; I couldn't face it again this year.'

'There's half a Chinese takeaway too, it's only a couple of weeks old.'

Jake put his hands over his face and groaned. 'A frozen Chinese, Mum? Are you okay?'

'What's wrong with that? We always freeze what we don't eat, don't we, Alf?'

Alf nodded; he wasn't even listening. He was lost in thought, wondering whether an eye twitch was a sign of dementia.

'Oh, and there's some lamb chops, they're a bit freezer-burnt but if you cover 'em in minty jelly, they should be fine – chewy but still fine.'

Just as Jake was mentally planning to flush this haul down the loo, Marnie came into the kitchen and tugged on Alf's arm. 'Grandad, please come and see my room – I need you to see my room.'

Jake winked at Marnie; she deserved to have her own room with her own en-suite, and she deserved to be a little bit spoiled every now and then. Marnie went back upstairs and gave her grandparents the grand tour – they oohed and aahed at her face masks and fairy lights, and lay on the new bedding, stroking the heated blanket. Alf even helped himself to a bottle of Volvic from the mini fridge.

Jake could tell his parents thought he might have gone a little overboard and were worried that Marnie might get used to this 'celebrity treatment' as Di called it. But, with Jake not drinking, she was in safe hands – and with Marnie being completely full-on, Jake would be kept very busy and wouldn't have the chance to even tiptoe off the wagon.

'Listen, we're off to the caravan in the morning, but we're only a phone call away – do you hear me?' Alf said sternly to Marnie. 'No pissing about, okay?'

Marnie nodded, but she wasn't really interested – she was too excited.

'Say it to me out loud, Marnie.'

Marnie stopped what she was doing at looked directly at Alf. 'No pissing about, Grandad.'

'Good girl – on you go.'

And after three cups of tea and an in-depth discussion about the origin of mulligatawny, Alf and Di left for an early night, because apparently you simply must get up at three a.m. to drive to the south coast of England.

As they were about to leave, Alf pulled Jake aside. 'Can you go and visit your uncle this week? I think he could do with seeing a fresh face.'

Jake groaned – he couldn't really be arsed with driving over to Burnley. 'Please, Jake – do that for me, son.'

Alf didn't often ask for favours, and he saw in his old man's eyes this was important to him. 'Okay, I'll go Friday afternoon with Martin, before the school run.'

'Thanks a lot, son. Take care now.'

Jake ordered a Chinese for Marnie, a sort of celebratory dinner for her first night – it was fresh from the takeaway, and not from zip-lock bags in the freezer. They watched two episodes of a strange thing called *Squid Games*, before Marnie took herself up to bed for a mango face mask and a bottle of refrigerated water.

'Moneybags' was a nickname that every single relative from Lancashire had given to Jake when he had once paid for a Chinese banquet for twenty people. It was New Year's Eve, and Jake had been too hungover to return to London after a particularly boozy Christmas at his parents'. He reluctantly attended the Oriental Pearl, a New Year's tradition for the Petersons and their extended family and friends. Five hundred quid was a small price to pay to make up for some of the moronic decisions Jake had made during the festive period of 2009. He'd put his Uncle Bert in a headlock during a game of Twister, which resulted in him having to wear a neck collar well into January. He had also taken a two-year-old Marnie for a walk in her buggy, and ended up leaving her at the urinals of The Admiral Nelson, a small pub in the next village.

It was a phone call to Alf from the landlady that shone a light on that particular mishap. 'There's a brown baby in the gents; I presume it's your Leanne's.' Alf was raging, and it was one of the only times Jake had ever heard his dad raise his voice.

So, once Jake had settled the bill for the set menu at the local Chinese, he'd hoped he would be forgiven but, alas, his Northern relatives just saw this as an opportunity for him to show off. Rather than being grateful for a free six-course meal with Cava, they glanced at each other uncomfortably. Mutters made their way around the table. 'We can pay for our own meals; we're not bloody paupers.' 'Fancy Pants flashing the cash, is he?'

But the one that really stuck was 'Moneybags from London'. Jake felt their disdain, and even though he'd had a skinful, he tried to rectify his decision by announcing that the twenty dinner guests were welcome to pay the tip. It took over fifteen minutes to organise that. People were digging deep into their pockets, while two people went out to their cars to look for change. Eventually, Mr Pang, the owner of the Oriental Pearl, was given £19.28 to share between his staff.

Jake was insulted by the 'Moneybags' nickname. He had worked hard and smart for his cash, and his family – particularly the older ones – thought of him as some sort of pools winner. It wasn't his fault that they hadn't shot for the stars, that they had settled for a beige life with just about enough to cover the mortgage. He didn't want a life that allowed for one holiday a year and a sensible car – he wanted to have options, and to be able to pay a restaurant bill to say sorry for breaking a pensioner's collarbone.

'I can't believe our parents still live in the same houses,' Jake said to Martin as he drove over to Uncle Bert's home.

'Yeah, well, you need to brace yourself – things are very different now.'

'How so?'

Martin offered Jake a cigarette, which he declined – he hated smoking in the car, plus Di would go mental if she knew. She said it made him look like a roughneck.

'Do you mind if I do? This is about to get really fucking stressful.'

Jake could feel Martin tightening up so decided to allow it. 'Hang it out of the window then, will you?'

Martin obliged, just grateful for a fix before the sadness. 'So, my dad, right. Basically, every time I go, there is less of him there. One day I'll go and visit and there will be nothing left of him at all – just a shell.' Martin sucked deeply on his fag and blew a long stream out of the window. 'It doesn't help that he sometimes seems himself, not often and not for long, but he remembers stuff really clearly, and then stupid me thinks he's coming back, that he's getting better.'

Jake had no words of comfort; there was nothing he could say. He would just have to support Martin through this, and be a sounding board when he needed it.

As they approached the familiar cul-de-sac, Martin flicked the cigarette butt out of the window into the face of an unsuspecting cyclist. They pulled up outside the house, and even without going in, you could tell that an ill person lived there. Nothing obvious – just a stale feeling about the place.

'Hello Uncle Bert, how are you?' Jake shouted at Martin's dad, who was sitting in an armchair in his stuffy lounge, twiddling with his hearing aid. Bert was a big man but had withered with age and was frail and bony – his glasses were almost as big as his face, but he still squinted as he attempted to focus on his nephew's face.

'Moneybags, is that you?'

'Yes, it's me – Moneybags.'

'What do you want? You want the money for that Chinese meal, do you?'

Jake laughed. 'No, Uncle Bert, that was my treat.'

'Well sit down then, I'm straining my neck here looking up at you, lanky streak of—'

Martin interrupted. 'I thought it would be nice for you to see Jake, Dad – he's back living up North now, not far from here.'

Bert's hands shook as he sipped his mug of tea. 'Run out of money, lad?' He laughed, his shoulders shook, and he spilt his tea on his lap.

Martin dabbed his trousers with a tea towel, and turned his head back towards Jake, whispering, 'At least he remembers you – that's pretty good.'

'You look well,' Jake shouted again.

Bert scowled; he didn't like bullshit. 'No I don't, you liar. I look horrible, but that's life isn't it, Moneybags? Old age happens to us all.'

Jake felt awkward – he did look absolutely terrible but you don't say that when you visit somebody, do you? Bert was only three years older than Alf, and the physical difference in the brothers was immense. There was an awkward silence; the bungalow smelt of urine and farts, and there was no fresh air since the electric fire was on full blast. Jake tried to continue the conversation.

'It's cold out today – good job you've got your fire to keep you warm.'

Bert looked at the glow of the bars and then back at Jake. 'Are you from the leccy company?'

'No Uncle Bert, it's me, Moneybags… from London.'

Bert hesitated for a while and he squinted at Jake, suddenly remembering who he was talking to.

'Oh, hello son, have you been at school today?'

CHIPS AND GRAVY

Jake looked to Martin for support – he had no experience with this, and he really didn't want to make it any worse.

'Dad, this is Jake, Alf's son – he's come for a visit.'

'Where's your mother, boy?' Bert suddenly blurted out at Martin. 'Tell her I want to go and see Frank Sinatra.'

'She's not here, Dad, she's gone, remember?' Martin said wearily.

'Gone where? I want to go and see Frank Sinatra.'

Martin sat down on the floor in front of the armchair and held one of his dad's skeletal hands. 'Mum's gone to heaven and so has Frank Sinatra, Dad.'

Bert took his glasses off and rubbed his eyes – Jake didn't know where to look. There was a sad pause as Bert processed this information.

'Have they gone there together?'

'Yes, Dad, they're waiting for you.'

'Not long now, our Martin, not long now.'

'Shall I put the CD on now, Dad? Are you ready?'

Uncle Bert slowly stood and leaned one of his elbows onto the mantlepiece as Martin pressed play on some ancient CD player that sat on a table in the corner. As the sound of Sinatra singing 'That's Life' filled the room, the old man clicked his fingers and swayed in time to the music with his eyes shut.

'Right, that's my cue to make him a buttie and then we'll get off – long visits stress him out.'

Jake buttered and Martin filled the bread with two slices of thick ham, a smear of English mustard, and two slices of beef tomato. 'He has to have the tomato in the middle of the two slices of ham, or the bread goes soggy and he'll freak out. And never triangles, always rectangles – that's how my mum used to do it.' Jake put a glass of water next to the plate on a small wooden tray. 'And he doesn't eat the crust, but I have to leave them on because he has a special use for them,' Martin said, trying to smile but almost breaking down.

'This is intense, mate. I had no idea it was this bad.' Jake was in shock; nothing could have prepared him for this.

'I can't talk about it, really. I just come in a few times a week and it's the same drill – same sandwich, music and conversation.'

'What about the other days?' Jake asked. Martin was an only child; there was literally nobody else.

'Michelle comes with the boys at the weekend, and we have a carer who puts him to bed and gives him his medication. I watch him on an app on my phone, and the whole place is alarmed, you know, in case he wanders off or has a fall.'

'What medication does he take?'

'Blood pressure tablets, blood thinners, pain killers for the arthritis and something to slow down the dementia.'

'And is it slowing down at all?' Jake wondered how bad things would be without it.

'Is it fuck,' Martin said angrily. 'To be honest, sometimes I wish he would just go – this is no life. They wouldn't let a dog live like this, would they?'

Jake had no answer for that – Martin made a good point. But what if they found a cure for this the year after 'putting down' a patient – would you ever get over that decision?

Bert ate the sandwich slowly; he then carefully crumbled the crusts onto the carpet in front of his chair. 'For the birds,' he said, whilst looking at the ceiling.

'Did you enjoy that, Dad?' Martin asked.

'No, it was shit! Where's your mother, boy?'

'She's not here, Dad, she's gone – remember?'

At this point, Jake moved into the hallway and waited for Frank Sinatra to start before he went and got into the car. He felt he was confusing things, and quite honestly he couldn't understand how this man was allowed to live alone.

As they drove over to the school to collect Marnie, Martin's phone rang and he took a sharp intake of breath. 'Ahh no, it's fucking HR, here we go.' Martin listened intently to the person on the other end of the phone. 'Okay, so I'll see you tomorrow then – thanks for the call.'

'Well?' Jake asked.

'I have to go in on Monday for a *chat*,' he said, using his fingers as speech marks.

'What you thinking?' Jake probed.

CHIPS AND GRAVY

'That was head office and they're sending someone up from HR; they've reviewed the evidence and the statements, and they will discuss their findings with me at the meeting.' He looked out of the car window and sneered. 'Statements, evidence – I'm not Richard fucking Hillman. It's all a bit much, don't you think?'

Jake shrugged. The term 'chub on' in reference to the length of a skirt was risqué in any place of work, never mind a child's bike shop. Martin needed to rethink his attitude to women, and he needed to make serious adjustments to his phrasing – the number of times he'd said the word 'knockers' that week would make even Bernard Manning wince. It really didn't look good.

But what Jake had witnessed that day – the patience Martin had shown to his dad and the level of care he took in making a simple sandwich – showed him that his cousin wasn't all bad, and when he needed to show up, he did. However, what did play on Jake's mind that day was just who the heck this Richard Hillman was.

Jake put some work into his client files that evening, straightening out their records and updating the information on their investments. Things were ticking along quite nicely, but one fund was underperforming and they expected more movement. Jake put together a short presentation on a small Mexican company looking for investment. They had discovered how to infuse concentrated amounts of caffeine with nicotine into a slow-release lozenge, keeping people perky and satisfied all day long. This little tablet had so far stopped three million people from smoking, and the tobacco companies were becoming concerned. There was a rumble from the coffee plantations, too – their sales were taking a dent. This was interesting, and Jake had one of his strong feelings. Even if it was just a novelty, once this hit Europe, there was big money to be made, and quickly. Imagine a pill that made you feel like you'd had a coffee and a cigarette, and you kept hold of that feeling all day long – someone had managed to bottle this, and it had been signed off as safe.

Jake recommended his client put half a million into this to help it get into Europe – they were almost there, and this cash injection would put it firmly on the market within months. It felt quite good to dip his toe back into this exciting world – choosing architrave and ceiling roses was nice and all, but investing huge amounts of cash and watching it grow was where Jake got his real thrills.

Sunday morning's meet-up with Lucy was something Jake kept to himself. The last thing he wanted was Marnie and Martin getting themselves all excited over nothing, so the dog walk was a sneaky affair, with Jake slipping out whilst his house guests slept. It wasn't difficult – Martin had had a skinful on Saturday night and would be feeling fragile, and Marnie had announced that Sunday was her day of rest after doing a forty-hour week at the hellhole that masqueraded as a school.

It was quite a crisp morning, and for once the sky was blue and there was no sign of the grey drizzle that seemed to live permanently over Lancashire. It was hard to chat freely in the rain, and even harder to hear somebody with your hood up. Jake carefully chose his outfit – countryside chic with a nod to Mayfair was the look he eventually went with. Lucy was waiting at the post office with a scruffy-looking Alsatian and wearing an equally scruffy outfit. Jake couldn't help being a little disappointed that perhaps this was not a date with sexual intercourse on the menu – was this really just a walk?

'Hi you,' Lucy beamed. 'This is Rita.'

Jake patted the dog's head. He wasn't really an animal person – London and investing wasn't really a good environment to become a pet owner so, apart from the racehorse he bought without ever meeting it, he was a virgin to all of this. 'She's friendly, I take it. Rita the dog?' He kept his distance until he got the green light.

'She's fourteen – she hasn't got the energy for attacking so you'll be fine.'

'Nice day for it,' Jake said as they started walking, suddenly feeling self-conscious. He was bad at this – he'd not wooed a woman in, well, had he ever wooed a woman? Nicky had just sort of latched on, and he'd allowed it so long as it didn't interfere with his schedule. He didn't even have a schedule now, nowhere to be and nothing significant to do.

Jake's confidence started to drop. What if she thought she was doing him a favour, taking him for a walk like she was his carer? Maybe his mum had asked her to 'get him out the house for some fresh air'. She was wearing a pair of Converse that had the laces missing with hiking socks, so certainly wasn't dressed to impress.

'You look nice, very cool. A bit too cool for dog-walking, if I'm honest. Are you going out after this?'

'No, this is my dog-walking outfit,' Jake said defensively.

'What, Chelsea boots and cashmere?' Lucy raised an eyebrow. 'Where do you think we're going, Sandringham?'

Jake broke into a smile. 'Can I let you into a secret? I've never been on a dog walk before – well, not a proper one in the countryside anyway.'

Lucy chuckled. 'Hence the incredibly expensive gear.'

'I wanted to make an effort.'

'This is all for me?' She blushed, and so did Jake.

'Well, I guess so – when a girl invites you out, I suppose you want to look your best.'

'I feel bad now, coming out in my scruffs – it's just normally so muddy and usually raining.'

'We'll know for next time; you smarten up and I'll dress down, and we'll meet in the middle.'

'Okay, deal, but for today and on account of our miscommunication, we'll stick to the paths and away from any swamps.'

And so she led the way through the village and out onto a gravel road that followed the River Ribble for miles.

After an hour of enjoying the scenery and chatting mainly about the perils of not drinking, Jake's phone rang three times on the bounce.

'Sorry, I need to get this – it's somebody who needs some support. Well, a kick up the arse actually.'

Lucy walked slightly ahead, allowing Jake to take the call.

'What, Martin?'

'Where are you?'
'Walking. Sunday morning walking.'
'Right, well, I've had a disaster.'
'Okay, I'm listening.'
'Got bladdered last night, ended up sending some messages.'
'Continue.'
'Called a few people a slag.'
'Who?'
'Michelle, obviously.'
'Obviously.'
'Janine.'
'Brave!'
'And then, unfortunately, that girl from Halfords with the short dress, the one who I "sexually harassed".'
'Martin! You absolute dick.'
'I know, you don't have to tell me. I've pretty much sealed my fate there now, eh?' There was a pause as a lightbulb moment occurred. 'Unless, Jake, we say you sent it from my phone?'

Jake groaned – Martin's stupidity was at an all-time high. 'No, we won't be saying that.'

'But now what, Jake? I'm lost, everything's crumbling.'

'You'll need to get job-hunting, starting tomorrow. And you better get round to your house and apologise to your wife *and* her sister today, okay?'

Martin sighed down the phone – his head was pounding, he was sweating, and his life was blowing up around him.

'I only meant to go for a couple of pints at the local, I was hoping to have a game of pool with some of the lads that prop up the bar.'

'Hmm, and did you play pool?'

Martin racked his brains. The last thing he remembered was being sick into his cupped hands, and then giving a white girl with dreadlocks a good seeing-to in an empty skip behind the pub. He really needed to get a handle on his life – plus, one of his Patrick Cox shoes was missing, and they didn't make them any more.

'I don't think I played pool, or maybe I did. Fuck only knows.'

'Martin, apologise. It's the only way.'

'Okay, fine. But Jake, can you please make a massive roast later? I'm hanging.'

It was at this point Jake realised how important it was to have a mum.

'Go on then – pick up a piece of beef from the butchers, and I'll be back around lunchtime to start prepping.'

'Thanks, Jake – thanks very much, mate.'

'Take some painkillers, have a shower and we'll get you sorted, you tosser.'

Lucy O was a little bemused – she'd picked up that Jake was making a roast dinner for a wet wipe of a person who'd had a skinful the night before.

'Sorry about that, Lucy – I have my cousin staying and he needs a bit of guidance.'

'So you're very caring – that ticks another box for me.'

'Another box... there's more?'

'Yeah, I've already ticked a few.'

'Let's hear it then.' Jake was a sucker for a compliment.

Lucy linked Jake's arm, a moment she'd been waiting for, and she executed it well. 'Good-looking, stylish, chilled and now we can add caring.'

Jake felt a warmth – not as warm as a hot toddy or an Irish coffee might make him, but a good feeling that was as close to a drink as he could get that day.

'Any negatives you want to share about yourself?' Lucy asked.

Jake took a deep breath and let her have it. 'I was a raging drunk, a cokehead, a shit partner and a cold-hearted bastard, but that was the old me. I'm hoping, but I can't guarantee, that the new me – the Sunday dog-walking me – is here to stay.'

'Are you looking for a friendship, a relationship or just a hook-up?'

'I don't know, Lucy. I'm still sort of pining for my ex but that would never work, and there hasn't been anyone significant since. I'm not sure what I want, but I like you, and you've definitely awoken something up in me.' Lucy's eyes involuntarily flicked down to Jake's groin, which somehow broke the ice. 'A tense moment can always be eased by gazing at some genitals, I find,' Jake said, deadpan.

Lucy laughed, then stopped and faced Jake. 'Honesty is the key for me here. I've been lied to by everyone I've ever known my entire life and, for once and quite refreshingly, somebody has told me exactly how it is. Thank you.'

'Look, I'm quite a simple guy – when I'm sober. I try to be open and honest too, what's the point otherwise?' Lucy nodded in agreement. 'What about you? Tell me more about the famous Lucy O.'

Lucy sighed – she could be there all day, but she decided to give Jake the shortened version. 'I was only fourteen when a talent scout spotted me in an am-dram performance of *My Fair Lady* where I was playing Eliza. They sent my parents a letter asking me to attend an audition for *Coronation Street* to play the illegitimate daughter of a factory owner.'

'Wow, you must have been so excited.'

'My parents were,' Lucy said cynically. 'Anyway, I got the part. It was between me and another girl, but she had a touch of acne starting, so she was eliminated after they saw that under the lights.'

'Oof, brutal.' Jake felt for that girl – being a teenager was hard enough without being rejected because of your face.

'Sometimes I wonder whether it would have been easier if I'd not got in – it's caused me a hell of a lot of grief.'

'How so?'

'I virtually lived on the *Corrie* set for the remainder of my childhood, being looked after by runners, fellow actors and producers. Within three years my parents split up, my mum died, and then I fell out with my dad.'

'My god, that's horrible, Lucy. How on earth did you cope?'

'I coped because I had a part in Britain's biggest soap and, as an actor, I'd hit gold. I had no choice but to keep it together.'

'But in terms of family, who did you have to help you?'

'My nan was my official guardian, who was alright back then when she got to meet the cast and go to events with a free bar.' Jake frowned – that didn't sound very grandmotherly. 'I got an apartment just a few minutes away from the set, and I lived with various friends and boyfriends. Looking back now, most of them were just leeches. Bags being packed and doors being slammed were a regular occurrence back in the day. I went through friends like hot dinners. Anyway, it all went to shit, so here I am – selling cheese and living in an armpit of a village with my nan.' Lucy laughed, but not happily.

Jake stopped, took Lucy in his arms and kissed her gently on the mouth, just once. She smiled at him shyly and they continued their walk, understanding one another a tiny bit more.

Tom Jones

How could one song be the reason that Jake had six virtual strangers sitting in his lounge, intermittently sobbing and sipping Mellow Bird's – a light brown powder that was used as a cheap substitute for coffee a few decades ago? The amount of caffeine in it was surely described as 'trace' on the label since it gave no high, no rush, and it tasted like a liquid Werther's Original. But, as Martin had nipped down to the corner shop, it was the cheapest on offer, and Martin was a tight arse.

Jake had arrived at Tuesday evening's meeting, and as per, all the usual suspects huddled in the doorway. Since the night was particularly cold, they were desperate for the doors to be opened. Lucy O emerged from the back of a minicab; she no longer had her licence after a nasty incident with a Mazda, a breathalyser and a rat-faced judge. She half-expected to be papped, so she pulled down her hood almost to her eyes, but nobody seemed to care she was a superstar. The focus at 6.50 p.m. on the freezing cold evening was why the fuck the church hall was in darkness, and where the hell was the chairman? Jake tried to hold back the satisfied smile as Lucy huddled up close to him. He liked the girl enough to feel a little bit of joy in her presence. He wasn't planning on anything serious, but she could certainly keep him amused on these dark winter nights.

'I'm a little bit nervous,' Lucy whispered to Jake.

'Don't be – it's going to help, I promise.'

'Shall I go and introduce myself to people?'

Jake shook his head. 'Save it for the meeting, then you can do it properly.'

At one minute past seven, it became apparent that this was not normal – not one person could remember Keith ever being late. In hushed whispers, the members speculated about his whereabouts. There were no positive suggestions, none whatsoever – a car crash, heart attack, alien abduction and one helpful suggestion he had been snared by an online paedo organisation.

Jake addressed the group, hoping to be the voice of reason.

'Guys, come on now, calm down – he's probably got a plausible reason for being late. Let's give it ten more minutes, and then we reconvene somewhere else, agreed?'

'I'll try his phone again, but I think it's switched off which is really concerning,' Peggy said, holding her pink glittery phone case to her ear. 'Hello Keith, darlin', it's me again. Where are you, sweetheart, have you forgotten the meeting? Please call back, we're worried about you.' She sighed before applying another layer of iced pink lipstick, using her phone camera as a mirror.

'What's the backup plan in these circumstances?' Lucy asked Jake with some desperation. She hadn't thought she needed a meeting, but now she was here and had made the effort to get ready, she wanted to see what she could get out of this. Plus, she really liked Jake, and wanted to spend some more time with him.

'I don't know, it's early days for me too. I sort of relied on Keith to hold it all together,' Jake admitted.

'What was the last thing he said in the WhatsApp group?' Dean asked. 'Maybe we've missed something.'

The entire group took to their phones, scrolling through the chat to see what Keith's last instructions were.

'See you Tuesday, stay safe, stay calm and, most importantly, stay sober,' Tyler read out. 'He wrote that on Friday afternoon, so we know he was still alive four days ago.' Tyler looked a little unusual that evening. His rockstar hairstyle – usually fashionably unkempt – was smooth and without any product. It didn't suit him, and it was clear he hadn't 'got ready' that evening. His statement leather jacket was nowhere to be seen, and had been replaced by a cardigan that was likely from Burton. Jake gave him a double glance, wondering if they had a new member. They were quite a pessimistic bunch, and Keith was the founder, the leader and the most together person Jake had met to date – perhaps he was assisting a group of nuns crossing the road, and it had taken a bit longer than he'd planned? Why must people always presume the worst?

Ten more minutes passed by and, eventually, due to the cold, the group piled into three cars, set the engines running and talked to each other through the windows.

'We'll need to find another venue, any suggestions?' Dean yelled from the furthest car away.

Lucy immediately ruled herself out. 'I live with my nan and we can't go there, she's in one of her moods.' Lucy couldn't piss her nan off again that day – she'd already broken an ornament that was apparently 'priceless'. And when Lucy pointed out that the sticker on the bottom of the porcelain horse with a brass chain around its neck had been priced at £2.99, her stinky nan told her to 'Get back to *Corrie*, for the love of god.'

'There's absolutely no way we can go to my house,' Dean said adamantly.

'Why not?' Jake asked.

'Because we have cream carpets, moron.'

Nobody questioned that – this was Lancashire, and there wasn't a clean shoe for miles. Jake thought ahead. Once The Coach House was renovated, the last thing he wanted was a group of locals stomping their muddy boots on his restored floors, so perhaps now would be a good time to show up and show support.

'Okay, let's go to mine and then, when Keith does appear, he can join us there. Follow me up to the house, it's only a few minutes.'

There were a few murmurs of discontent. People didn't generally like to be taken out of their comfort zones, but they relied on this meeting to keep them sober, so a change in location was simply something they would have to cope with. Plus, nosiness trumps all, so off they went, up to this Jake guy's house, to see if the rumours were true. Dean typed the address and change of plan onto the WhatsApp group, so Keith and a missing Janine would know what was happening, and a convoy of cars holding the damaged and the dry drove up the hill to Jake's abode.

As they arrived, Martin was positioned in the driveway in his dressing gown, holding a half-pint of milk that he'd no doubt been swigging from the carton. He had heard some cars arriving and, as a self-appointed security guard, decided to make his presence known by standing wide-legged, which is what he had seen bouncers do to show authority. Jake pulled alongside his clown of a cousin, and glared at him through the window.

'Go inside and put some clothes on right now, Martin; my addiction meeting is happening here tonight. Stay out of the way – remember it's anonymous, so none of your wisecracks.'

Lucy O was seated in the front next to Jake, and she gave Martin a friendly nod. A little bit of excitement and a smidgen of embarrassment hit Martin as he realised she was within groping distance. Yes, she had seen him in his sixteen-year-old dressing gown, but he'd washed his hair the night before, so the smell of Vosene might well have her mesmerised.

'Pleased to meet you, gorgeous,' Martin said in the most alluring tone he could muster up. Jake felt that same hideous feeling he'd had when his mum had turned up at the school disco with a flask of milky coffee and some smelly egg sandwiches which made people retch. He didn't want Lucy to make presumptions based on his gene pool, and with pervy Martin and his semi wandering the corridors, his chances were shrinking.

'Err, don't worry about him, he's just my cousin. He's got lots of problems of his own. Oh, and my niece is around somewhere, but she's just a kid – she's nice and not a gossip.'

Nobody even acknowledged Martin pegging it back inside, the rotten dressing gown, or what Jake had said. They all just stood back in absolute amazement at this beautiful property that belonged to Jake, the aloof posh bloke from big, dirty London.

The group settled into Jake's lounge – some on the floor, some on the arms of the sofas. Jake brought in the kitchen chairs and hissed at Martin, who was hovering on the landing. 'Can you make some drinks, mate, make yourself useful?'

Martin, who had changed into his flared jeans and stripey shirt combo, was happy to oblige. The closer he got to the soap star, the more chance he had of appearing on the front pages.

'What are we going to talk about? Keith is the one who does the meeting plan,' Jake asked, by no means wanted to lead this thing – he was only three meetings in, and felt a bit nervous. When no one responded and everyone continued to look to him, Jake decided he would have to improvise. 'Erm, well, we'll just have to wing it. Why don't we talk about what we all take from these meetings – the reason we have all agreed to change location, rather than cancel.'

It was a good idea. It was quite telling that this had happened – there had to be a reason they had all co-operated, and talking about the benefits of group therapy may help, especially for the newbies.

'Before we begin, everybody, this is Lucy. Perhaps she could share her story.'

Lucy wasn't fazed – she was used to the limelight and her favourite subject happened to be herself. All eyes went to Lucy, and she began her tale of woe.

'I'm Lucy O'Callaghan, but my friends call me Lucy O.' She waited for a gasp as people realised they had a star in their midst, but no one reacted. 'Anyway, yeah, so, I'm an addict of alcohol and sometimes drugs. I'm an actress, you see, and the business is highly pressurised so turning to substance abuse is par for the course.' She threw back her head and dabbed her tear ducts delicately with her middle fingers. 'My life has been a soap opera even without "the show I will not name".' She added that just in case anybody was still trying to piece together who she was. 'I don't have a strong support network, so coming here is a way of me asking for help. I've done rehab loads of times, but somehow, I can't keep it up once I'm out.' She turned to Jake and grabbed his hand. 'I just can't do this alone,' she whispered with her eyes shut.

Peggy stood and patted Lucy on the shoulder. 'Thank you, Lucy – well done for sharing your story and welcome to the group.' Lucy beamed her £20k smile around the room.

'Okay, let's move on shall we?' Peggy stood up and began. 'I'm here because this is part of my routine. From the minute I got sober,

I had to have a regular routine, and I've stuck to it. I do breathing exercises each morning, meditation in the evening before bed, and I generally practice gratitude whilst I am cooking the tea. Monday, Wednesday and Friday, I do some sort of class – yoga, watercolours, pottery, that sort of thing. Tuesdays are for this meeting, and if I'm completely honest I find them exhausting, sometimes upsetting, but I know that this is part of my journey and, come rain or shine, it must be done.'

Frank whooped as he always did each time Peggy said anything. It was involuntary, he insisted. Okay, so she had an American accent, and the yanks did a hell of a lot of whooping, but he had a crush – a crush on a lady who was out of his league, and completely unobtainable.

Peggy sat back down, leaving the space empty for Dean, who stood and bit his nails before admitting, 'I'm not going to bullshit you guys. I am here primarily because I wanted to see what Jake's house was like.' Most shrugged and nodded – that was okay they were all human. 'However, I do feel a sense of belonging, and this is a comfort.' He inhaled deeply. 'The fact we're all strangers fighting the same demon must mean something. I don't really like the sharing, but I do like listening to you all.' He threw his hands up as if to say, 'That's all, folks', and sat back down.

Tyler stood and played with his hair – he felt uncomfortable in his skin that night. Nobody had asked him why this guy who normally channelled rockstar had suddenly turned into a young Donny Osmond.

'Before I share, I think I should address my new look.' Tyler screwed up his face. 'Mum thought – well, so did all of my family actually – that my presentation was adding to the problem, the eyeliner and leather apparently reducing my chances of getting a job, and maybe even a girlfriend.'

'Well, they're right. You did look like an absolute menace; I'd cross the street if I saw you in the village and I didn't know you,' Frank admitted.

'Well, that's rude, Frank – you should never judge somebody like that.' Jake felt a responsibility to keep the group positive.

This wasn't TikTok – nobody should be berated for their choice of clothing.

'A man wearing make-up and ripped jeans only says one thing to me.'

'What does it say, Frank?' Tyley asked with agitation.

Frank wasn't going to hold back – it was about time someone listened to him. His own daughter had had her nose pierced, and it knocked him sick.

'In my day, people like that were outcasts, classed as weirdos. You know what I mean, surely?' There was an awkward silence; Frank was the oldest and could be forgiven for these assumptions, but nobody in an addiction group was getting on board with it. 'Who's that guy that ate a canary live on stage – come on, one of you must know who I mean?'

Nobody replied, although they all knew he was referring to Ozzy Osbourne.

'That was one of your lot. I blame the headbanging music – I think it's got subliminal messages that send people totally mental. You don't want to end up like that, son, eating pets in the name of entertainment.'

Frank folded his arms – he'd made his point and done his bit for the youth of today.

'Right, I think we've heard enough of this – and you need to stop chipping in, Frank. What does this group mean to you, Tyler? Does it help you in any way?' Jake asked calmly.

'Being here, doing this and wearing this...' He tugged at his freshly ironed cotton shirt. 'It means my mum gets a break from the worry; she can relax a little bit. She's the one who has suffered most with my addiction, not me. I quite enjoyed getting wrecked every day.'

The room fell silent. Jake wasn't expecting an answer of any substance, but Tyler hit home. Drinking and being drunk wasn't the only problem. It was the ripple effect on others – that was where the trouble really started. Sure, general health took a good kicking mentally and physically, but let's be honest here – it was the actions and decisions that impacted their nearest and dearest that brought them to these meetings.

Tyler had seen a huge decline in his mum recently. A week ago, she had found a half-bottle of peach schnapps stuffed into a hole in the mattress – that was the blow that triggered her third breakdown in as many years. Her ex-husband, Tyler's father, had been an addict, and it didn't end well for him. He had died six years before on the operating table after his body rejected a new liver. She didn't want to lose her little boy to this, but the demon seemed to be following her family around like a bad smell. Her face had crumpled, the deep lines under her eyes soaked up the concealer, and she was losing her already thinning hair in fistfuls. The stress of being her only son's constant support had finally consumed her, and it was her hitting rock bottom that had caused Tyler to really try this time.

Dean patted Tyler on the knee as he sat down, recognising that this could be crunch-time for the young fool. At least he had caught it early, and realised that something had to give – at least there was that, thought Dean. If only he himself had clocked it in his twenties instead of spending thirty years building up the tolerance of a rugby team.

Jake had prepared himself to talk but, just as he was about to embark on a lovely story about finding solace in numbers, a boiler suit-wearing Janine burst into the lounge, caked in mud.

'Err, shoes, Janine.' Jake stared at her shabby Doc Martens, hoping and praying it was mud and not rat excrement.

'Ooh, disgusting,' Lucy O recoiled as she looked Janine up and down.

'Fuck me, is that Lucy O?' Janine responded. 'Err shit, sorry, you just caught me by surprise.'

Lucy put her hand out as if Janine might kiss it, but she instead received a fist bump.

'I need to sit down, Jake – shift, mate.'

Jake stood from his seat, since he had been brought up with manners, but the woman was late, dirty and downright ridiculous.

'I need to tell you all something – I have some news.'

'It's not your turn to speak yet, and you don't even know how we're doing things, Janine,' Peggy snapped.

'I'm not sharing, Peggy – I have news on Keith.' Janine tried to catch her breath – she'd been rushing, and her heart rate was up. She wasn't great with words, and she needed to try and get this right. 'You know Keith?' she said, and everybody nodded. 'Well, he's dead.'

'I'm sorry, what?' Jake said.

She put her hands over her face. 'Sorry, sorry to come out with it like that. Shit, I practised this all the way here. Fuck, sorry if there was a better way to say it, but there isn't – he's definitely dead.'

Peggy immediately dialled Keith's number, refusing to believe this. Janine was a nutter, so she wouldn't accept it until a normal person confirmed it. The group watched as Peggy shook her head. 'He's not answering, guys.'

Janine frowned. 'Yeah, because he's dead, Peggy – and dead people can't answer the phone.'

Jake gathered himself. 'Janine, how do you know this?'

'His daughter called me. Keith had me as his emergency contact, probably because I live closest to him.'

'And what did she say, Janine?' Dean got onto his knees in front of her; it was slowly dawning on everyone that she was possibly in shock. He held her hand, and she didn't even flinch.

'She said, "Just to let you know, my dad won't be running the meetings any more". Then I said, "Why not?" And she said, "Because he's dead".'

'Dead how? Surely you have more details?' Frank sank into his chair – this was a real blow. Keith wasn't exactly Mr Personality, but he was a solid part of his recovery, and a good egg.

'His daughter said they think he had an aneurysm, and that the Amazon delivery guy found him this morning on the path outside his shed.'

'Outside all night, alone,' Dean shuddered – that was a sad and lonely way to depart.

Janine wiped her nose with her sleeve. 'She did say that we should play "It's Not Unusual" by Tom Jones at the funeral. Apparently it was his favourite song.'

'Great song, good choice.' Tyler nodded in approval.

'Isn't she going to organise the funeral? What's she telling you for? I may have been in London for a while, but I'm pretty sure the custom is that family sort out their own dead.'

Jake was flabbergasted by the way this was being told, but Janine insisted.

'She said she works in retail and that they're very busy coming up to Christmas, so she's asked me – well, us – to sort it all out.'

Peggy let out a sob. Keith had been an absolute rock to her – he'd been kind and forgiving, and had listened and never judged.

'He was only seventy-three – such a beautiful soul. I will miss him so much – I can't believe that he's gone.' Frank moved closer to Peggy and put his arm around her, taking this chance to smell her platinum hair.

'I hadn't known him long, but he seemed like a thoroughly decent guy – he made me so welcome. RIP mate.' Jake joined his hands and looked to the sky; he presumed that was an appropriate motion in these circumstances.

'Also,' Janine sniffed, 'his daughter said there would be absolutely no family at the funeral, and that they won't be paying a penny towards it. She said it's up to his drinking club to give him a send-off.'

It was then that Jake recalled Keith's story about how he'd alienated his children, been disgraced in his career and, by his own admission, hadn't been a support to his wife through terminal cancer. There were a few dark moments where nobody said a word, but everybody knew that Keith must have caused irreparable damage.

'I'm not really sure what we do now – do we say a prayer, light a candle? I just don't know.' Peggy dropped her head onto Frank's shoulder in devastation.

Tyler started to slowly click his fingers rhythmically, and the group looked at one another, wondering what was going on. Lucy O was quite enjoying this – it felt very soap land, and it was the most interesting thing that had happened since her final scenes on *Corrie*. Besides, she'd never met Keith, so she felt nothing really.

'Can I join in?' she asked Tyler.

He nodded, and before long the group were all clicking, even Janine, who didn't manage to stay in rhythm but tried anyway. Once they were all in some sort of sync, Tyler slowly sang 'It's Not Unusual' in his rock-star voice from beginning to end.

Misery Loves Company

Getting Marnie up for school was no easy feat. It was separated into three sections: first, the gentle knock and the obligatory 'good morning' in a soft voice. Ten minutes later, a sterner approach, accompanied by a warm mug of tea and a pat on the shoulder. Ten minutes after that, it was lights on, curtains open and a lecture on what it would be like to enter today's world with no qualifications, and how life on benefits may look like a laugh, but once the leccy meter goes off and the bailiffs arrive, it'll be a homeless shelter, and that's what she'll deserve. Jake had basically turned into Di – before long, he'd be wearing an elasticated skirt with pop socks.

Once the teenager had dragged herself downstairs, Jake caught himself telling her to 'eat her breakfast or she'd waste away.' This parenting thing was hard work. You were literally responsible for another person's welfare for a full quarter of their lives – it was no wonder Leanne was shit at it, and it made total sense that Michelle had gone off the rails too. She had two of them to deal with, and they were feral.

Once he had dropped Marnie off at school, Jake would wander the supermarket wondering what to get for tea, trying to ensure he didn't double up and make the same thing twice in a week. He'd also spent at least twenty minutes in the chemist that week discussing periods with the pharmacist, and how much pain relief he could administer without her getting high, or 'ketty' as Marnie liked to call it.

It was the first of December, and a buzz had descended upon the village – people had a festive spring in their step, but Jake didn't feel it that year. He always associated Christmas with partying. The ritual of putting up a tree wasn't worth doing without a glass of something naughty, even in the morning. So, this particular year felt flat, and almost pointless. As far as Jake was concerned, Santa could go fuck himself.

'What do you mean we're not having a tree?' Marnie was absolutely horrified when Jake announced during their evening meal that he didn't mind a bit of holly, but that he couldn't be arsed to buy a tree.

'You won't be here anyway. Nan and Grandad will be back, and Christmas will be at their house as it always is.'

'Yeah, but I'm here right now, and Christmas lasts for a whole month, doesn't it, Martin?'

Martin looked up from his chicken Kiev. 'Are there any beans? I always have beans with this – Michelle always does beans with everything, 'cause I like beans.'

Jake massaged both his temples, trying to release some frustration. To give Martin his due, he had just been through the week from hell. As instructed, he'd been home on the Sunday to apologise for the slag messages, only to find Janine alone at the house. Michelle, the boys and Ste had gone to the Chill Factore followed by Frankie & Benny's and wouldn't be back until at least ten. Martin had then attempted to barge past Janine, planning to be waiting in his marital bed when his wife and her boyfriend returned home. Janine had stopped him entering by poking him in the eye with her index finger and crushing his foot in the front door.

On the Monday, Halfords had called first thing to forcefully insist that Martin did not to attend the HR meeting. Until further notice he was banned from all Halfords stores across the country. A complaint had been made about threatening messages sent by him at two a.m. on Sunday morning. The victim was apparently now on pills.

On the Tuesday, Halfords then sent an official email asking for his pass, badge and two XXL company fleeces to be returned within seven days or he would face legal action.

By Wednesday, Martin was at his lowest ebb. He got another taxi back home, ready to succumb to any of Michelle's demands – even if it meant him learning how to iron, he really was prepared to do anything. Unfortunately, when he arrived, every single item of Martin's was packed neatly into boxes and stacked in the garden with an envelope containing divorce papers sellotaped to the top one. 'Irreconcilable differences' was the reason cited; Michelle didn't even mention his perversions. It was clear she couldn't be bothered to fight, and that she'd simply had enough.

Martin had whinged and whined to anyone who'd listen that week – the builders, the plumber, even the white dreadlock girl had taken an earful in the chippy. After listening to Martin drone on about years of marriage 'going up the swanny', she told him it was no fucking wonder, 'cause he was a shit shag and he smelled of sick. Martin took that on the chin – it was very hard to create friction on the bottom of a wet skip wearing only one shoe.

Jake and Marnie did their best to cheer him up – cups of tea, whole packets of biscuits and letting him have *Top Gear* on whenever he wanted. But it was dawning on Martin that he had thrown his life away carelessly, and now somebody else lay on his side of the bed. Richard Hammond flipping yet another car was not enough to sort this out.

'I don't give a shit about Christmas, Marnie, not any more. I just want some beans.'

Marnie put down her cutlery and stood up. 'I'm going to bed, see you both tomorrow.' She left a full Taste the Difference chicken Kiev with a side of triple-cooked chips barely touched. She'd had a gutful of these men today, and they'd cancelled Christmas all because one was a drunk, and the other a pervert.

'What a bloody waste – there's people starving,' Martin called after her.

But Jake had a good think. This was a young girl, her mother was off sampling the delights of the Costa del Cock, her grandparents had buggered off camping, and here she was with two middle-aged losers who wouldn't even put a Christmas tree up.

He turned to Martin. 'This is all wrong, hurry up and eat that

– we're going out.' Jake scraped his dinner into the bin, before grabbing his jacket and car keys.

'I'm too tired, and very depressed. I just want four cans of cider and bed,' Martin protested, his head almost resting on the Kiev.

'Tough shit, Martin. We're going to Homebase, and whilst we're there, you can ask them for a job.'

Jake: Hey Lucy, not sure if you're busy, but do you fancy coming over? I need a woman's touch. 😊
Lucy: How could I refuse an offer like that?
Jake: Pick you up in an hour?
Lucy: Okay cool. Will send you my address. x

Forty minutes and £380 later, Jake and Martin had filled the boot of the Land Rover with everything Christmassy Homebase had to offer. It wasn't classy, and was a far cry from the carefully selected Nordic decorations Jake had been used to when he'd lived in London. Nicky had been very particular when it came to the festive season, and Jake hadn't batted an eyelid when branches and intertwined twigs costing hundreds of pounds had been carefully placed around the home. This was different, a proper Northern affair: twinkling lights, a snowman that bellowed 'Merry Christmas', and a plug-in tree pre-decorated with plastic stripey candy canes – all probably created by a small child in a sweatshop who had never even seen snow. It was the tackiest set of trimmings, and once the house was renovated, Jake would palm them off on Martin so the boys could endure the grotto.

Martin had been told at the tills that they were only taking on warehouse staff, and he should apply online quickly if he was interested.

'Twelve pound an hour, forty hours a week shifting boxes,' Martin said glumly as they drove away.

'The boys will want gifts, I presume, this Christmas?' Jake reminded him.

'They want a new Xbox and these mega-pricey hoodies, been going on about them for months.'

'Shifting a few boxes in a warehouse needs to happen then. They're your kids, you need to keep being a parent.'

'You're right – I want to see my kids smile. I want to be the one who made that happen.'

Martin scrolled through pictures of the boys on his phone, recalling Christmases gone by as they drove back to the village. 'Tommy, my youngest, he put a small bauble up his arse one year. Ended up in A&E on Boxing Day. Brilliant Christmas, that,' he said fondly.

Jake grimaced.

'Another year, when Janine was drinking, she turned up pissed in a sexy Mrs Claus outfit on Christmas morning. My Michelle were fuming. Crotchless it was, with flashing lights round the tits.' He laughed – really belly-laughed. 'Me dad's eyes popped out of his head. This was before, you know, he lost his marbles.'

Jake smiled. The thought of Janine in anything like that was very strange – he didn't quite see her as a sexual being.

'Everything's changed now, though,' Martin sighed. 'Janine's sober, you're sober, me dad's nuts and my Michelle's knocking off some gym dick... It's going to take some getting used to.'

Jake just listened. This was going to be a hard transition for Martin – he'd been left behind and he didn't really fit in anywhere, not even Halfords.

'I've got something that might cheer you up,' Jake said.

'What?'

'Now don't get stupid, but I'm picking up Lucy O and she's going to help put the decs up.'

Martin sat up straight in the passenger seat, and pulled the mirror down. 'Christ, I look like shit.'

'Forget about that, Martin. Look, I'm sort of seeing her, mate. Me and Lucy, we went on a date – it might turn into something.'

Martin slumped back into the seat, and slammed the mirror up aggressively. 'What about Nicky? Thought you were trying to get her back?'

'She never replied to my email – and she's with someone else, time I moved on I reckon.'

'You're always the lucky one.' Martin shook his head in disbelief. 'I'm happy for you though, cuz – deep down. At least one of us can get off with a celeb. Anyway, I won't take her off you – I'm not like that.'

'You couldn't, but thanks for not trying,' Jake laughed.

'She'd be mine if I did one of my *Little Britain* impressions.'

'She would not, but feel free to give it a go.'

Back at the house, and after giving Lucy a quick explanation about Marnie – her affliction of saying it exactly how it was – Jake called her down from her room. She was wearing a pair of pyjamas that were far too small, and she had three spot stickers in various places on her chin.

Marnie sat on the stairs, tucking her knees up to her chin. 'I've just been on FaceTime to my mum – she reckons you're a right old Scrooge for not having a tree.'

'Your mum should get her arse back here and try putting a tree up herself, then!' Martin barked.

'Errr, she's working, Martin – you should try it. Oh no, you can't, 'cause you've been sacked.'

Just before Martin had a chance to launch into his 'it was just bantz' defence, Jake butted in, 'I have a surprise for you, Marnie.'

'What is it?'

'Well shut your eyes, and open them on three.'

On three, Lucy came through the door, holding the talking snowman up like a trophy.

'Ta-da!' Jake said, gesturing towards them both.

Marnie opened her eyes without smiling.

'What, an ex-*Corrie* star who works at Booths?' she said without any excitement. 'I didn't even watch it when she was in it.'

'Cheeky little cow – send her to bed,' Martin said curtly.

'It's not Lucy O from *Coronation Street*, Marnie. It's Lucy, my friend, who has come to help decorate this whole house so it feels like some sort of Blackpool Christmas grotto – my boot is full of this shit.'

Marnie smiled a little, then narrowed her eyes. 'What, really? A tree and everything?'

'Yes. I'll make the hot chocolate, and you three get started.'

Marnie was in her element that evening – she chatted away to Lucy about periods, spots, school and living with the losers. Martin stood on a step ladder, pinning lights to trees and regaling Jake with stories from happier times. He even took a picture of the tree and sent it to his boys, who sent back a 'thumbs up' emoji. Lucy had escaped the clutches of her nan for the night – no toenail clippings flying across the lounge, and no lectures on putting the heating on when 'you don't pay the bleeding bill'.

Jake did wonder how a glass of red would have gone down at the end of all this, but that feeling disintegrated quickly when Lucy O asked if she could stay over. By the end of the evening, with every corner of the house flashing and twinkling, Marnie said to Jake on her way to bed, 'That was good, that was.'

All it took to make four people temporarily happy was a trip to Homebase and a mug of hot chocolate.

Full Of It

The following week, things were busy but positive in Jake's unconventional world. Marnie was on the countdown to the Christmas break, and that meant minimal schoolwork, almost zero homework and a huge lapse in effort in terms of anything educational. It had only taken three days for Martin to get on the payroll at Homebase – they were so desperate, they didn't even check his references. Jake had watched him fill out the online application form and tried to keep a straight face after seeing some of the bullshit Martin had entered.

'A GCSE in music, Martin? Just remind me of the instrument you played apart from your own dick.'

Martin was concentrating hard on filling in each box rather than leaving them blank.

'And what about this? A Duke of Edinburgh award – since when?'

Martin took his glasses off and sighed. 'Jake, mate, nobody is going to check whether or not I picked up a few dog shits in 1995.'

'I suppose not, but what will you say about Maths and English? That's what they'll want to see – whether you can read and add up.'

'Already sorted – A-stars in both. Oh, and I studied logistics at Preston University in case anyone asks.'

'Fucking hell, Martin – at least make it believable.'

Anyway, the lies made it through the system, and the warehouse manager started Martin on a zero-hours contract within twenty-four hours of receiving the application form of lies – but at least he was working, and the kids wouldn't go short at Christmas as they paid their staff weekly. It was baby steps for Martin – he was basically learning to walk again. Jake showered him with praise as he left for his first day, and handed him a packed lunch full of all his favourite snacks.

Di and Alf were due back later that day, and Jake knew for sure they would be desperate to see how the house was coming along, and to check in on Marnie. Each time he heard the distant noise of an engine at the bottom of the hill, he was convinced it would be them, but a phone call mid-morning changed all that.

After answering the phone, there was at least a minute of phlegm being moved around in a nasal passage, into the throat and then onto a tissue. Alf finally spoke. 'Your mother and me are full of it, son.'

Jake sighed. 'Yes, I can hear that, Dad. Nasty cold by the sounds of it.'

'No, it's not a cold, son – it's full-on flu.'

'How do you know it's flu?'

Alf coughed before saying, 'Freezing, then boiling, then freezing again.'

Jake groaned. 'Yeah, that's the same as a bad cold, Dad – same symptoms.'

Di sneezed loudly in the background, and then there was a rustle as she grabbed the handset from Alf.

'This is no cold, son, this is the flu. I said to your dad a couple of days ago, "I don't feel right" – you know when you don't feel right? I said to him, "Something's coming", didn't I Alf?'

There was more rustling as Alf reappeared.

'She did – she said something's not right, and something's coming.'

'Well, you were right, Mum, and I'm sure caravanning at this time of year didn't help,' Jake said in a 'told you so' moment. What was wrong with the Caribbean? Even Tenerife was surely a better option than the south coast in December.

'Nothing to do with that, Jake – actually, there was a man in the service station on the M5 who was clammy as a toad. He was sweating all over the pumps just before we filled up. I knew I should have worn gloves.'

'Me and your mum just thought this guy was hungover – he had a look of a drunkard, you see.'

'A drunkard, you say?' Jake said. 'What does a drunkard look like exactly, Dad?'

The parents went quiet – Jake heard Di thump Alf's arm, and he quickly changed the subject.

'How's my girl doing? Is everything okay?'

'Marnie is doing great – she's a good kid, nice to have around.'

'Any news from her bloody mother?' Alf asked scornfully.

'She's been FaceTiming Marnie – I think she's doing okay, and Marnie seems fine without her to be fair.'

Alf grumbled something to himself.

'Erm anyway, we're off home now to cancel my eye operation, and then we're going straight up to bed to try and shake this thing off.'

'Woah, woah – don't cancel your eye op, Dad, don't be silly.' Jake felt this was overkill – that operation had been booked in for months.

'It says on the leaflet that if you are suffering from any of the following symptoms, please reschedule your procedure. Read 'em out, Di.'

Di cleared her throat. 'Recurring cough, sore throat, aching muscles, a high temperature,' she croaked into the receiver.

'Check, check, check, check,' Alf said, like they were his lottery numbers coming in. 'Read some more, Di, it'll be a full house.'

'No, Mum, stop reading that now. Okay, you cancel the op if you think that's best. I'll come over and bring some shopping, shall I? Save you having to go out.'

'That would be great, son, we'll send you a list,' Alf shouted. 'But don't come upstairs, you don't want to catch this. Leave it in the kitchen, son, stay safe.'

The extensive list followed quite quickly afterwards, and it was headed: GO TO MORRISONS JAKE. On it was an assortment of tinned fruit and meats, an extraordinarily large selection of cold and flu medication, including two tubs of Vicks Vapour Rub, twenty-four Morrisons own-brand rolls of loo paper and, rather bizarrely, a box of Cornettos – any flavour would do, apparently.

Jake read the list with dismay. It was too late to make changes to his parents' diets; nothing could be gained from a lecture on why pears in syrup may not speed up their recovery. They'd done it their way for this long, so he would follow the instructions and hope for the best.

Lucy had stayed over twice more since they trimmed up the house. The first evening had been quite natural and relaxed. She'd borrowed one of Jake's t-shirts to sleep in, and the two of them had huddled up and watched *When a Man Loves a Woman*, a film about addiction that resonated and made them feel close. When it finished, Jake turned off the lamp and they had sex – quite good sex, but it didn't blow any doors off due to the fact he had to keep telling her to shush in case Marnie heard them. Being a parent of sorts involved having silent sex, or facing an excruciating and awkward feeling the following morning.

Two nights afterwards, Lucy had offered to cook dinner for 'the family' as she called them. Jake agreed, but admittedly felt it was all a bit too soon and claustrophobic for her to be playing wifey. Marnie seemed to get along with her, though, and it was one less meal for him to think about, so he allowed Lucy O to potter about in his kitchen, creating something she called 'cowboy pie'. Martin was ecstatic – it turned out that this dish contained baked beans – not on the side, actually inside it.

Afterwards, Lucy quietly slipped upstairs and put her overnight bag in Jake's room. There was no conversation; she took it as read that if she cooked, then she stayed over. It would have been far too uncomfortable for Jake to question it, so he said nothing.

Lucy had cried after sex that night. It started as a small sob, which Jake tried to ignore because he was knackered. When the sob became a wail, he had no choice but to ask, 'What's the matter, Lucy, did I hurt you?' He knew for sure he didn't have the apparatus to cause any permanent physical damage – Ron Jeremy he was not – but anything was better than an emotional conversation at that time of night.

'Just hold me tight,' Lucy had said as she curled up in his arms. 'I just feel so safe with you; it's the happiest I've felt in a long time.'

'So... happy tears?' Jake asked in confusion.
'Yes, these are tears of joy,' she whispered.

Two nights later, Lucy and Jake went to an improv night at a local comedy club. It was her idea as, apparently, she was considering moving over to stand-up as a sideline to her acting. Jake felt obliged to go, even though he hated forced jokes, and being in a club reminded him of drinking. Still, he picked her up, bought her dinner and then fake-laughed for over two hours. Unfortunately, when they pulled up outside Lucy's nan's afterwards, she'd lost her door keys and apparently couldn't consider waking up her grumpy grandmother. And so it was back to The Coach House for another borrowed t-shirt and even more silent sex.

'It's amazing being your girlfriend,' Lucy said to Jake the following morning as he handed her a cup of tea.

Jake gulped. He had promised to be honest, so he couldn't let that one slide.

'Not sure we're quite there yet, Lucy.' He was as direct as he dared to be.

Lucy covered her face with her hands. 'Oh my god, I can't believe I just said that. I'm such a twat.'

Jake sat down on the bed, immediately worried he'd been too harsh. 'No, you're not a twat. I just don't like putting labels and pressure on stuff – we don't want to spoil it, do we?'

Lucy pushed out her bottom lip slightly. 'I'm sorry Jake, it was just a throwaway comment – I meant nothing by it. You brought me tea and that's boyfriend territory, in my book anyway.'

Jake left the room feeling a little strange. The whole thing felt staged, almost as if she was testing his reaction. He wasn't ready for a girlfriend and, if anything, his feelings for Lucy were rapidly reducing.

So, on this Thursday, Jake was all sexed out and looking forward to a quiet night in with no conversation. He just had a few errands to run, and then he would sit by the gas fire and watch mindless telly.

He had an hour or two before the school run, which he would combine with the Morrisons shop, so he decided to have a look over some work and update Lucas on his client's latest investment before he left. It was a wonderful feeling to see that things were going well, and the forecast on the investment almost guaranteed a very profitable period. Jake's inbox was full of new information on research that had been released on this product, and its name had been decided for Europe. Zing25 would be marketed and advertised the following year, and the company predicted a market takeover. It was to be as big as vaping – in fact, it would squash the industry and bring it to its knees. It would have Starbucks trembling at every board meeting, and the likes of Jake – and anyone else who relied on such substances to function – would be able to feed their habit with a simple and healthy lozenge.

Jake paced the garden, sipping an espresso and smoking a Marlboro. Opportunities like this were one-offs, and if he'd have been present when whoever it was who got the planet to believe that sucking a battery was better than cigarettes, then he'd have sold his house and invested himself. Of course, vapers were now wishing they'd stuck to the cigs, but only after billions had been made by the creators and investors. Perhaps this was Jake's chance to make a few quid, to really hit the big time and be able to send his parents somewhere further than a muddy beach in the sideways rain. He could hire tutors for Marnie, and then send her to university – nobody else would! Perhaps he could even help Martin out by getting Uncle Bert into a decent home where his needs would be met properly until the end.

All of this could be done without Jake batting an eyelid or worrying about his own future – there were millions to be made, and why on earth wouldn't he take a slice of that pie? This could be life-changing.

Jake checked his junk mail, as he did once a week or so, and immediately noticed something very interesting halfway down the page. An email from an address that he didn't recognise – but he certainly recognised the name. It had been sent to him four days ago. It was from Nicky, the lovely Nicky.

Hi Jake – wow, it's been a while. I'm so pleased to hear from you, I've thought about you quite a lot recently. Gosh, so much has happened in the last year for both of us, and you being clean has really made me smile. I had heard you'd sorted yourself out, but you tried so many times when we were together, I just wasn't convinced you could keep at it – but you have, so well done you. Perhaps it was me who fuelled the lifestyle. I wasn't tough enough, maybe?

I always knew there was a good and kind soul in there; that's why I think I stayed so long, just hoping I would get to see the real you. I sound bitter, don't I? I'm not, nothing of the sort in fact, I honestly believe you had to be alone to realise you were wasting yourself. So, I am only happy to hear that you got there, in the end, you really deserve to live a life and one that isn't constantly soiled with the poison that had a grip on you.

My life is very different – it feels strange to tell you this in an email, but I'm getting married, and I'm pregnant, two things that I wanted more than anything since I was ten years old. I won't sugarcoat this and tell you it's perfect because life never is, but I'm about to become a wife and mother, and I intend to make a damn good job of it. I won't go into too much detail about my relationship, as I feel that may be a little raw for me so soon after us, but I will say he's a good man with a kind heart and soul – sound familiar? Ha ha.

I truly hope that your dreams are coming true, and that you have found a safe haven in the North close to your warm family. I did enjoy their company – yes, sometimes they were a little rough around the edges for a posh girl like me, but anybody could see they all adored you. Do pass on my regards – I think of them often.

In terms of us meeting up, I'm not moving too far away from London until the baby is born, so it's unlikely I'll be anywhere but here. Do feel free to email me at this address if you're ever in London, and perhaps it would be cathartic to catch up over a coffee.

Thank you for getting in touch – it really was lovely to hear from you, Jake.

N xxx

Jake bowed his head after reading this email. Nicky was so eloquent, so classy and just so bloody lovely. She had a way of being honest, blaming herself for everything and making him feel good all at the same time. Jake could have murdered somebody, and she would have found a way to look on the bright side. This woman was wife material – she was the mother you'd want for your children. Educated, non-judgmental, posh without being snobby, she was perfect, and he'd lost her. He decided not to reply immediately; he had no intention of legging it to London, nor was she going anywhere. His response needed careful consideration, and that would take time. Besides, he would only allow himself to be honest with the woman he relentlessly lied to for years – she at least deserved that. How would he tell her that he was reluctantly in a relationship with a disgraced soap star who was barely out of her school uniform?

Jake played Coldplay in the car on the way to Morrisons. Nicky had liked the song 'Fix You', and she'd listen to it glassy-eyed all the time whilst they were together. He'd never really taken much notice of the lyrics, but that day he did. He'd be shaking in bed, shrouded in guilt and shame, wondering what time would be appropriate to open a fruity red whilst Nicky would make his breakfast on a tray listening to this very song. He wondered what would have happened, and where they would be, had he just got his act together earlier. Would they be waiting to meet their baby, perhaps having conceived in the Seychelles on their honeymoon? Maybe they'd have twins, a boy and a girl, covering all bases – the boy could have been a banker, taking on Jake's financial prowess, and the girl, well, also a banker but a kind one, like her mother.

His phone rang, interrupting his imaginary life.

'Jakey boy, it's Janine.'

'Yes, Janine, I know it's you – how are you?'

'Okay, I guess – a lot going on right now as I'm sure you know.'

'Well, the divorce papers haven't gone down well at my house, but he's sorting himself out.'

There was a silence. 'Not talking about *him* actually, and anyway I don't think there's much we can do there – that is one hundred percent done.'

'What are you referring to then?'

'Err, Keith, the funeral, the lack of a chairman for our meetings.'

'Christ, I'm sorry, Janine – how you getting on with the funeral? Do you need any help?'

'Bit late to ask now, it's been a week.'

Jake went red – he'd left Janine and the group to deal with the aftermath of Keith's death, but he had an excuse ready all the same. 'I've got a teenager living with me, plus Martin who's a right handful, and time has run away with me.'

Janine wasn't impressed; she too had her hands full. 'The funeral is next week at the crem – I'll put the details on the group. And actually, I'm not just ringing about that, Jake – I need to ask a favour.'

'Go on,' he said. What was one more job to add to the ever-growing list?

'Tell you what, I need to pop out to your house and take a closer look at your floors. Can we talk about it later tonight, say seven?'

Jake sighed – would he ever get five minutes to himself? 'Okay, sure, see you later Janine.'

'I'll bring a chippy tea – will that do you?'

'Well, bring gravy then,' Jake said rather bluntly. He was slipping back into a Northern way of life without even noticing.

The Devil Makes Work

Considering Jake had arrived back in the North with no friends, no job and an empty diary, he was pretty bleeding busy, and he wasn't sure how he felt about that. On the one hand, it was good, and what he needed. On the other, he felt harassed and annoyed that he couldn't put his feet up and do nothing. Between Marnie, Martin, his parents, Lucy O and now Janine, his days were back-to-back.

Janine arrived with two hot parcels of cod and chips, and two polystyrene cups of thick, chip-shop gravy – she wasn't in her work stuff and looked presentable, in Jake's opinion. Even though denim was considered casual clothing, Janine had teamed hers with a blazer and a rather colourful pair of trainers, managing to look feminine and possibly almost stylish. She still stomped, though – her beastly walk would never change.

'Where's the boilersuit, getting fumigated?' he asked cheekily as he plated up the supper.

'I've been to the solicitors with our Michelle,' she said grimly. 'I had to make some sort of effort to look serious.' She sank into the kitchen chair like it was the first time that day she had managed to get her breath. 'I didn't want this to be the case – if only Martin had shown willing.'

Janine looked genuinely upset – having her sister going through a divorce was stressful, plus adding in two impressionable boys to the mix, it had to be hard on them.

'But he *has* shown willing – you know he's working now. He's

'Well, what do you want then, 'cause he's taken.'

'Never mind why Janine is here – I thought you were eating with your dad tonight? I haven't made anything. Janine's bought the two of us a fish supper – there's nothing else.'

Martin's top lip curled, as he'd been looking forward to a hot dinner all day. 'I had a buttie with me dad but that's it, he wasn't so good tonight. I was hoping we'd be having tea together – me, you and Marnie. Where is she?'

'She's at her mate's tonight.'

'Oh, okay then – I'll have some beans when this one's gone home.' He nodded his head towards Janine.

'Look, Martin, I think there's something you should know – sit down a minute, mate.'

'Is it Michelle or the kids?' he said, panicking. 'Are they okay?'

'It's nothing like that, they're all fine,' Janine reassured him.

Martin sat and faced his cousin and sister-in-law. Jake led the way – he felt Janine might take too much pleasure in revealing that the internet had witnessed Martin 'shit shag' Peterson in all his glory.

'There's a video going round on TikTok,' Jake said tentatively. 'Now don't panic, we can try and get it taken down.'

'Good luck with that!' Janine said, smirking. 'It's already been shared thousands of times.'

'What video?'

Jake took a deep breath. 'Well, it's from the back of the pub – more specifically, the empty skip at the back of the pub. Ring any bells?' Jake almost shut his eyes; Martin would surely implode at this point.

'Seen it already,' Martin said casually. 'What of it?'

Jake and Janine looked at one another in disbelief.

'And you're okay with it?' Janine asked. 'You're not upset… or worried?'

'I could have gone on a bit longer, I reckon, but I'd had an absolute skinful so I wasn't at my best.'

'You know our Michelle has seen it – she's furious!' Janine hoped this would at least resonate.

Martin laughed. '*She's* furious? At least it wasn't in our bed, in our house! Cheeky mare.'

'So what – you don't mind that this is out there, and people know it's you?'

Martin shrugged cockily. 'As they said in *Friends*, "We were on a break!" Now if that's your big news, I'm going for a bath – regards to the boys, Janine.' And off he went upstairs, completely unbothered that his big bare arse was being viewed by the nation.

'Wow, just wow!' Jake had no excuses for his cousin this time. He had to just hope that somehow, at some point, Martin would grow up. Jake tucked into his food and changed the subject.

'So, what's this favour you wanted?'

Janine looked uncomfortable. 'Look, it's not something I really want to ask of you, but suppose I'm hoping you'll do the decent thing. So, we were wondering – the group, that is. Help is at Hand...'

Jake put his fork down. 'Go on,' he said, presuming he was going to be asked to be the chairman in dead Keith's place – something he would accept graciously, and with pride.

'Erm, well, the church hall is denying us the rental, and we all found it quite comfortable here the other week, so we figured we could make this our headquarters – going forward, we would like to meet here every week.'

Jake almost choked.

'Wait, what? You're kidding? Why are the church stopping us using their hall?'

'Fucking Keith didn't pay the fees for the year – nobody knows why.'

'Well, how much is that? It can't be much.'

Subs were only a quid a week, and Jake was prepared to cover it – that was surely the answer.

'It doesn't matter; they've had enough of us and want rid. We're not the official AA, are we? We're just a group that Keith made up and, apparently, with the number of incidents over the past year, we aren't worth the fifteen quid a week or whatever it is.'

'What incidents?' Jake asked. He was furious that a so-called religious establishment was denying a bunch of thoroughly decent human beings a place to air their troubles. Janine then reeled off a few damn good reasons why no fucker would want this group anywhere near their church.

'A few months before you joined, we had a guy who was really unwell with the drink, but also a bit of a wanker. He left a full adult nappy in the biscuit cupboard – they didn't find it for a week.'

Janine gagged, remembering the day of the discovery – she could still smell it in her thoughts.

'Oh, and when Frank was still driving, his wing mirror managed to hook itself to the handle of a parishioner's wheelchair, and ended up dragging her halfway home without noticing.'

Jake's eyes widened. Frank driving was a shocking thought – he could barely walk in a straight line.

'The woman had to have counselling, she thought she was a goner – at one point he was doing forty on the back roads.'

Jake's eyes widened.

'We've had communion wine go missing, physical fights in the car park, and now it turns out Keith was pocketing the subs. I think the priest has seen his death as a chance to get rid of us once and for all.'

Jake was clueless that there had been so much drama. 'For fuck's sake.'

Janine lowered her voice. 'You do know that's the reason he set up the group, don't you?'

Jake frowned. 'What do you mean?'

'He was treasurer at the local AA group, and there was a discrepancy with the contributions. Rumour has it he was ousted.'

Jake raised his eyebrows; Keith was a troubled soul for sure.

'He set up Help is at Hand because he had nowhere else to go. He needed a support group and it took off. Well, apart from the stealing and the nappies and the fighting,' Janine added with a sheepish grin.

'And now you want me to have all that going on here, in my home?' Jake said rather sarcastically.

Janine looked around the kitchen and nodded. 'It's warm and friendly, it's got character, it's a special place and more importantly...' Jake waited for an incoming compliment about him being a wonderful host and stand-up guy. 'More importantly, Jakey boy, it's free!'

His shoulders dropped. 'And the chairman's position, I suppose you want me to step into that role, run things like Keith did?'

Janine laughed and spat her tea out slightly. 'Christ no, you've not been sober for long enough, pal. No, that would go to Peggy – she's Keith's obvious replacement.'

Jake rubbed his eyes; this had been a hell of a week. He'd thought of drinking often, and there had been no meeting – perhaps there was a connection. He didn't relish the thought of his house being used in this way but really, before he had it looking super-classy and stylish, what harm could it do?

'Okay, but only until we find somewhere more suitable. And not after the floors have been restored – I'm not having them stamped on by nappy-wearing pissheads.'

Janine beamed – that was one more thing ticked off her extensive list of things to do. 'I can't thank you enough. I'm really starting to like you, Jake, you swanky bastard. Right, let's get these floors measured, and then I need to go and make sure the boys are in bed. Michelle's out tonight and they could be doing anything.'

Jake started to clear the plates and left Janine to get on with her job in the next room, but as she walked towards the hallway, she turned and asked, 'What was that Martin said about you being taken? Have you managed to get your ex back?'

'No, that's not happening,' Jake shouted back through the dividing wall.

'So why did he say you were taken then?'

Jake stopped scrubbing the plates, frantically trying to think of what to say. 'I am sort of seeing someone, but it's probably nothing.'

'Anyone we know?' Janine kept wiggling the tape measure to create the illusion that she was taking measurements.

'No, just someone I met online, nobody you know.' Jake felt his cheeks going red – he was unsure why.

And then, just when he hoped that would be the end of it, Martin shouted from the top of the stairs, 'He's been banging that Lucy O from *Corrie*. I'm surprised the bed's still standing if I'm honest.'

Janine left soon after. She was flustered and annoyed – she was unsure why.

British Gas

Jake's finances were pretty steady. He'd purchased the house outright, and he'd divided his money into three separate accounts. First was his current account, for living off, covering him for about two years comfortably without any huge purchases such as world tours, Maserati's or Louis Vuitton luggage sets. The second was for savings – this was a fund that would cover big purchases such as building works, a new kitchen, a new roof and three new bathrooms. The third was an investment account – he played around with the cash in here, watching it grow and sometimes deplete depending on what the world was doing. During COVID, that account took a nasty hit, but slowly and surely it had levelled itself out, and was only there to be accessed in apocalyptic circumstances. If the banks fell after an invasion from Putin, this was the money that 'fingers crossed' would be safe.

He had thought long and hard about the decision he was about to make, and although of course absolutely everything was a risk, this was going to be worth it in the end.

A few days before, Jake had dedicated an entire day to the investigation of replacement nicotine. He'd also made calls to several old colleagues to sound them out about Zing25.

'Sounds like it's gonna go off mate!' one guy had said. 'Any room for another investor?'

'Not now. I'll let you know if they decide to open it up again.' Jake had batted him away, not prepared to share the wealth just yet.

He also jumped on a Zoom with Lucas – it only seemed fair that he knew that this could be 'the one' in terms of investment. Lucas was in the office behind his desk, looking very businesslike in his sharp suit and tie. Jake felt a little embarrassed doing a meeting from his kitchen table, wearing a t-shirt splattered with paint.

'So, you're going to throw some of your own cash in, Jake? Christ, you really do think this is a goer?' Lucas leaned back in his big leather chair, pen behind his ear.

Jake nodded. 'Yes, I really do – did you see the projections I sent over? The numbers are incredible.'

Lucas squinted at his laptop and tapped the keyboard a few times. 'Yeah, yeah, amazing – I think I'll shove some in too.'

'Shall we go through a couple of the details, then? There's a deadline for investing, so we need to get going.'

Lucas looked under the desk and smiled. 'Err no mate, I can't right now. I've got a client waiting in reception, so just send it all over by email.'

Jake almost challenged that – they had booked an hour for this update, and it had been less than twenty minutes. He decided to let it go as Lucas seemed incredibly distracted.

And so, the following morning after sleeping on it, Jake made a huge financial decision. He transferred £250k, the entire balance of his savings account, into the investment fund of Zing25. He would have at least quadrupled his investment within two years – all he had to do was wait. He could manage the refurb using his current account and perhaps even dip into the third account, if needed. It was all doable, and well worth it.

It was a Saturday morning, and Jake had reluctantly agreed to go Christmas shopping with Lucy O – she'd specifically taken the day off work, so it would have been cruel to tell her that he'd rather hang out with Martin or help the builders drain the septic tank again.

It wasn't that Jake didn't like Lucy – he did – and had things not become so intense so quickly, then perhaps he wouldn't feel tired every time she spoke.

Marnie had gone back home to help her grandparents for the day. They'd felt she was young enough to fight it off if, God forbid, she caught the 'proper flu'.

Lucy almost skipped down the path of her nan's before she climbed into Jake's car and kissed him on the cheek. She was looking forward to a day out, with a long lunch and then hopefully a sleepover, which she'd string out until Monday if she could. Jake felt utterly exhausted with it all – even the sex wasn't enough to keep him fully interested.

'Ooh this is exciting, Christmas shopping with my man,' Lucy said, smiling her cutest smile with her expensive teeth. 'I thought we'd get some of those posh pies whilst we're in town, and have them on our knees tonight.'

Jake swallowed back a gulp. He had planned on dropping Lucy off and then swinging by his parents' to pick Marnie up for a night of shit telly on the sofa. The last thing he wanted to do on a Saturday evening was to hold in farts and talk about Deirdre and fucking Ken. Jake said nothing – he would have to deal with this strategically once he'd filled his boot with crap for the family.

Walking around Manchester with a local 'soap star' was an eye-opener for sure. At least ten people asked for a selfie with Lucy, whilst Jake stood quietly holding the bags, wishing a tram would flatten him.

By the time they walked into the restaurant for lunch, Lucy was glowing with pride. She had proved to herself, and more importantly to Jake, that she was still a somebody, and that the people hadn't forgotten her. Even when a rather dopey man asked, 'Are you feeling any better dear? Falling asleep in the bath is very dangerous, you know,' Lucy made a quip about getting back on her feet, and signed the man's bus ticket with her eyeliner.

Jake found the whole thing preposterous – even if he'd bumped into Elvis Presley himself, he would never lower himself to ask for a selfie.

They sat by the doorway of a small tapas restaurant just on the corner of Deansgate. Lucy faced the window and intentionally sat slightly to the left so the shoppers could get a glimpse of her as they passed. It was all a bit naff in Jake's view. This did not make him think any more of Lucy – in fact, he couldn't wait to get away from her and all her dickhead fans.

'So, what I was thinking is that on Christmas Day, I know you'll probably have family commitments, but at night we could meet at yours and I can give you your pressie.' Lucy winked in what she thought was a sexy way.

'Are we doing presents?' Jake fought to hide a wince.

'You don't have to get me anything – this is something we can both enjoy.' Jake smiled blankly. 'Do you want a clue, Jake?'

He almost shook his head. 'Go on then.'

'It's lacy, it's furry and it's festive.' Lucy jiggled her breasts, but Jake felt absolutely nothing.

'The thing is, Lucy, my parents have this whole thing planned that goes from Christmas Eve until well past Boxing Day, so I won't be free, unfortunately.'

Lucy's face fell – she'd been relying on Jake to make this year half decent. 'Oh, okay, I just thought… with this being such a tricky time for those of us that don't… well, can't drink, I would be able to lean on you a bit. Do you see what I'm saying?' She gazed out of the window, doing her best impression of a newly widowed Hollywood great.

Jake immediately felt bad. It was possible he was Lucy's only friend, and they did share the same demon after all.

'Aren't you spending it with your nan?' Jake asked, hoping to salvage this somehow.

'Yes, during the day, but she goes to bed at eight o'clock,' Lucy said glumly.

Jake failed to see the problem with that – an eight o'clock bedtime sounded like heaven.

'Oh okay, so it's just me, Nan and the dog then. We'll probably have a microwave meal. Nan's not a cook, and she doesn't like washing up.'

'You could cook!' Jake enthused. 'Let your old nan put her feet up.'

The waiter came over to take the order, and Lucy shooed him away and replied through gritted teeth, 'She doesn't really like me to use the kitchen. She gets a bit funny and territorial.'

'Still, it must be nice for her to have company?' Jake had recently learned that loneliness was a bigger killer than smoking, according to an advert he'd seen. He happened to like both, so his days were numbered.

'Not really, she's a very angry person and quite shallow, my nan. She was proud as punch when I was working on *Corrie*, showing me off and asking me to cut ribbons at local events, but after I was axed – *temporarily* – she seems to be ashamed more than anything else. I don't feel very welcome there.'

'Shit, that's not good.' Jake wondered why so many old people were bitter and nasty these days – surely they'd gotten over the war by now.

Lucy realised this was a battle she couldn't win, so she pulled herself together. 'Anyway, not to worry, I'll keep myself busy somehow. Tell you what, we'll do something on New Year's Eve, something special – just the two of us.' And then she snapped out of her dark patch and began googling hotels in Scotland.

Jake nibbled miserably on the rubbish tapas; it was as far from Spanish food as you could get. A dish called 'Angry Potatoes' pretending to be *patatas bravas* was basically fat chips drowning in tinned tomatoes, apparently rendered fuming by a sprinkling of paprika. The *gambas pil pil*, a dish usually consisting of plump prawns sizzling in chilli oil were, in this case, shrimp the size of maggots swimming in a tepid liquid. Jake didn't feel any joy from this lunch or this relationship – in fact he felt cornered. However, he and Lucy were cut from the same cloth, and he didn't want to send her back to square one, so he endured a couple more hours of their gruelling day before leaving Manchester empty-handed. He would do his Christmas shopping at TK Maxx in Oldham one night the following week – alone!

'Okey dokey then, see you soon, thanks for a nice day,' Jake said as he pulled up outside Lucy's nan's house. She hadn't noticed which turning he had taken, because she was busy on her Instagram account posting the pictures of her fans. Lucy looked up, realising she had been brought back home, which was not the plan at all.

'Oh, I was thinking I'd come back to yours tonight – make a weekend of it,' she said with disappointment.

Jake shook his head. 'Sorry, I need to pick Marnie up, she's been at my parents'. They've had a cold, I mean proper flu, and she's been there helping out.'

'Well, I can come with you. I'd love to meet your mum and dad.'

Jake paused – why couldn't she read the room? If he'd wanted her to meet his parents, he would have asked. They were nowhere close to a meeting of relatives and he knew, deep down, they never would be.

'Do you mind if we don't, Lucy? I'm absolutely knackered and I'm going to have an early night.' Jake avoided eye contact; he didn't want to see sad eyes or a bottom lip trembling. He'd put his shift in for the day, and could do no more.

Lucy left the car feeling deflated. She'd packed for two nights and had told her nan that it wouldn't be long before she'd be out of her hair for good, to which Nasty Nan had replied, 'Thank fuck, there is a god!'

Jake pulled up outside his parents' home – it didn't feel as depressing as it had when he'd first arrived back. He had once associated their blue front door with failure and misery; the door he had walked through after London had chewed him up and spat him out onto the pavement. But now, this was just Alf and Di's house that he could visit anytime if he wanted a brew, a bollocking and access to all the frozen leftovers he could ever want.

'Jake, is that you, son?' Alf shouted from the bedroom as Jake entered their cluttered hallway.

'Yes, Dad, how are you both feeling?'

'We're on the mend, but my legs are still like jelly, son,' Di croaked.

Marnie appeared from the kitchen; she had her coat on and her hood up.

'Looks like someone's ready for the off,' Jake smiled. Marnie had also put a shift in that day.

'Them two,' she said in a whisper, 'are a fucking nightmare.'

'Jake, can you ring British Gas and let them know the bill is going to be higher this month?' Di yelled.

'Why?'

'Because we've had the electric blanket on during the day.'

'Why do I need to call British Gas?'

'Because it says in the pamphlet that if there are going to be significant changes to usage, they should be informed.'

'They won't give a flying fuck, Mum.'

'Eh, potty mouth,' Alf bellowed.

'And Jake?'

'Yes, Dad?'

'We'll need to have Christmas dinner at yours this year.'

Jake felt sick, and narrowed his eyes. 'Wait what, why?'

'I'll still be weak by then – peeling potatoes and stuffing a turkey will wipe me clean out.'

'It's two weeks away, Mum, you'll be fine by then.'

There was silence for a while, and then somebody got out of bed and shuffled to the top of the stairs. Alf stood and shouted down, 'Jesus Christ, son, we're in bits here. Surely you can rustle up a meal in your massive mansion for the seven of us?'

Jake huffed. 'Seven, where you getting seven from?'

The bannister creaked as Alf leaned back against it to free up his fingers for counting.

'So, there's me, your mum, our Marnie, that great lummox Martin, my brother Bert, you and Pat Bayley, our neighbour – that's seven.'

'Actually Dad, Martin will be seeing his kids that day, and why the heck is Pat Bayley coming?'

'No, son, Michelle and the kids are off to Euro Disney for a week, and Martin ain't invited. Pat normally goes to family in Southport, but her daughter is having a hysterectomy on Boxing Day, so she'll be nil by mouth on the twenty-fifth.'

'And that is our problem why?'

'You can't expect someone to cook a dinner, watch everyone else eat it whilst you contemplate having your womb removed, son – that's not on.'

'You're killing me, Dad – this is my worst nightmare,' Jake shouted up.

'You could have no legs, stop moaning,' Alf said, and then he dragged his feet back to the sick bay to turn up the blanket and give British Gas the shock of their life.

Marnie and Jake giggled all the way home as Marnie broke down her day. 'They've had me up and down those stairs like a nurse on speed,' she yawned. 'You'd think they had smallpox,' she added, having just covered it in History for her GCSE. 'I was sent to inform the neighbours that flu was in the vicinity. And then they asked me to warm up their socks in the microwave – nearly threw up, I did.'

'For fuck's sake.' Jake's stomach turned – this was the very same microwave they used to heat up all the tinned shit he'd bought them in the Morrisons shop. 'It's no joke getting old, Marnie. They used to be fairly normal, would you believe?'

Marnie frowned. 'I can't imagine my grandparents not being weird.'

Jake didn't have that luxury – they'd been off the wall as long as he could remember, but he embraced it most of the time. 'They've always had their quirks, but it's accelerating at an alarming rate.'

By the time they pulled up at the house it was dark, freezing cold, and a thick coating of frost covered the valley and the roof of The Coach House. The lights that Martin had pinned to the oak tree flickered, and the place couldn't have looked more festive.

'Look at our house, Jake – it's like something from a film. I can't wait to get in and put my PJs on.'

The fact that Marnie said 'our house' made Jake feel good, and not in the slightest bit claustrophobic. This was somebody that he didn't have to put any effort into being around; it felt right. Okay, she wasn't his daughter, but making the kid feel at home and looked after was a special feeling, and one that was new to him. He had never really looked after anybody before, only himself, and he'd done a piss-poor job at that.

Martin was waiting in the kitchen. He looked quite tired, and Jake suspected he may have been crying; the swollen eyes and puffed-up cheeks could, however, have been an indication of a 'big night out'.

'Good god, you look rough,' Marnie said as she saw Martin slumped at the table, nursing what looked like a cup of tea.

'Is that Baileys, Martin? Are you drinking Baileys out of a mug?' Jake picked it up and smelt it.

'No, it's tea, dickhead. I've given up the booze for a bit.'

'Bollocks!' Marnie laughed. 'As if!'

Jake felt the shift in Martin's mood and decided that, although he agreed this was probably nonsense, he would be supportive.

'Marnie, go and get changed and ring the Indian and order a takeaway – anything you want.'

Marnie's huge eyes lit up – she loved a takeaway with no limits. There were never any limits when Jake was buying. Nan and Grandad always insisted they share this and that, and would try and force her to finish the whole thing even when she was full.

'They're going away for Christmas, Michelle and the kids,' Martin said flatly.

'Yeah, I heard. Disneyland, right?' Jake sat across from Martin. 'Look, it's just one year, and it'll take the sting out of their parents splitting up.'

'Her mum and dad have paid for it – they want me out of the picture.'

'You can see their point, Martin. You've been fired for sexual harassment, and then had sex with a woman in a skip on camera. It's not ideal.'

Martin nodded – the penny had finally dropped that he was public enemy number one for good reason.

'So, you'll spend Christmas here with my family. Your dad's coming, and we'll make the best of it.'

Martin looked up and smiled. 'Really? You don't mind?'

'You're family, mate. We'll have a laugh, and the boys will be back before you know it.'

Martin nodded – he felt a bit better. 'I really didn't want it to be just me and my dad. I know it sounds selfish, but he's not great company – not any more, anyway.'

Jake couldn't disagree – who could relish the thought of spending Christmas in a smelly lounge, explaining that Frank Sinatra was dead on repeat?

'Go on up, Martin, and put your pyjamas on – we'll eat some food and watch a film.'

By half-eight, the three tucked into a massive Indian. Marnie only ate naan bread, rice and chips but Jake said nothing – so long as she ate something was all that mattered. Marnie showed Martin the latest phones, iPads and headphones whilst they ate as gift ideas for the lads. He was adding up how much this little lot would cost when a car pulled up on the driveway.

'Who the hell is that at this time?' Martin said as he peeked through the gap in the curtains. He turned around with one eyebrow raised. 'Fuck's sake, it's the Doberman – probably come to break my jaw.'

Marnie giggled. Martin was hysterical, especially when he was pissed off. Jake was secretly pleased Janine had turned up; he'd really enjoyed their chippy tea, and was disappointed that she'd left so abruptly. He also felt happy when her name appeared on his screen, be it a text or a call. Something told him that she felt the same. He checked his reflection in the handle of his knife to make sure there was no food on his chin.

'What do you want this time, Janine?' he heard Martin say from the doorway. It was extremely unwelcoming, but her reply really made Jake smile.

'Definitely not you, Fatso,' she said, before barging past him and walking into the kitchen dressed like Scott of the Antarctic.

'Janine, to what do we owe this pleasure?' Jake asked whilst continuing to eat his food.

Janine leaned against the worktop and observed. 'Proper little set up you have here – what is this, a pyjama party? Look at you all,' she laughed. To be fair, they all had checked nightwear on with dressing gowns and massive slippers, essential attire in this old and cold house. There were currently only two working radiators downstairs due to the plumber being slow as a slug, and upstairs relied on plug-in heaters that Jake had hired for the duration of the renovation.

'I tried calling but it went straight to voicemail. I left you a message,' Janine said, pointing at Jake's phone on the side.

'Oh, it must be dead, sorry – was it important?' Jake had purposely switched his phone off the minute he'd left Lucy's. He didn't want to spend the evening responding to romantic messages with sickening emojis.

'Just to say I wanted to pop round and try a treatment on the corner of your floor before I ordered a job lot of the stuff. And I was passing, so...'

Martin looked up from his loaded poppadom. 'You were passing a house that sits on a hill with no neighbours?'

Janine looked away uncomfortably. 'Well, sort of passing – I had to look at a job round the corner.'

Martin narrowed his eyes suspiciously. 'What job, and what corner?'

Jake came to Janine's rescue. 'Pull up a pew. There's a Madras on the go here, join us, please.'

'She's had her tea, surely?' Martin muttered grumpily, putting his hand firmly on his garlic naan.

Janine began to take off her coat and gloves. 'I haven't actually, and I'd love some, thanks.'

Apart from Martin intermittently scowling at Janine, it was a nice meal. There was laughter – mainly at Di and Alf's expense – plus good banter between the Masters of the Universe. Marnie ate her white rice, observing three messed-up adults successfully getting through a curry without a lager in sight.

'It's snowing, oh my god, look at it!' Marnie shouted as the plates were being cleared.

Sure enough, in the time they'd taken to eat their meal, the Lancashire skies had dumped a white velvet coat on the valley as far as you could see. There was no sign of it stopping either, as snowflakes pelted the ground silently.

'You can't drive home in this, Janine,' Marnie said. 'You should stay and watch a movie until it's stopped – come on, you can wear some of Jake's pyjamas, so you don't feel left out.'

Janine thought for a moment – it was true, her old van would struggle getting down the hill and, with it being so cold, the snow was turning to ice almost as it landed.

'Is that okay?' she asked Jake shyly.

Jake nodded. 'Sure, can't have you going out in this, can we?'

Marnie and Janine went upstairs to root through Jake's drawers whilst he and Martin cleared away.

'She's not so bad – she's only looking out for her sister. She's quite nice, Janine.'

Martin raised his eyebrows. 'See if you still think that once she's chinned you.'

'She's good with your boys.'

'Yeah, suppose.'

'And she's loyal – definitely got her family's back.'

'Not my back,' Martin said firmly. 'Definitely not my back.'

'That's unfair, Martin – she tried to get you and Michelle back together, and then you went and did your porn movie.'

Martin shut his eyes. 'Yep, starting to realise that was not my finest moment.'

'Let's work with her, not against her. She could really be a help for the boys right now.'

Martin nodded. Jake was right, Janine was right – they were all right.

Because it was snowing and close to Christmas, Marnie asked to choose a film that suited the evening. With the gas fire blasting out its filthy chemicals and the curtains open so they could watch the weather, the four settled down to watch *The Shining* – a terrifying film from the 1980s that, if you read between the lines, is basically about severe mental illness. Jake let it happen. Marnie had some funny ideas – she could be quite childlike in so many ways, but more mature than all the adults put together in another. It was a particularly jumpy film, and Jake and Janine sat side by side on the sofa in the corner with a blanket over their legs.

'This is fucking terrifying,' Janine whispered to Jake as Jack Nicholson slowly started to lose his mind in a house on a hill covered in snow.

'It's going to get a lot darker, I warn you now,' Jake whispered back. 'Can't believe you haven't seen it.'

'I probably have, but I saw loads of films drunk and fell asleep halfway through or I don't remember watching them,' Janine admitted.

Jake nodded knowingly. He had attended cinemas and London shows in the same state. He even flew to New York to watch *The Lion King* on Broadway – he'd been so lamped he never even saw the ending.

'Here we go, this when it gets really scary,' Martin shouted from his bean bag on the floor.

Janine immediately grabbed Jake's hand under the blanket. She was a tough cookie, but spooky shit was something you couldn't fight your way out of. Jake squeezed her hand reassuringly, and neither let go even once the scene ended – in fact they stayed like that for the next half-hour.

It was a funny thing: with the curry, the film and the hand-holding, Jake hadn't thought about drinking or Nicky, not once. Just as Jack Nicholson was about to show his wife how to open a door with an axe, another car pulled up onto the driveway, the headlights blasting through the open curtains. Martin jumped up.

'It's a taxi – who the fuck is this?' He was quite the charming host. He went off to answer the door for a second time that evening, and Marnie paused the film so they could hear who it was.

'Well well well, what do we have here?' Martin said flirtatiously.

Jake wondered if that dreadlocked barmaid had crawled her way up the hill for the sequel of 'Sex Skip'. He hoped not, as Janine would have to free up her hands for a scrap.

The tune for *Coronation Street* can be achieved quite effectively by puffing out the cheeks, opening each side of the mouth slightly and humming the tune – it creates the sound of a trombone, which is what Martin did as Lucy O made her entrance to the living room.

Jake immediately removed his hand from Janine's and threw the blanket to the floor. 'Lucy, what are you doing here?'

Lucy O was wearing a onesie and a bobble hat – a sort of ski outfit for people who didn't ski. 'You said you were having an early night, so I thought fuck it, I'll have one with you.'

Jake was stunned. Either she was unbelievably stupid and didn't understand a brush off when it slapped her in the face, or this was calculated.

'I brought hot chocolate, the posh stuff.' She pulled out a tub of Fortnum & Mason drinking chocolate that was secretly Cadbury's decanted into a fancy tin.

Jake said nothing; he could think of nothing.

'Look at you, you *are* tired. Let's go up, come on.' Lucy stroked Jake's cheek before noticing Janine. 'Oh, hello – you're the cousin, are you?'

Janine stood, towering over Lucy in an awkward-giant type of way.

'Erm, no – I'm Jake's cousin's wife's sister. Not sure what that makes me,' Janine said meekly. 'We met at the meeting here the other night – Lucy, right?'

Lucy shut her eyes, for effect. 'Oh crikey, my memory is shocking. Yes, I think I remember. Did you want an autograph, was that you?'

'No, that wasn't me.' Janine then yawned, for effect. 'Right, I think I'll try and get down that hill now – it's getting late.'

Jake gulped. Neither of these women was his girlfriend, and neither was in any way his type – yet here he was, feeling extremely uncomfortable in between them both.

'See ya later, Jakey boy – bye guys.' Janine gathered her coat, hat and gloves and bolted out of the front door, missing the end of yet another film.

The household watched as she faced the blizzard, managed to get into her van and then basically skidded down the hill with no seatbelt on, and with no certainty the brakes would work at the bottom.

Martin then piped up, 'Hey, she never did that patch test on the floor.'

To which Marnie replied, 'She never intended to.'

The Final Curtain

If Jake was given the job of designing a crematorium, he'd do a damn sight better than this, he thought to himself as he gazed around the bleak room. It had no character whatsoever. If you really must send your loved one into a furnace, then at least do it with style. He was sure this place doubled up as a conference room on the days they weren't barbequing.

'Look at the chairs,' he whispered to Dean, 'they're so cheap.'

Dean ran his finger across the plastic. 'And sticky,' he grimaced. 'Still, at least there's a few here.' Dean looked behind him and smiled a little. 'A decent turn out, but who are all these people? I don't think there's enough buffet.'

Jake felt a tap on the shoulder, and turned to see Frank wearing a tracksuit and slippers. Jake looked him up and down. 'Glad to see you made the effort, Frank.'

'Couldn't fit into my suit – it's those Ginsters pasties they do at the local shop. I first started on them about three months ago...' Frank stopped talking – his mouth had dropped open as a lady in a wide-brimmed black hat, a fitted black shift dress and sporting a bright red lip elegantly glided past him. 'Peggy, is that you?' Frank smoothed his hair and smelt his own breath inside his t-shirt.

Peggy turned, smiled gracefully at Frank, and then took her seat just in front of them with her husband.

'Now *that* is what you call a woman,' Frank loudly said to Dean and Jake before sighing.

'Jesus, you've got it bad. You know she's married, Frank, and like two decades younger than you?' Dean reminded him.

'A man can dream – let me be.'

'Frank, who are all these random people – do you know any of them?'

Frank scanned the room and nodded at a few of the guests. He then turned back to Jake and Dean. 'These are all ex-members of Help is at Hand – some moved away, some joined AA, and some went back to the drink, but Keith helped them all out in one way or another.'

Jake felt a swell; it was lovely that Keith had started this group over ten years ago and had been a constant support to his members, and now they had come to pay their respects. Never mind that his kids weren't there – almost every seat was full.

'Hey, how's things going with Lucy? I heard you two were getting, err, close if you get my meaning.'

Jake didn't mind Dean asking – in fact, it could be good to get an opinion from somebody else. He whispered into Dean's ear, 'To be honest mate, I wish it had never started. I'm just not feeling it and she really is – feeling it, I mean.'

Dean relaxed immediately – he couldn't be doing with Lucy. 'She's annoying, right? Totally full of herself.'

Jake nodded. He didn't want to be disloyal, but fuck, she was irritating. 'I can't exactly kick her out of the group, can I? I'm scared to end it because she seems so vulnerable.'

Dean rolled his eyes – he knew only too well what it was to be trapped. 'And now it makes sense,' he said knowingly.

'What does?'

'AA forbids relationships with other members – this is why, it's a minefield.'

Jake nodded slowly. 'Yeah, you're right – this is exactly why. It doesn't help that we're meeting at my house as of Tuesday. How awkward is that?'

'Fucking hell,' Dean said, almost laughing. 'What a quandary – shouldn't be so irresistible, should you?'

'So no sage advice?'

Dean thought for a few moments. 'We may have just hit on something that could get you out – why not end it with her and say it's because you're in the same group. It's a conflict of interest, and AA frowns upon it, so we do too. That way she doesn't feel hurt – it's not you, it's the group type thing.'

Jake's eyes lit up – this was a damn good point. 'That works, that totally works – sobriety over everything, right?' Jake obviously didn't reveal that he had been 'holding hands' with another group member who he had developed some unexplainable feelings for. There was only Peggy left before he would have to move on to the men, but he kept that one to himself.

Right on cue, Lucy O made her entrance. She sat at the back on her own and nodded to Jake, but that was all. She knew she'd been walking on thin ice by muscling her way into Jake's on Saturday night, but things had got so unbearable at her nan's she felt the ten-minute taxi ride to Jake's would be worth it. She didn't get the warm welcome she'd hoped for, and when Jake made a wall out of blankets and didn't touch her once during the night, she knew she could be on her way out. Why did this always happen to her? What was she doing so wrong? Yes, she could be a bit much – sometimes she was too full-on too early – and she did tend to become attached to people quite quickly, but for pity's sake, she was a star, and stars have flaws – her agent had told her that when he released her.

Lucy just hoped that this time, this one would be different. 'A wealthy older man with a big house' was her destiny according to her clairvoyant, and she'd been on the money with absolutely everything apart from her getting a Bafta – but that was still possible, especially if they brought her back to *Corrie* with an uncontrollable tic. She would just have to put in the groundwork, try a bit harder and play on Jake's weaknesses until he fell for her properly. It wouldn't be long before she was lady of the manor, and perhaps *Emmerdale* would have an opening – their set was only an hour and a half away.

Lucy really shouldn't have been there – she'd never even met Keith, but Janine had insisted the whole group go to make up the numbers. Ideally, she'd have arrived on Jake's arm and people would nudge each other, wondering if it was really her. She'd have to make sure the funeral was about the deceased, and not herself. But on this day, Lucy went against the grain and kept her head down, wore barely any make-up, and planned to leave just before the end so as not to draw attention to herself – Jake would respect that, he would see that she could tone it down, and that would impress him.

The service was nice enough – Peggy did the eulogy as she had known Keith a few years, and had been closest to him. It was an emotional tribute, but Peggy sniffling and stopping to say, 'Poor old Keith' every few seconds was quite distracting. Eventually, Peggy's husband, who was an extremely dapper gentleman in a three-piece suit including a pocket watch, led Peggy down from the microphone and said, 'Settle down,' loud enough for everyone to hear.

Just as the coffin was about to be sent on the conveyor belt to the oven, a small man with a receding hairline and a woman with almost the same face but with more hair made their way unexpectedly towards the poor excuse for an altar.

The man grabbed the microphone, and began a tale that was worthy of a Facebook post.

'Hello. My name is Steve, this is my twin sister Susan – over there are our partners and our children.' A scruffy-looking group waved from their seats, like something from *Family Fortunes*.

'Susan and I are Keith's children. Keith's secret children, might I add.' The funeral guests gave each other nervous looks – what on earth was going on? Susan then grabbed the microphone. 'I just can't let my dad go without saying a few words, it wouldn't be right. You see, you all know him as Keith the addict, Keith the disgraced teacher and Keith the failed father and husband. Well, we know different.'

Peggy put her hands over her face. 'Poor Keith,' she wailed again.

'We just want to say that although he made some poor errors of judgement, he did his best. He was a good dad to us and a kind man; he was under a lot of pressure trying to juggle two families. It took its toll.'

Frank shouted out, 'Scum!' very loudly, and Jake jabbed him in the shoulder. 'Well, he come across all holy than thou,' Frank angrily pointed out.

The twins ignored Frank – they had expected more heckling so this was tolerable.

'We just wanted to say goodbye to our dad, to let people know he was loved, we're not a dirty secret any more.' Susan let out a sob, and her twin comforted her.

'Do his other family know you exist?' Peggy enquired. This had really shaken her, and although 'poor Keith' had been a good friend, she didn't condone this at all.

'They do – they have for a while, us being the reason he was pretty much shunted out of the family.'

'And does your mother make a habit of sleeping with married men?' Frank blurted out.

Susan and Steve looked at one another. 'Our mother is dead,' they said in unison.

Peggy could take no more – she threw off her hat and sprinted up the altar to hug them both. 'You poor babies, orphaned at such a young age.'

Dean said out of the side of his mouth, 'They're over thirty, hardly babies for fuck's sake.'

Whether or not Keith had been a drunken philanderer who'd left an absolute mess in his wake, it was still rather sad to watch him burn. Tom Jones blasted out of a speaker, and that was it – he was gone.

The wake was a typically Northern affair. Soggy sausage rolls, massive pork pies you could break a window with, and coleslaw where the mayonnaise had turned to water around the edges. It wasn't exactly an afternoon at The Ritz, but it was all the group could afford.

'I wonder who gets Keith's house?' Peggy said in a hushed tone. 'This could be tricky – I mean, really tricky. Wonder what he's left and who to. We'll need to check the will and make sure the right thing happens.'

Janine looked flustered – she'd been responsible for this 'event' and she'd really done her best to make sure that she gave Keith the send-off that he deserved, and that's exactly what he'd got. But she would not be around for divvying up the estate – that was not on her.

'Hi, Janine, you look nice,' Jake said, taking in her lack of overalls and presence of black jeans.

'Thank you!' she said curtly, without looking up.

Janine barely made any eye contact with Jake at all that day. After Saturday night, she'd felt embarrassed, a little confused and super-awkward. There had been no message, no call. He went very quiet after the hand-holding, and it would seem that it had meant much more to her than it did him.

It was possibly the first time ever that Janine had really felt something genuine for a man. She wasn't a virgin, of course not. She'd been around the block a fair few times, sometimes even backwards. But she was a virgin in the field of feelings, and this was uncharted territory for a girl who could drink a sailor under the table, and beat a thick armed farmer in a fist fight. This was an uncomfortable place for Janine to be, and she wasn't entirely sure what it meant. So, she dealt with it by avoiding eye contact, ridiculous as it sounds. It sort of worked.

Jake, on the other hand, found this rather frustrating. He'd thought of nothing else but Janine since Saturday night – he'd built a bedding wall between himself and the soap star so that he could think of her without interruption. She hadn't messaged him, she'd barely said goodbye and, although this wasn't as important, she'd taken his favourite pyjama bottoms. He'd waited for Keith's cremation so he could continue that connection, explore it more and perhaps instigate another scary movie night without small blonde visitors. He, too, was confused. Having feelings for a woman who scared him physically, with all the grace of a dump truck, was quite odd. If somebody had told Jake a few years ago that he'd have romantic feelings for a woman whose first choice of outfit was a boiler suit, he'd have pissed his pants laughing.

Jake spotted Tyler at the back of the hall – he was still channelling a Christian youth worker. With the weather still well below zero, he wore a chunky knit and hat to match – there was no sign of his skull-and-crossbones jewellery that had once deemed him a menace to society. Jake beckoned him over, and Tyler grabbed onto a lady's sleeve – a very slim lady verging on underweight – who he led proudly over to the group.

'This is my mum, Lorraine.'

Lorraine smiled – it was a blank, strained expression, the sort of smile that told a thousand stories, none with a happy ending.

'It's so good to meet you all. I wish it were under better circumstances,' Lorraine said. 'But I'm glad to be able to thank you, really.' She paused and caught her breath. 'For taking Tyler under your wing. He's been better since coming to group. It has really helped him having some kindred spirits to share with.'

'You're welcome, dear – it's not been easy, he's a little tyke.'

Jake frowned at Frank's response, since he'd done fuck all to help Tyler – he'd insulted his attire, booed at his singing and told him that the only hope for him was to join the Marines and learn the hard way.

But Lorraine continued, 'Don't get me wrong, he's not perfect, I still have to check behind the boiler, and inside the cistern, and in the boot of my car.' Tyler rolled his eyes; there weren't many hiding places left at this rate. 'But we're getting there, aren't we Ty? Can't lose you too. And I'm so grateful to you, Jake, for opening up your home – these meetings are very important.'

Jake felt a sense of pride. He really thought Tyler was a good kid, somebody who maybe lost his way too early in life. Perhaps becoming a victim of his surroundings. All you had to do was look at Martin to know that if you never leave a place, the boredom will get you eventually.

Lorraine suddenly glanced over Jake's shoulder. 'Hey, where did that Lucy O get to? I meant to ask her for an autograph for my mother – she's in a home, and she could use that as currency.'

'Don't know, but it's not like her to miss an opportunity to shine,' Dean muttered.

'This is a wake, Dean, people don't shine at a wake,' Peggy admonished him. 'She left after the service – gone to the chemist for her nan before it shuts apparently. She won't be back.'

Jake was relieved – at least he wouldn't have to fight her off in the car park. He tried to catch Janine's eye, hoping that the lack of Lucy may create an opportunity for her to visit that evening, but Janine continued to stare ahead, pretending that she didn't hear, but was secretly thrilled that shitty little Lucy wasn't around to make her feel ugly and unwanted.

As the buffet disappeared and the crowd thinned out, Keith's twins and their family approached the group.

'We're leaving now, and we wanted to say that Dad found much comfort in running this group. We'd also like to thank you for arranging it, and wondered who we owed money to. We can't have you paying for Dad's funeral – that's our job.'

'Quite right,' Frank said, folding his arms. He'd only put a tenner towards it, and he'd eaten at least that much worth of Stilton.

At last, Janine spoke – it was, after all, her gig. 'If you leave your number, I'll send you a WhatsApp and I'll let you know, if that's okay. So sorry for your loss – he was a good bloke and he helped a lot of people.'

The group said their goodbyes, and watched as Keith's secret family left the building.

'Wow, what an absolute farce. Long lost kids showing up, his other kids not bothering. I hope my funeral goes more smoothly than that,' Dean smirked. 'He was a sly one for sure – came across so godly and wise. You just never can tell.'

'Hold your horses a minute there, Deano. Weren't you having an affair with a man behind your wife's back? Not sure you can talk,' Peggy barked. 'None of us is blameless, are we? Some of the things we did when we drank were pretty darned terrible. People in glass houses should shut their god damn blinds.'

Frank whooped – he felt this certainly deserved a big whoop.

Peggy's words transported them all back to darker times. Car crashes, infidelity, the time a certain person ruined a child's pantomime. The list was endless – impregnating somebody whilst being married could be classed as tame. Peggy was right – judgment day would come to them all, and when it did, they should be ready, or else.

Jake arrived home ready to take on the world. Keith's unexpected exit had proved that life was too short, that it could end at any time – just like that, on the path outside of your shed. Not giving you any time to tidy up your misdemeanours, pay your subs or even check if you're wearing clean undies.

Life was for living and for Jake, the time was now. He would end things with Lucy, he would send Nicky a reply wishing her the best, and he would tell Janine that he didn't know why but he liked her, quite a lot. He would have all of his family for Christmas lunch and he would do it with a smile. And, as of Tuesday night, he would hold the meetings for Help is at Hand in his lounge, and he would provide the biscuits.

She's Dead

Jake sat in front of his laptop the following morning and began to type.

Hi Nicky,

Wow – firstly, congratulations on the engagement and the pregnancy. I always knew you would make a fantastic wife and mother; it's such a shame that I couldn't have been the one to give you the life you deserved. As you know, I'm based in the North now and haven't been further than Oldham since arriving.

It would be great to get together, but I'm trying to stay away from London for a while – it has too many temptations for me as I'm sure you'll remember. I meant what I said though – if you're ever in the vicinity, I'd love to show you the house I bought and what I am doing with it. Mum and Dad think it's perfect the way it is, but you know their taste is akin to a doctor's waiting room. I'm going for muted colours, country chic, lots of bare wood and wellies. I guess it's got a Cotswolds vibe, somewhere I know you love and can relate to.

Anyway, I'm about a year into this project and it will probably be another six months to a year before it's finally finished. I'm really enjoying watching it change. Leanne has temporarily moved to Fuengirola to open some English pub, so in the meantime I've been given the task of looking after Marnie.

She lives here at the house and, in some other jaw-dropping news, my cousin Martin has also moved in. I was hoping it would be for a very short period but Michelle, his wife, has filed for divorce, so I'm not sure how long he's staying.

My life is busy which is good, it distracts me from thinking about the booze and I think I'm finding a way to be me without it. I'm always free on email and on the phone if you ever want to chat properly.

Hope all is well with you.

Jake x

After pressing send, Jake grabbed his keys, jumped in the Land Rover and drove to Lucy's nan's house without prior arrangement. If nothing else, sobriety had allowed Jake's manners to resurface. He was a polite boy when he'd been younger, and it was only when he became an alcoholic did he change into a rude knobhead with no inhibitions. With this in mind, he'd decided to break things off with Lucy face-to-face, like a man.

The house was a small mid-terrace two villages away. Jake had planned his speech on the way, and Help is at Hand would be the excuse he would give to save Lucy's feelings.

A gnarled woman who could have played a witch in a play with absolutely no need for make-up stood in the doorway, sizing up Jake. 'Are you this boyfriend she's been harping on about?'

'I'm not sure, to be honest. Is she about?'

'She's in her room, using up all my electricity and gas.'

'Would you mind telling her that Jake is here to see her?'

'Is that your car, is it?'

'Yes, is it in the way? Do I need to move it?'

'No, no. I just expected something a bit more glamourous. They normally have better cars than that.'

'Who do?'

'The men – our Lucy's other victims,' her nan said, smiling wryly.

Jake wasn't sure how he felt about this interaction; this woman was weird as hell.

'So, can I talk to her? Is that okay?'

'Guess so. What do you want her for anyway? Does she owe you money? 'Cause she ain't got a pot to piss in.'

'No, she's a friend of mine, actually.'

Her nan burst out laughing. 'Okay, but for how long? That's the question.'

Just as Jake was considering running away, Lucy appeared at the bottom of the stairs.

'Oh Jake, thank god. I really needed to see a friendly face today.'

'Why, what's the matter?'

Lucy burst into tears and threw herself into Jake's arms. She sobbed and sobbed; she was almost retching as she struggled to get any words out.

'Can we sit down please... Nan?' Jake didn't know what else to call her.

'I'm not *your* nan,' she said scornfully.

'I know that, but I don't know your name.'

Nan thought about it for a moment, as though she was giving her account details to an online scammer. 'Well, I suppose it's Anne – come through.'

Jake placed Lucy onto a sofa next to Rita the dog, and sat in an armchair facing her. 'What's happened? Try and tell me calmly?'

Lucy turned and screamed, 'She's dead.' And then she put her face into a cushion and howled.

'Who's dead?' he asked Anne. 'Help me out here, what's she on about?'

Anne sank into her chair and picked up her knitting. Casually, she said, 'Her character from *Corrie* – they've killed her. Last night, news hit The Street that she'd slipped away peacefully in her sleep.'

Lucy lowered the cushion, revealing swollen, red-raw eyes. 'I've got nothing left, I'm finished.'

Jake really had no idea how to react to this. 'Maybe it's for the best – you can move on and maybe get another acting job.'

'Don't be so fucking stupid, I was in it that long, nobody will see past her.'

Anne began twisting the lemon-coloured wool around her finger and gazed out of the window wistfully. 'She's right – I heard that Pam St Clement went for a part as a chief inspector in *Line of Duty*, and do you know what they said?'

Jake shook his head.

'They said there's no point even doing the audition, Pam, because in the eyes of the viewer, you'll only ever be Pat Butcher.'

Lucy glared at her nan. 'You're loving this, aren't you?'

'Not really – you're making a right racket and still not a penny in rent, and me a pensioner.'

Lucy stood and wiped her eyes with her sleeve. 'Look, Nan, I'm trying – you know I'm really trying.'

Anne sighed and rolled her eyes toward Jake. This woman had reached the end of the line with her granddaughter, and she'd run out of sympathy – there was literally not a shred of emotion left inside her.

'Jake, that's your name, isn't it? Can you take her for a drive or something and calm her down? I've been listening to this carry-on all bastard day.'

Jake nodded – the situation was unbearable, the house was unbearable, and Anne really was a hideous old wanker.

'Lucy, grab a bag. You can stay with me tonight, and things will seem better in the morning.'

Lucy didn't have to be asked twice – she was packed and in the car within five minutes.

Back at the house and whilst Lucy had a bath, Jake explained to Marnie and Martin what had happened.

'So, she can never go back to The Street?' Marnie asked.

'Well, not unless they're in the habit of bringing back the dead,' Martin said. 'She'll get another job. She could do *Celebrity Big Brother*, they like addicts and mentalists on that.'

Jake jumped up to shut the kitchen door. 'Shh, try and keep it down, you two. She keeps crying and hugging me, don't set her off again.'

'You've gone off her already!' Martin sneered. 'Pumped and dumped, poor Lucy O.'

'Never say pumped and dumped again, Martin, for god's sake.'

'Why?'

'The fact you have to ask is very worrying. Anyway, help me out – keep her busy tonight, will you? This is a three-man job, and I've got stuff to do.'

Martin and Marnie did just that – they taught Lucy to play 'Shithead', a card game the Peterson family had played since the dawn of time, they then sat and watched her perform 'Consider Yourself' from *Oliver!*, a defining moment in her early career.

Jake sat in his study and contemplated how to approach Janine sensitively, but with the full intention of letting her know how he felt. Eventually, he began communication.

Jake: Hi, it's Jake. x
Janine: I know...
Jake: So, I enjoyed the other night, the movie and stuff. x
Janine: Okay.
Jake: So, do you fancy doing it again, maybe tomorrow night?
Janine: Will your girlfriend be there?
Jake: She was never my girlfriend, and no, that's done.
Janine: Is this a date, 'cause that's what it sounds like?
Jake: Yes, I think it is.
Janine: See you tomorrow then, Jakey boy. x

That night, Jake slept in the spare room. He knew Lucy would be waiting for him on what she deemed to be her side of the bed, but he never appeared. He didn't feel it appropriate to upset her any further, but the blatant avoidance of physical contact should at least let her know he was checked out in a romantic way. He would wait until morning and, after he'd broken things off, he would offer his friendship, his support within the group, but that was as far as it would go.

Well, that was the plan anyway.

The following morning, Lucy was in a darker place than before. She'd spent the night pacing the corridors, contemplating her next move. It was clear that Jake was not interested, and she had her suspicions that 'Big Janine' was about to launch a takeover. On top of that, she was completely skint and her return to the nation's best-loved soap had been snatched away without any warning. She realised this may have been what rock bottom looked like.

Jake, however, awoke with a spring in his step – he'd finally got some sort of closure with Nicky, and losing her was becoming less painful. His new life wasn't so bad and finally, a life without booze looked bearable. It was Marnie's last day at school, and it was a non-uniform day followed by some sort of naff end-of-term disco in the school hall. Jake promised to pick her up at nine p.m.

Marnie chattered away as she buttered a crumpet for breakfast. 'Want one, Uncle Jake?'

He shook his head. He was busy checking his emails, and crumpets did nothing for his waistline.

'Apparently there's a rumour going around school that one of the teachers is on "the list". Mr Palmer, the science teacher – do you know him?'

Jake didn't respond, so she put forward her case.

'According to Poppy Jenkins, her dad's brother is a community police officer – well, he said that she should avoid him at all costs.'

Jake sort of listened. 'Well, don't go throwing accusations around until you have actual proof.'

'Ah, but that's not it.'

'No?'

'No – he went to Legoland in the Easter holidays and he hasn't got any kids.'

Jake stopped what he was doing and looked up. 'Is that it?'

She sat down at the table, alarmed that Jake wasn't into this theory a little bit more. 'You explain it, then – it's a bit strange, don't you think?'

'Maybe he just likes Lego – some adults do.'

Marnie shrugged. She hadn't thought of that.

'Right, go and brush your teeth and I'll drop you off.'

She stuffed the second crumpet into her mouth, and left the kitchen.

Jake quickly logged into his work accounts – he wanted to see if there had been any movements on Zing25, but he hit a problem almost immediately. Why had the spreadsheet on that account become inaccessible? He tried a few times, but each time drew a blank. It was as though it had been removed from the system. He looked at his watch – it was only 8.20, so it was unlikely he'd be able to get hold of Lucas, as he'd either be in bed or on the tube, but he gave it a go anyway. The call went straight to voicemail. Jake moved towards the window of the cottage, and left a voice note.

'Lucas, mate, call me back ASAP – just wanted to check Zing25 and can't access this spreadsheet. Any reason why? Let me know. Thanks, pal.'

There was only one tick. He would have to wait until he got above ground before he could get an answer.

It was 11.45 by the time Lucas got back to Jake – he was in a pub in east London, waiting to meet a client.

'What's that you said about Zing25?' Lucas shouted down the phone.

'What's going on with the spreadsheet? I can't access it.'

'I can't hear you, mate. Hang on one minute.' There was a rustle and then a door opened as Lucas stepped out onto the London pavement. 'Sorry about that mate, right okay yeah Zing25. Erm yeah, that's gone, mate – that's not happening, I meant to call you actually.'

Jake sat down at his kitchen table, his heart racing. 'What do you mean it's gone?'

'Err yeah, they found something in it during the testing – something carcinogenic, apparently.'

Jake shut his eyes and put his head on the table.

'Some guy got really sick, ended up going into a coma, then they did tests and traced it back to Zing25. Then, when that news became public, others came forward and revealed they'd suffered the same side effects. They'd been in and out of whatever the

South American equivalent of A&E is with palpitations – you know the score.'

Jake had slipped down from his chair and was sitting with his back to the oven on the floor by this point.

Jake heard Lucas spark a cigarette and blow a puff of smoke. 'So, they pulled it, mate – they pulled it from the shelves over there, and there's no chance of it getting over here, not now. Shame really, I quite fancied having a razz on that myself.'

'What, and you didn't? I thought you were going in with some personal cash.'

'Yah, I didn't bother. I heard a rumble that it may not be the goldmine we first thought.'

'And you didn't think to mention that to me, Lucas, during our meeting?'

There was a pause as Lucas scrabbled through his memory of the Zoom meeting when his PA was on her knees under the desk. 'I thought I did, mate – I was so totally high that day.'

Jake was speechless. His client had signed a clause accepting that there was a risk of losing their investment, and that they could afford to lose it, but Jake had thrown all of his savings at it.

Lucas continued to spout his shit in his boarding-school accent. 'It's the same with all of this sort of stuff – there's just no long-term research. And Europe won't accept just anything; they're always spoiling the party for someone. Jake, are you there mate, can you hear me?'

'Yes, I'm here,' Jake said quietly.

'Yeah so, they're facing lawsuits and all sorts of shit. Glad I didn't put any of my dollar into that, Christ. Anyway, I've got to go, my lunch date has turned up and she's fit as.'

'Lucas?'

'Yes, mate?'

'I'm done, you're on your own. Don't contact me again.'

Jake ended the call, the realisation that he'd just lost a quarter of a million of his own money almost causing his heart to stop. He was frozen to the spot, trying to put this catastrophic event into some sort of perspective. He stayed on the kitchen floor for possibly more than an hour processing it. He only snapped out of it when Lucy made an appearance and almost tripped over him.

'What the hell are you doing down there?' She was still in her nightwear and looked even worse than yesterday.

'Thinking.'

'About what?' she asked, flicking the kettle on.

'I just had some very bad news, very bad financial news.'

Lucy joined him on the floor while she waited for her water to boil.

'Looks like we're both having a bad day.'

Jake didn't feel that there was any comparison, but he allowed her to wallow with him.

'It's bad, Lucy, I've really fucked up.'

'Will you have to sell this house?'

'Well, either that or live in it like it is. I can't afford to keep throwing money at it, not now I've lost my life savings.'

'Oh!' Lucy said – she knew that renovating The Coach House had been Jake's number-one priority. 'You'll have to get a job, like me.'

Jake scowled. 'I had a three-year plan – I was financially secure. That's all gone to the dogs now. I might even have to move back to London and earn some money.'

'Is that so bad? I love the city. This place is so uninspiring, Jake. We're go-getters, we were at the top of our game once. I mean, what's the long-term plan, Jake – this?' She opened her hands out, gesturing to the dated kitchen he sat in.

'They said to take this one step at a time, didn't they? The people at The Meadows.'

Lucy scoffed. 'Yeah, that's because they had no aspirations to do anything even remotely interesting. Look where we live, there's literally one chippy, two pubs and a shop that shuts at five,' she sneered.

Jake thought back to ordering Vietnamese food at three a.m. to rolling out of the casino at six, his pockets brimming with cash, to Michelin-starred business lunches paid for on the company card. London certainly was alive, and there was plenty of money to be made there.

'And I could come with you so you're not on your own. Not as your girlfriend or anything, but as a flatmate. I could maybe see if *EastEnders* are hiring.' Mentally, she was already on the train.

Jake's mind was racing – perhaps he could nip back for six months, leave Marnie and Martin at the house, and try and recoup the lost funds. He wasn't a man to give up – he couldn't work on a cheese counter or push trolleys, he'd been to university for god's sake, and he was clever.

'Maybe I could get a flat near the office and put it through the company,' he thought aloud.

Lucy nodded excitedly. 'I could get a new agent and go to auditions – maybe all of this is meant to be.'

Jake grabbed his laptop and opened Rightmove. 'I'm going to see what's available – perhaps you're right.'

Lucy watched as Jake scrolled through apartments near the city. She saw a fire in his eyes and an energy grow, and she liked it. And then she had an idea that would change everything.

'Wait here, I've got something that will help.' She left the room and bolted up the stairs, leaving Jake looking for rentals.

Within ten minutes, Lucy had set out two beakers and opened a warm bottle of prosecco.

'Where did you get that?' Jake asked, making eye contact with the bottle.

'My bag – I carry it around in case things get bad, never go anywhere without it. It's a coping mechanism.'

'Lucy, that's a really bad idea for both of us.'

'Is it though?' She had persuasion in her voice. 'We're both facing some really tough times, and we've proven that we don't need to drink all the time. If ever there was a day when we needed this, it's today.'

Jake continued to scroll, trying to avoid the bottle of magic that would allow him to let go for a little while. An uncomfortable feeling developed in his chest and stomach, but that turned to a warm excitement. What harm could it do? Nobody would know. It was just a one-off, and perhaps this was the fuel he needed to make things happen.

'Go on then, pour me a glass.'

White Spirit

'Drink that, mate, it's a nice milky Mellow Bird's, should settle your stomach.'

Jake had awoken in his own bed with Martin perched on the end of it, pointing to a big, steaming mug. He groaned and pulled the quilt over his head; he really didn't want guests in his room, especially when he felt this fragile. The door burst open, and Di edged her way in backwards, holding a huge tray laden with food.

'Right, we've got all sorts here. I basically defrosted a few different Tupperwares, so he'll at least find something he likes. Sit up, son, and let's start with this Spanish Chicken – at least, that's what I think it is.' Di sniffed the dish of red mush and then corrected herself. 'Actually, that's a Tikka Masala – what am I like?' She stuck a spoon into the food and nodded to Jake. 'Come on, you know the drill. At least three mouthfuls, let's go.'

Jake knew the drill alright – he'd been in this home prison for three days, guarded by Martin and basically force-fed by his mother. And there was no escape as Alf was on the front door, and Janine on the back. Marnie oversaw admin – Jake's phone and laptop etcetera – so as a family, they had it all covered.

'What day is it this time?' Jake asked wearily as he forced down a mouthful of spicy gunk.

'It's Saturday – only five days until Christmas, but we'll have you right for then.'

'Whoopee,' Jake said miserably. Christmas was the last thing he needed.

'Are you feeling a little bit better at least, mate?' Martin asked nervously – he really didn't like Jake in this way. Weak Jake, almost a pathetic Jake, made Martin feel unsafe. In the last few months, he had found a huge comfort in the support and wise words he'd had from his cousin. Without Jake, he'd be in the shit.

'I'm getting there, I was probably doing too well.' Jake forced a smile.

'Bollocks,' Marnie said from the landing. 'You were sabotaged and you know it.'

'I'm an adult, Marnie, nobody can force you to drink, you know. I put that glass to my lips.'

Di clenched her fists. 'Ooh, I could ring that little runt's neck, I really could.' 'Little runt' was now the only way Di would refer to Lucy and, after the week they'd all had, she had a huge knot of rage boiling inside her. It was all going so well – she and Alf were recovering nicely from the flu until they got the call.

'Tell me again, Martin, what the police said.' Di put her head in her hands, ready for this one more time.

'They said that Jake was negligent and Lucy is in serious trouble.'

'Well, she was the one who was driving,' Marnie added, sitting on the end of the bed to join the others.

Di got really angry again. 'He was in no fit state to give permission – isn't it called something? What's the term for it?'

'Diminished responsibility,' Marnie said confidently, having investigated the law using Google.

'Yes, but Jake let her drive his car knowing full well she was over the limit *and* also banned, plus he got into the car with her, so that makes it even worse.' Martin had also become a paralegal by watching YouTube in the middle of the night.

Di shook her head; this was her worst nightmare. Just when she thought she had him back, he'd gone and messed things up.

'You're a moron, son. What are you?'

'A moron, Mum,' Jake said glumly.

'But why, Jake? What made you go on a bender? You were doing so well.'

This had been his first opportunity to explain things properly as he'd been on a ward for a few days, and was barely mentally present owing to the colossal hangover and banging head that set in ten minutes after he'd been admitted to A&E, and the booze had worn off.

Alf popped his head round the door just as he was about to begin. 'Oh, you're awake – right, you've got some explaining to do, sunshine. You've nearly killed your mother with all this.' Alf pulled out a chair from the corner of the room and perched on the edge. He was still recovering from his 'super cold' so he sported a rolled-up tissue sticking out of one nostril.

'And you've got *her* to think about,' he said, pointing at Marnie. 'The little girl we entrusted you with. You can't carry on like that when you're responsible for a child.'

Jake bowed his head; he felt terrible about Marnie. He wondered what she'd seen, and whether she'd ever trust him again.

'I'm sorry. I'm so sorry, everyone.'

Marnie dragged the tray up the quilt towards her, and picked it up. 'You don't have to apologise for being sick. It's not your fault.'

'Bless her – she's been really worried about you.' Martin watched as Marnie took the tray of former takeaways down the stairs.

Jake began his ale tale. 'I had some really bad news that day. I was pretty low.'

'What news?' Alf frowned.

'It was financial. I lost quite a bit of money.'

'Gambling?'

'No, investing.'

'Same bloody thing,' Alf said angrily.

'Anyway, it knocked me for six – it really was a huge blow for my personal wealth.'

Di rolled her eyes. The term 'personal wealth' was completely alien to her; it was only for toffs and snobs.

'Lucy was here, and she was in a mess. They'd killed off her character in *Corrie*, meaning she could never go back.'

'She was shite anyway, wooden as a bleeding horse,' Alf snarled.

'Anyway, we ended up drowning our sorrows. It was only

supposed to be the one bottle, but we all know, when it comes to me, there's no such thing as just one.'

It was the first time that Martin had realised that Jake was an actual, proper alcoholic, and not somebody who liked a few too many drinks now and again – he had never understood the gravity of how bad it actually was until he saw Jake that day.

'Do you remember seeing me in the pub?' Martin asked.

Jake furrowed his brow. 'Sort of, just remind me.'

'I was in there having a drink at the bar with a friend, and you came crashing in with Lucy. You were both pretty merry, but you were okay, still standing.'

Jake nodded – he did have a recollection of the pub and the dreadful dreadlocked girl sitting with Martin.

'And then what happened?'

Martin went a bit red. 'Well, you started getting stupid, like, making all kinds of inappropriate suggestions on the microphone which was being used for the general knowledge quiz, actually.'

'What do you mean, what did he say?' Di asked.

'Oh, just asking if he could hire the skip for the night – that sort of thing.'

Di and Alf looked at each other in total confusion, but let it go.

'And then what?' Jake was waiting for the part where it all went wrong, and what had happened to result in six stitches above his right eye.

'Well, you and Lucy started helping yourself to the optics – at one point, you went down to the cellar and tried to drag a barrel up.'

Jake turned on his side – this was horrific.

'The bar staff tried reasoning with you, but you were too strong for them. In the end, it took two of the locals to get you out of the door – you were being quite physical and a bit of a nuisance.'

'And what did you do about it, you great lummox? Didn't you step in and help your cousin?' Di asked Martin through pursed lips.

'Of course I did – and I ended up being slapped in the face and shoved out of the door too. They said I was just as bad the week before. I hadn't even started my pint – it's probably still there,' he said sadly.

Alf's arms were folded; he was not happy. 'So how is it they ended up driving away together, drunk?'

'The bar staff called the police; they said that somebody was out of control, and they should get down there pronto before somebody got really hurt. That Lucy O jumped into the driver's seat of Jake's car, and he got in the passenger seat. Lucy said she wasn't getting nicked again for no one, and before I could stop them, they'd sped off.'

'But where to?' Jake asked – he had absolutely no recollection of this whatsoever.

Alf stood up, a very serious look in his eyes. 'Well, I think I can take over from here because I know exactly where you ended up, Sonny Jim.'

'Where?' Jake held his breath as Alf delivered the worst news possible.

'Marnie's school disco – in all your drunken glory.'

Jake's brain suddenly began to tease him – showing him blurry flashbacks of a middle-aged man doing a Noddy Holder and screaming 'It's Christmas!' using a megaphone across a school assembly hall to a crowd of highly amused teenagers, and some very angry teachers.

That man was Jake.

'Oh my god, I want to die,' Jake groaned. This was not the classy affair of falling off the wagon he had planned.

'You fell on the buffet table and it collapsed in the middle, bending the hinges, so you'll need to get that repaired,' Di said furiously.

'And you defaced a whiteboard using a permanent marker,' Alf added. 'You wrote "Mr Palmer is a paedo" in block capitals for some reason, so you'll need to get in there with some white spirit over the holidays.'

Jake nodded shamefully.

'After you'd caused holy hell at your niece's school, you went on your way to the next disaster.'

Alf paced the bedroom, wringing his hands in despair.

Jake suddenly remembered Marnie and two boys – Martin's

boys, actually – pleading with him not to get back into the car with a drunk driver.'

'Hey, I saw your kids, Martin. I saw Tommy and Dylan – I remember that.'

Martin nodded. 'Yes, you did – they tried to stop you leaving, they called me for help, but by the time I got there, you were well gone.'

Jake felt revolting – even the children had more fucking sense than him.

'That's when Marnie called us, wasn't it, Di? Poor girl was beside herself. She kept saying, "Uncle Jake's pissed, Uncle Jake's pissed," over and over again.'

Jake grimaced; he didn't really need the script reading out. 'And is this when we had the accident?' he asked – he definitely couldn't remember anything after seeing the kids, only waking up in hospital with a gash on his head, and murmurs about a collision.

Alf spluttered in disdain. 'Now hang on, you can't call it "the accident", Jake. An accident is unintentional.'

Jake looked at the three faces around his bed, each one utterly disgusted by what happened next. 'Intentional, what do you mean – we did this on purpose?'

He touched the gash on his head with two fingers – it still really hurt.

'You and Lucy drove the car into the front doors of Granada Studios – you know, the old set of *Coronation Street*?'

Jake sat up bolt upright, his eyes widening. A flashback of a demented Lucy hurtling past the Trafford Centre, shouting, 'Let's see what the cocksuckers think of this.' He did remember trying to grab the wheel, but then he also recalled singing along to 'Jingle Bells' outside Selfridges. It was all a muddle.

Finally, as reality set in, he asked, 'Jesus, was anyone hurt? Did we hurt anybody?'

Martin shook his head reassuringly, 'It was midnight, nobody was there, but you got a concussion and she broke her arm.'

'Serves her right, little runt,' Di muttered. 'I'll break her legs when I get my hands on her.'

'It was on the news, Jake; it's been all over social media. She'll get on *Big Brother* now, no problem,' Martin said, as if it were a good thing. 'The headline was "Crash on the Cobbles" – there's a meme doing the rounds.'

'Poor Lucy. She's really messed up, you know, and she hasn't got anyone at all. Where is she now?' Jake did feel bad for her – what a desperate thing to do.

Di's mouth dropped open in total shock. '*Poor* Lucy? She's literally a terrorist – she could have killed you both, and others. Imagine if it had been during the day, kiddies go there all the time! Poor Lucy, my arse.'

Jake sighed. Yes, it was pretty reckless and very stupid – and it could have been life-changing for them both – but she had problems, big ones. 'She's an alcoholic, Mum – we do terrible things, we make horrible choices, you know how it is.'

Janine had been listening on the landing to Jake's version of events, and felt now would be a good time to step in and deliver her news, as sensitively as she knew how. She knocked lightly on the open door.

'Hello, mind if I come in?'

'Please join the party, I've just ordered a tray of shots,' Jake said sarcastically.

'I thought you should know that I went to see Lucy's nan a few days ago,' Janine said.

'Why?' Jake asked in confusion.

'Well, I called you on that day, the day that you fell off the wagon. We were supposed to be meeting that night, remember?'

Jake did remember; he'd been looking forward to it. 'Did we speak?' he asked, hoping he'd not made a tit of himself.

'No, Lucy answered your phone with plenty to tell me.'

'Lucy, on my phone?' Jake shook his head – that made no sense.

'Yes, she said you and her were moving in together, somewhere in London?'

Jake rubbed his eyes: yes Rightmove, yes apartments, and yes London all rang some sort of a bell, but he'd never agreed to her going with him.

'No, we're not moving together, and I'm not sure why she answered my phone – it's all really blurry.'

Janine raised her eyebrows and tilted her head to one side. 'When I asked where you were, she said you were in the shower and that you were both spending the day in bed together.'

Jake narrowed his eyes – this could have happened, he wasn't entirely sure, but this all felt quite stalky, something he suspected Lucy of being.

'Okay, well, I'm not sure about that, Janine. My memory is really fuzzy, and if I did do that, it was because of alcohol and nothing else.'

'Luckily, I'm sure that didn't happen,' Janine said confidently. 'At the time I called you, you were in the pub causing a ruckus, and she was in the ladies' with your phone. I've got mates everywhere, and this is a small place.'

'What a nasty little madam,' Alf shouted.

'Yeah, she was playing games – not sure what she was trying to achieve by winding me up. Everyone knows that's a bad idea.'

Di nodded – she'd been witness to one or two brawls where Janine had walked away unscathed, holding a ponytail as a memento.

'Anyway, I decided I would go and speak to her nan to let her know about the drinking – that's the right thing to do when someone falls off the wagon, let their family know so they can be helped.'

'I bet she wasn't happy, poor woman. I bet she's devastated,' Di said, imagining the reaction of any normal grandparent.

'No, not really,' Janine said. 'She really wasn't that bothered.'

'Yeah, well, the nan's a bitch, Janine. I've met her and she's horrible.' Jake recalled all her cackling and sarcasm whilst knitting a tea cosy.

'Look, Jake, Lucy is not an alcoholic,' Janine said firmly.

'Yes, she is! I actually met her in rehab.' The code of anonymity had to be broken temporarily; needs must. His parents glanced at one another, thinking exactly the same thing – rehab, an expensive hotel without any booze for London cranks was what that was.

'No she isn't, Jake. She said she was an alcoholic as an excuse for her last drink-driving charge, and the judge insisted she get treatment. Her lawyer advised her to say she had an addiction problem – the courts are easier on you, as are the press, more importantly.'

'But what about the group? She joined Help is at Hand,' Jake argued. Nobody would go there unless they had to, would they?

Janine smiled sympathetically. 'Yeah, her nan said she joined that to get her claws into some guy. She's not got a problem with alcohol – she drinks a glass of wine with her dinner most nights – but her nan is just fed up with all the bullshit.'

Jake sank back into his pillow; it was a very dark day.

Filthy Knickers

The accident was hugely prominent in the local press; people were almost giddy about the fact a very expensive window needed replacing after a local star and her 'boyfriend' attempted to 'blow up' Granada Studios and were maimed in the process. Di had called the *Lancashire Evening Post* to try and get the story dropped, or at least changed so it told the truth, but they were on skeleton staff as the Christmas party was a two-day affair including a trip to the Blackpool illuminations *and* the dizzy heights of Funny Girls – so she got nowhere.

Jake was still under armed guard after a week of being out of hospital – the guard being Janine, and the weapon being Janine also. The family had googled the living shit out of this situation, and the general consensus was that the thirty days after the subject had poisoned their bloodstream was when they were most susceptible to another relapse.

'You're not staying here for thirty days, Mum. That's absurd.'

Di had allowed Jake down the stairs that morning so long as he held Alf's arm when he was upright in case of a dizzy spell.

'Well, you're not to be left alone at any point – what if that little troll Lucy comes back, peddling her filthy wares?'

'She's not a wench from the Middle Ages, Mum. Besides, I think her filthy wares would be wasted on me anyway – I'm exhausted.'

'When you say filthy wares, Di, do you mean a full bar or her upstairs and downstairs?' Martin said, pointing to Di's lady bits.

'Get to work, Martin, and focus on yourself,' Di snapped.

Alf couldn't help but laugh; Martin must have been dropped on his head more than once with a comment like that. He quickly got back to the serious point of his messed-up son.

'Jake, just remember who got themselves in this state – listen to your mother, please son.' Alf put his feet up on the sofa without taking his shoes off.

Di got Jake settled on the other sofa, and threw a blanket over his legs. 'There's so much temptation, we have to keep an eye on you.' She then shut the curtains, plunging the room into darkness.

'What the…' Jake exclaimed. 'Why am I being denied the daylight?'

'What if you see the brewery truck in the distance, delivering to one of the pubs? You'll be off like a whippet on a rabbit.'

Martin popped his head around the door. 'He's barred from the local… for life,' he said as he put on his work fleece. 'And so am I, for some reason.'

Di nodded at Alf – their plan had worked. Jake had been banned for his behaviour, obviously, and although technically Martin hadn't sucked the optics or rolled a barrel across the floor, he was Jake's cousin and best friend, so it wouldn't be fair to treat them differently. She and Alf had gone down there, met with the brewery, and ensured that all the Petersons would get the same treatment. That included Leanne, who happened to work there when she wasn't in Fuengirola.

'He could intercept the wagon, club the driver over the head, and then where would we be – an addict driving around with a ginormous pint attached to his back?'

Jake groaned – this was one of the most ridiculous scenarios he'd ever heard. Not even Shane MacGowan had held up a beer lorry.

'We've got a rota, son; you will never be left alone until mid-January. We have to give you a fighting chance of slaying this beast.' Alf put on *Homes Under the Hammer* and gestured to Jake, 'We've got loads of these recorded, and the houses are absolutely shit.' He smiled. 'Just go with it, son, let us look after you.'

Jake gave in; his family had come to the rescue. He wondered if, without them here, he would perhaps throw a bottle of wine in his trolley. Would he swig a nip of brandy from the bottle Di had kept to make the puddings? Perhaps he would. His bender had certainly awoken his awareness of alcohol, and with it being such a boozy time of year, he couldn't say – with his hand on his heart – that he didn't fancy another. He may not have remembered much about that night, but he did remember letting go and not giving a fuck – that was the feeling that he missed.

Around lunchtime, Marnie came into the lounge and handed Jake his mobile phone. He hadn't seen it since before the very bad day, and the doctor on duty had given it to Di in a plastic bag. Di hadn't wanted him to have it at all because something may be on there that triggered him, but as a family – and that included Janine – they felt Jake should have his phone.

'On account of this house not being in North Korea, give him the bleeding thing, will you, Di?' Alf had shouted when she stuffed it into the back of the bread bin behind a loaf of Soreen.

As soon a Jake switched it on, it started to ping. Multiple messages from various members of the group, asking whether the meeting was definitely on, and what should they bring, and can they bring a new member – questions came in thick and fast.

The first meeting at the house was less than twenty-four hours away, and Jake had a head injury and a plethora of family milling around like Securicor – he would have to have a think about whether this was appropriate. There were thirty-two separate messages from Lucy O. He read a couple and then he deleted the rest. He couldn't and shouldn't forgive her; yes, this went against the advice from the big dogs at AA, but Lucy had brought that bottle of prosecco (which was a crime in itself) and she had sabotaged Jake's sobriety for her own gain. He couldn't help her – he had to put himself first.

After an afternoon nap on account of all the painkillers Jake was being fed, he awoke to find the lounge empty. He pulled back the curtain to see that Alf and Di's car was gone.

Janine appeared, covered in flour. 'Don't get excited, you're still under surveillance.'

'I'm certainly not even close to excited,' Jake said wearily. 'Where have they gone?'

'Just nipped home to get more clothes and check the house.'

'You been on the sniff?' Jake gestured to the white powder Janine had on her face.

'We're attempting mince pies, Marnie and me,' she said.

'A successful attempt?' Jake asked.

'I won't be having one if that's an indication. Your dad coughed up in the mixture.'

Jake nodded – that was exactly what he expected.

'Cup of tea?' Janine asked as she went to leave the room.

'Don't go yet,' Jake said, 'stay with me for a little while.'

Janine sat down on the armchair, and put her hands behind her head.

'Thank you,' Jake said genuinely.

'You're welcome – but what you saying thank you for?'

'Everything. Being here, supporting Mum and Dad, making infected pies, opening my eyes about Lucy.'

'We're family, right? We look out for each other.'

Jake observed Janine for a moment. She was a gruff character, rough around the edges, with a really strange sense of style. Most of the time, it was difficult to know whether she'd pounce and rip out your jugular. But somewhere, deep in her eyes, there was softness that was more beautiful than anything he'd ever seen in a person.

He snapped out of his daze. 'I feel bad taking you away from home, Michelle and the boys.'

'They've gone to Disney with me mum and dad, not back until New Year.'

'Didn't you fancy it?'

Janine laughed loudly. 'Did I bollocks. Hate theme parks, hate travelling and I need a break from the bleeding hooligans.'

'Why, have they been testing your patience?'

'Just a bit.' Janine pushed the door shut so Marnie didn't hear what Martin's lads had been up to this time. 'You won't believe what they've done.'

'Go on then, give me a laugh.'

'They've been selling my used knickers to perverts online – thirty-five quid they made in the first week.'

'Excuse me?' Jake's eyes bulged.

Janine sat closer to Jake, regaling him with a mad story she'd not had a chance to tell anyone about as of yet. 'My pants kept disappearing, and at first I thought the dog was taking them and eating them – some dogs like a strong smell,' she laughed, and Jake joined her nervously. 'Anyway, the little dickheads left the laptop open one day, and I saw a message from someone called Playful Percy to be specific.'

Jake was intrigued. 'What did it say?'

'"Just received the yellow ones, but they weren't as pungent as I'd hoped. Could you get me some more?" The cheek of it.'

'So, what do these people do with them – wear them, sniff them, what?'

Janine shrugged. 'Whatever it is, hopefully they'll wash them after and send them back. To be fair to the boys, they used the money to buy me and their mum a Christmas pressie, so I didn't go in too hard. And don't tell Martin – this is right up his street.'

Jake and Janine chewed the fat for a while, chatting about the weather, how much they both disliked turkey, and whether a booze-free pub would work in the centre of Manchester. She eventually had to leave, as Marnie had grilled the mince pies by accident and the smoke alarm went off.

At teatime, Jake felt much better physically. The booze had left his system, and his head was clearer. Di had made a corned beef hash, which Jake normally found abhorrent, but today the smell made him feel safe. Martin had put in a shift at the warehouse, and a plate of steaming home-cooked food was all he'd been looking forward to all day. He'd seen the boys the day before, and given them their presents and his love. He hadn't made a scene; he'd even given Michelle a Christmas card. Yes, okay, it said 'Hoe Hoe Hoe' on the front, but he'd made the effort in his own way. He was picking up the boys on New Year's Day, and they were going to Winter Wonderland in London, where he would try to outdo their time in Paris.

'I'm holding the addiction meetings here at the house for the time being. Tuesday evenings, seven 'til eight-thirty in the lounge,' Jake said loudly.

Janine beamed – she was glad this was still happening. Alf, however, was quite concerned.

'I think you should give yourself until the new year before you take that on, son.'

'No, Dad, people need it – *I* need it. Especially now at this time of year. If anything, what just happened to me makes me understand the importance of it.'

Alf had a think. 'But we'll all be here, and we'll see the members; I thought it was all supposed to be a secret.'

Di's eyes lit up. 'I wonder if we'll see that postman, Alf, remember? I suppose we'll have to hide upstairs, will we?' She was more excited than appropriate.

'No, Mum. I've explained to everyone it's my home and there will be family around from time to time. If anyone is uncomfortable, there's always AA.'

'So, you're not the AA?' Alf asked, screwing up his face. 'What are you then?'

Janine stepped in, 'We're a group called Help is at Hand that a man called Keith set up a few years ago.'

'Well, why can't this Keith have it as his house?' Di asked.

'Because he's dead,' Janine said directly.

'Jeez, that's not a good advert for this group,' Alf muttered.

'Look, I really want to do it, so can someone please get a shitload of custard creams and make sure we have enough milk for the brews?' Jake had thought about this all day, and he knew that this was one positive he could add into a very negative week.

'I'll do that – I like shopping and I'll catch the corner shop if I go now.' Marnie jumped up from her chair and began to put her coat on before adding, 'We can also give the alcoholics the mince pies we made – there's no booze in them, and it is Christmas.'

Janine shook her head at Jake and looked away – those little black grenades were not for human consumption.

With Marnie off on the biscuit run, Jake felt this was the time to open up about his financial situation. He didn't mind Janine being there – it wasn't a secret, and people would all know soon enough.

'You know I told you I'd had some bad news, financially.'

They all looked up in unison.

'Go on,' Martin said.

'Well, I lost all my savings.'

Alf threw his knife and fork down. 'What, all of your money?'

'Yes, almost all of my money. I have a bit put by, but that's it.'

'How much we talking, Jake?' Janine asked with genuine concern.

Jake took a deep breath. 'A quarter of a million pounds exactly.'

There was corned beef hash dropping out of mouths as the diners got their heads around this news. Shouting, wailing, thumping of tables and a sort of giddiness came over Martin who shouted 'you dickhead' a few times over. Jake sat quietly, waiting for the madness to stop.

'If you all calm down, I will explain the situation.'

Di held Jake's hand as he started at the beginning and told them all about the Zing25 debacle.

The first comment came from Alf. 'Right, what date does your mortgage need paying, son. We'll have a whip round.'

'I don't have a mortgage.'

'So, what do you call it then? You know the loan you get when you buy a house?'

Jake shook his head. 'I bought the house outright; I own the whole house.'

Janine, Alf, Di and Martin all threw their hands in the air.

'Well, what's the problem then? Either sell up, or get a job,' Di said, heaving a huge sigh of relief. 'No mortgage? People wait 'til they get to our age to get to that position,' she shrieked. Silly Jake – all was not lost.

Jake was a little put out. 'Hang on, guys – I needed that money.'

'Yeah, but you've got a roof over your head, and food on the table. What else do you need?' Alf said, now relieved that the bank wouldn't repossess his son's house.

'The small matter of a new kitchen and new bathrooms, plus I'm halfway through having the heating replaced. I want all the floors doing, plus some of the window frames are rotten. There's so much I want doing here.'

'Is it a want or a need, Jake? Maybe get things prioritised,' Janine said sensibly.

'I've always said it's a gorgeous house just like it is now,' Di said, admiring a radiator that was half on and half off.

'Homebase do some gorgeous furniture,' Martin said seriously.

'I'll do your floors for nothing,' Janine said, 'if that helps.'

'Pat Bayley makes curtains – she did some smashing ones for the caravan, so that's the windows dressed.'

'And we've still got that old toilet I saved from your skip in our garage. Go and get that tonight, Alf, will you?'

Alf nodded.

Jake sat there and listened to many, many suggestions which he thoroughly hated, but also thoroughly appreciated.

The Drunk Tank

Peggy arrived at Jake's about half an hour before anyone else. As the new chair, she would lead the meeting at their new location after 'Poor Keith's' untimely death. As usual, she was impeccably turned out but, with it being the twenty-third of December, she'd added a white fur stole to her outfit. Di and Alf watched as Peggy stepped out of her little Porsche 911 before bending over to lift a box out of the boot.

'And so it begins – it takes all sorts, don't it, Di?'

Di glared at Alf. 'Get your eyes in your head before I pluck 'em out, Alf Peterson.'

It was true – Peggy was a fine-looking woman. She was the right side of sixty-five and still moved liked a sports car. Quite the opposite of Jake's mum, who was in her mid-seventies and moved like a Waltzer.

'Some glamour-puss is at the door, Jake,' Alf shouted from the bedroom that he and Di had been stuffed into for the evening. 'Send her up here after the meeting, I think I might have a problem that needs attending to.' He winked at Di, who clouted him around the back of the head.

Martin had taken Marnie to see his dad that evening. He didn't normally go that late, but the carer who usually put him to bed had fallen on the ice so would struggle to lift him. Marnie agreed to go and help in exchange for a full English the following morning, plus £8.75, which is what Martin had found in the pocket of his jeans.

Peggy looked Jake up and down, and then hugged him hard

– she'd heard about his troubles, there weren't many who hadn't, and she was absolutely disgusted in Lucy O.

'Oh, look at your head, you poor thing.' She had tears in her eyes as she saw the nasty cut. 'You could have lost your life, or worse, your sight.'

Jake waited for an appropriate time to step away from Peggy's grip.

'You're so good for doing this, a really top bloke,' she said, mixing California and Lancashire together in the one sentence.

'What's in the box – is it Lucy's head?'

Peggy chuckled; she enjoyed the local humour. 'I have new starter forms that my husband kindly printed out; I have twelve packets of tissues because you know there's always someone crying – usually me.' She laughed and slapped Jake's arm. 'And I have a couple of bottles of bleach, because all these strangers defecating in your lovely bathroom is really quite triggering.'

Jake gulped. He recalled Janine's dirty nappy story, and prayed everybody had gone for number twos at their own home that day.

'So, let's get set up, shall we?' Peggy opened the lounge door to find candles lit, the fire glowing, and all the chairs in the house sitting nicely, awaiting the group. There was a table in the corner for refreshments, and it looked very inviting. 'Oh wow, you did it already – I could have done this.'

Jake shook his head. 'I can't take the credit – my family did it all. They've been brilliant.'

Peggy smiled. 'Family is everything, Jake – that's the reason I'm here, remember?'

He and Peggy carried in the coffee and teapots, took their seats and waited for the others to turn up. Jake left the front door slightly ajar; he felt it was too formal, expecting people to knock and be let in.

First to arrive was Dean, dropped off by his ex-wife, but he didn't come alone. Dean had brought a neighbour who had come to him a week or two before, and revealed she was struggling. Dean had told her about his journey, and suggested she join the group and attend the next meeting with him.

Claudia was a black lady with the smoothest, most flawless skin Jake had ever seen. She smiled shyly at Jake and sat down next to Dean. Frank arrived next – they knew it was him because he made so many bodily noises without even talking, grunting, sighing and groaning as he walked up the drive, before eventually belching after his first gulp of tea.

'Well, you've had quite the week, Drunky,' he said to Jake with one eyebrow raised.

Peggy immediately laid down the law. 'Frank, *no*! Tonight, we play by the rules. You don't talk unless it's your turn. You can chat away after the meeting, but for now just keep your mouth shut.'

Frank was about to whoop and then he stopped himself – he wanted to stay in this group, and he liked its new location, so he behaved and kept as quiet as he could.

'Hello everybody, hope you don't mind but I brought my uncle.' Tyler arrived with an older, red-faced, shaky man who looked absolutely broken. 'This is my mum's brother, Charlie.'

Jake nodded to Charlie who tried to nod back, but he was shifting so uncomfortably, the nod was more of a wobble.

'First meeting?' Jake asked.

Charlie shook his head. 'That's not why I'm shaking, mate.'

The familiar roar of Janine's van could be heard chugging up the hill, and Jake immediately felt more comfortable. Janine being there made him feel good – he just wished that she didn't have to keep going home. Once Janine had stuffed three custard creams into her pocket and sat down across from Jake, they were ready to go.

'Shall we make a start?' Peggy said and took to her feet. It was almost seven, and she knew there would be a lot to discuss. 'Okay, my name is Peggy – I was cabin crew for Emirates, I couldn't have any children, so I replaced it with drink...'

'My name is Frank. I have a dog named Stella, for obvious reasons. I was head gardener at a stately home until they let me go, so I drank...'

'My name is Tyler. I'm literally still just a kid. I don't know why I drink; I just like it. I went to university, and it got a hold of me, before I knew it, I drank in the mornings...'

'My name is Dean – I'm a gay man, but I was married to my wife for many years, and I lived a lie. I thought that coming out would heal me, but it didn't – if anything, it accelerated the problem. I kept on going, until eventually my family staged an intervention...'

'My name is Claudia; I'm a part-time nurse. I have one daughter at university, and the other one is travelling Southeast Asia. I miss them so much that I can't see the point in staying sober. I don't have a school run, or endless piles of washing; I don't have to drive into town at midnight to pick them up from a bar; I don't have anyone to argue with about the trays of food in their bedrooms.' Claudia expected somebody to chip in and say something, but today everybody played completely by the rules, and let her share without a word.

'I have a husband, you know – I bet you all thought I was on my own the way I'm talking, but I'm not. He's completely normal, a good guy, and he sees this as a natural part of life. That our daughters are doing their thing, and we should do ours. But I don't feel like this is me – only thinking of myself every day feels wrong, and actually unnatural. Sometimes they don't reply to my messages for days, and I'm not coping. Anyway, drinking has kept me company these last couple of years, and I do it in secret. A bottle in the bath, a mug in the garden, but I'm losing control – I'm taking days off work – so I am here to find a reason to stop. Is that okay? Dean said it would be.' Claudia looked to Peggy for confirmation, who nodded.

'You're here because you don't want to be dependent on alcohol, so yes, that's totally okay.'

Claudia smiled with relief; this really did feel like a safe space.

'My name is Charlie, and I'm an alcoholic. Sorry, not sure if we have to say that here. I've done AA, I've done the steps, but I keep relapsing and that's why I thought I'd try this meeting. Tyler's done pretty good since he started here and his mam, my sister, is at her wits' end with the pair of us. So here I am, still shaking from the three-day bender I had last week. I'm kind of fucked up, if you want the truth. I went through something as a kid, and drinking just makes it all feel better – until it doesn't. You all know how it goes.'

There was a veteran in the group – not a successful one like Keith who had managed sobriety for years; this was a man who had failed but was still trying. It was hard to know how to feel because the drink had certainly taken its toll on Charlie – you could see it in his skin, in his speech, it was deeply engraved in the crevices of his face, and it didn't fill the others with much hope.

'I'm Janine. I think of alcohol every day and have to talk myself down. I'm not okay, I'm not in control, and I have some extremely deep-rooted issues. On the surface, I look like I've got it together, but underneath I am weak and vulnerable and scared. That's my Tinder bio – thoughts please?' There were some laughs and some big grins at this; Janine had an honest way of making people feel completely at ease with the truth.

'I haven't had a drink in over four years, but even now, after all that time, I'm still fragile enough to know that it could take a death in my family or maybe a health scare, or something small that hits on the wrong day at the wrong time, and then I would be back in it. I do *not* want to go through day one again, and that fear is what has got me to day 1,538.'

Frank clapped – he didn't whoop or yell, he just clapped with genuine pride for a teammate. And it wasn't even the fact that Janine had achieved these numbers, it was the way she explained it: raw, real, honest and exactly what each and every person in that room needed to hear that night.

'I'm Jake. I guess I'm last because my fall from grace was very recent and very public.'

A few knowing smiles made their way onto the faces of the group members.

'No excuses here, no blame and absolutely all responsibility for this,' he pointed to his eye, 'is on me. I had some shit news – I was with somebody who wanted to drink, and I used those reasons as an excuse to join in. I haven't done any Christmas shopping, and my parents have moved into my house because they are so terrified that I'll drink without supervision. I scared the shit out of my niece who I'm responsible for, and fucking hell, she is one person that doesn't deserve that. I'm waiting to hear if I'll be charged with whatever they throw at you when you lend your car to someone who is also drunk. I've had a concussion; my vision is still a bit off and *apparently* I was completely on board with blowing up Granada Studios.'

People couldn't stifle their laughter at that – that was a line literally straight out of a soap opera.

'And I achieved all of the above in less than twenty-four hours.'

Peggy's agenda was very fitting – she got the group to map out how they would get to New Year's Day without drinking. She'd printed out a week's plan, and brought coloured pens so each person could figure out how to navigate the trickiest seven days of the entire year. It really helped, and when Peggy discovered that the whole group were most worried about New Year's Eve, they organised a meet-up for a walk and talk, in the hope that they could keep the wolf from the door.

'Let's meet here, at the house – that way we can just have a meeting if the weather is bad,' Jake suggested, as they put their coats on, ready to battle the elements.

'Beautiful house you have,' Claudia said as she admired the half-stripped bannisters.

'It's getting there,' Jake replied, remembering he would have to put the brakes on his spending.

'Does it have a name?' she asked. 'Houses like this always have a name.'

Just before Jake could tell her a little bit of history on why his home had been named The Coach House, Charlie piped up, 'I'm just gonna call it The Drunk Tank.'

Before Jake could respond, the group, led by Tyler, all began to sing 'Fairytale of New York' as they walked out of the door. Jake had no choice but to join in – it was Christmas Eve-eve after all.

Big Bird

Even though Di and Alf were still suffering the back lash of the dreaded winter lurgy, they wouldn't allow Jake to leave the house or pitch in for the big day. Getting a turkey on Christmas Eve was no problem, Alf had told him, as he skidded off the driveway to meet his butcher friend who had promised to come up with the goods.

Di had gone to the twenty-four-hour Tesco in Blackburn at four a.m. to beat the crowds – she also knew that Jake would be asleep, so she left quietly, meaning he was less likely to escape. By 8.30 that morning, the kitchen was a sea of peelings and pans. Jake rubbed his eyes, wondering how all of this could have happened whilst he was sleeping.

Di had her snowman apron on and blue curlers in her hair – this was Di's Christmas Eve look, and it would be until she was under the ground.

'I feel so bad, Mum, I should have sorted all this out.'

'We expected too much of you too soon, Jake. It's me that's sorry.' Di checked her watch, and then pulled two paracetamols out of her apron pocket, putting them into Jake's hand.

'Can I help at all? Shall I do starters? Have you even got a turkey?' Jake felt useless and guilty – it was his home, and ultimately his job to host. But Di sat him at the table, put a warm cup of tea in front of him, and reassured him that it was all in hand.

'Your dad is meeting a guy about a bird right now – we did have one in the freezer, but the feet looked a bit green so we've left that for now.'

'Phew,' Jake muttered.

'And Pat is doing the starters – she does a wonderful split pea soup so she's defrosting a big tub right now, and I picked up a massive trifle from Tesco's this morning, and of course we've got my Christmas puddings from last year.'

Jake gulped the tea – it all sounded absolutely inedible without wine to wash it down, or a Baileys to line his stomach.

'How did you get on with Uncle Bert?' Jake asked Marnie as she joined him for a brew at the table.

Marnie shook her head. 'Please shoot me if I ever get that way.'

Di looked up from the carrot she was peeling. 'Eh lady, that's your grandad's brother you're suggesting needs putting down.'

'Well, Grandad said he's a racist and that it couldn't have happened to a nicer bloke,' Marnie replied.

'Grandad was angry that day – we all say things we don't mean,' Di retorted.

'I don't say anything I don't mean,' Marnie said factually.

Di sighed – it had been such a shame that Alf and Bert had lost their brotherly bond when Bert still had his faculties. Marnie being born had brought some very unfortunate opinions to the surface, and had caused a real rift in the family. Alf had said more than once, 'Some things cannot be forgiven, Di – now leave it, will you.'

Eventually, after many attempts, she'd given in and stopped trying to mend their relationship. At the beginning, she was sure that Bert would realise that his comments about Marnie being the 'little black sheep' and 'what we got instead of a Korma' were unacceptable, but he never did apologise, and by the time Bert's wife – who was the real Nazi – had died, he was already starting to lose it. The irony was that Bert's favourite carer was a Pakistani lady called Amina, and his eyes lit up when she walked into the room. Perhaps it took the brain to decline for Bert to actually think straight.

'Martin was crying on the way home – he said it was hay fever, but it's December,' Marnie said with sadness.

'Crying about what?' Di asked – it wasn't like Martin to show any emotion other than banter.

'Uncle Bert took off his wedding ring and told Martin to have it. He said his time would be soon, and he didn't want some gay nurse slipping it in his pocket in the back of the ambulance.'

'A rare lucid moment,' Jake said, smiling.

'It must be awful for him – all alone and suffering like that. I wish your dad would visit more. Whatever has happened, he's family – you work through it, you find a way. I'm just glad he's coming for Christmas, because this could be his last one.'

'He asked if you still looked like Les Dawson, Nan,' Marnie said innocently.

Jake exploded into laughter; he couldn't stop himself.

'Looks like it might be his last bleeding Christmas!' Di said as she drove the peeler straight through the carrot in her hand.

'Grandad's back!' Marnie said, running to the window and waving. 'He's got the turkey, Nan, he's sorted it.'

Di cleared the kitchen counter with her arm, making space for the centre piece. 'Bring him in,' she shouted, 'let's get a look at him.'

Alf plonked down the biggest turkey Jake had ever seen. 'Ta da! I waited in a layby for two hours to get my hands on this bad boy.'

'Can I ask why we didn't just use a supermarket? Why are we meeting dealers in shady places for massive birds, Dad? You could have got a stuffed one covered in streaky from M&S.'

Alf's mouth dropped open. 'Considering you're now on the breadline, son, you'll need to hustle a bit more. M&S! Charging through the nose, and there'll not be as fresh as this. My guy said this was still squawking this morning.'

Jake and Marnie looked at one another dismally, that was information they didn't need to know.

'Leave it with me, I'll have this dressed and stuffed and looking better than any supermarket bird in no time. Right, you'll need to go for a lie down now Jake, doctor said to rest.' Di pushed him out of the door into the hallway.

Alf stopped him before he went up the stairs. 'Before you go, Jake, I wanted to run something past you.' Alf lowered his voice even more. 'It's about Janine – she's on her own tomorrow. Now she's insisting that she wants a day by herself, but she's been bloody marvellous with you and all your issues, and she's really helped us out too. So, we think she should spend it here with us – nobody should be alone at Christmas.'

Jake nodded. 'I agree – that turkey could feed the village. Of course let's invite Janine.'

'But do you think Martin will cope with that? They're not exactly the best of friends.' The last thing Alf wanted was Martin having to eat this turkey through a straw.

'I'll sort it, Dad, leave it with me – at least let me do that. Now, I know I'm not to drive or leave the house, but I need to get some gifts for tomorrow.'

'Who for?'

'Well, all of you. I've not had a chance, and I'll feel horrible on Christmas morning without anything to give.'

Alf had a think – Di had all their gifts wrapped by September, and he'd never been a last-minute person. If this generation would just plan in advance and start paying for things over the year, there would be a lot less need for payday loans.

'It's not necessary, son. You've had a tough time, your bank account's virtually empty, and nobody expects anything from you this year.'

Jake shook his head in shame. He simply couldn't be that person, not again – one who chose booze over people. He'd ruined too many Christmases in the past, and the cycle had to be broken.

'I've still got some cash, Dad – I just can't be as lavish.'

Alf wasn't having it. 'Me and your mum want for nothing, the only present we want is for you to be well.'

Jake rolled his eyes – why did parents always request ceasefires and cures for diseases instead of fucking air fryers?

'Okay fine, but can you please do me a favour and nip to this address for me? It's close by, and I've bought something for Marnie. I can't let her down again, Dad.' Jake placed an envelope of cash with an address written on the front into Alf's hand, and left him to it.

Jake: Can you please join us for Christmas lunch, my sober friend?
Janine: Do I have to? I'm kind of loving the peace.
Jake: No, of course not. But we'd all like you there, be nice to see you. Nobody should spend Christmas alone.
Janine: I take it your mum has been in your ear.
Jake: My dad, actually, but it's probably come from her.
Janine: What shall I bring?
Jake: Definitely no food, we've got a turkey the size of a bus in the kitchen. Just bring yourself!

Even with a sore head, a house filled with uninvited bossy people and decorations that Jake would normally associate with the pound shop, this was the most Christmassy he had felt since his childhood. Every surface of the kitchen was taken up with a plate or a bowl filled with something that had been prepped for the following day. The shabby table that Jake had inherited was set for eight people. Nothing matched, there were chips in the plates and, notably, there were no wine glasses on the table. Marnie had written out name cards for all the diners with a fountain pen, and Di had tied tartan ribbon around the rickety chairs. It wasn't fancy – it was thrown together by a family at the last minute in a time of crisis. Without wanting to sound wanky, Jake was touched.

Marnie was giddy that evening – she was still young enough to feel that Christmas Eve warmth. She and Alf sat and watched some Christmas telly, and ate endless Quality Streets in the lounge. Di had her special Christmas Eve soak in the tub with a gingerbread bubble bath and a copy of *Woman's Own*. Martin FaceTimed his kids from the back garden – it was a hard call, particularly when both boys said this was the best Christmas they'd ever had.

Meanwhile, Jake sat quietly in the kitchen, contemplating. The last time he'd relapsed, he went to rehab alone. Specially cooked food, state-of-the-art facilities and world-renowned therapy – it cost Morris, Webb & Butler a small fortune. But what Jake's family had done for him that week was priceless. He went to bed that Christmas Eve filled with hope.

The next morning, Marnie opened her gifts first as the family watched. Di and Alf had filled a sack full of bits and pieces – huge noise-cancelling headphones which would have her run over if she wore them on the high street, a glowing face mask that was unnervingly similar to Hannibal Lecter's muzzle, various bits of stationery including a pen that was also a calculator and a compass, and other nonsense to pad out the sack. She appreciated it all, and not once did she seem sad her mum wasn't there.

Martin reached into his coat pocket and handed her an envelope filled with paint charts.

'What's all that about?' Jake asked, frowning. Surely that couldn't have been it.

'Well, as you all know, I'm skint at the moment, but I had a think and it turns out, it doesn't have to cost the earth to give a gift worth having,' he said proudly.

'What's she supposed to do with this lot?' Di said.

'If she picks a colour she likes, I'll get it from Homebase at a massive discount, and then me and her will decorate her room together. We'll do it properly, woodwork and everything. What do you think, Jake?'

Jake grinned. 'That's actually a great idea, Martin.'

'And I can do any colour I want, Uncle Jake, because it's my room?'

Jake nodded. 'Fuck it – I can't afford to pay a decorator any more, and if I don't like the colour, you can keep the door shut.'

'Thanks, Martin,' Marnie said, getting up to hug him. 'You're alright, you know.'

'Are you ever going to come home, Marnie? Your mother will be back next month,' Di said.

Marnie stopped smiling – she didn't want to be reminded of that. 'What's next?' she said, changing the subject whilst eyeing up the large box wrapped in gold paper.

'Well, that one's from me.' Jake handed it to her.

'Don't worry, I don't expect much – I know you're not rich any more.'

'Thanks for bringing that up.'

As Marnie opened the gift Jake had found on Facebook Marketplace for a very reasonable price, she put her head in her hands. 'Oh my god, is this really for me?'

Jake nodded. 'Of course it is.'

'I never had a laptop before – not of my own, anyway.'

'Well, I figured you've got your GCSEs coming up, and you're going to need to be properly prepared. Then you can go to college and then university, because you've got the ability to do it, and I'm not having you waste that massive brain of yours.'

'And then I can be rich and successful like you... used to be,' she added awkwardly. 'I'm going to put this on charge in my room, then later I'll connect it to my phone. You know you can connect Apple devices to one another, Nan, did you know that?'

Di shook her head – she knew how to make an apple turnover, and that's as close as she could get. 'Don't you go breaking that or dropping it in the bath, lady.'

Marnie ran upstairs with her new Mac – she wouldn't have dreamed of asking for something so expensive, and this was a huge surprise.

Di started stuffing the wrapping paper into bin bags with a worried look in her eyes. 'You can't afford that, Jake. We've got the big computer in the back bedroom she could use.'

'Oh Mum, calm down, it's fine. That, right there, is an investment in her future.'

Alf and Di were both acting as though he'd gifted her an apartment in Mayfair.

'She could use it for gambling, or trolling,' Martin unhelpfully suggested. 'The clever ones always seem to be caught in an attic with a laptop. Who was that guy who infiltrated the Pentagon? Can't think of his name.'

'Enough, Martin, you're making it worse.'

'Anyway, cuz, I didn't forget you, and I know you didn't get me anything because you've been unwell, so don't feel bad.'

Jake laughed. 'I don't feel bad – you've lived here rent-free with no sign of leaving.'

'Yes, there is that. Anyway, here is your present from me.'

'Let us guess, it's from Homebase,' Di said.

Martin went red. 'It's not actually – well, not all of it, anyway.'

He handed Jake another envelope, and inside was a handwritten note:

This is a voucher for 100 hours of free labour. Also 40% off any product that's not on sale at Homebase for as long as I am employed there.

Merry Christmas!

Martin Peterson, esq.

'Thanks, Martin, I'll hold you to this. On your next free day, you can strip all the windowsills with a heat gun.'

Martin gulped.

Janine had very kindly offered to pick Pat up on her way up to the house, or that was the story Di had cooked up and fed to a gullible Jake. The truth was, she'd asked Janine to give her a lift but she had an ulterior motive. Pat was instructed to use the journey to prise out as much information as she could about Janine's love life, and whether Jake could be a good fit for her. Pat had obliged, and promised to fill Di in on her findings at the first opportunity they had to be alone.

Pat was a good woman – perhaps a little bit on the opinionated side and the root of all village gossip – but she had been a damn good friend to Di over the years, and she trusted her like a sister.

'Go out and help Pat bring that soup in, will you? We can't have it spilling all over the gravel.'

Jake looked out of the window to see Janine's big van pulling up. As he got to the front door, Pat shouted out of the window, 'Can somebody help me down? This vehicle is very high. Have you got a step ladder, Jake?'

Jake assessed the situation; Pat wasn't the lightest of women, and Jake had no experience of lifting larger ladies out of vans, so he yelled for Martin, who was used to all this, to come and give him a hand.

Martin immediately obliged. 'Right, come on girl, let's be having ya.' He skilfully heaved Pat out of her seat and set her down onto the gravel. Jake took her hand, and guided her towards the door.

'Thank you, boys. Ooh, I remember you two toe-rags when you were teenagers, always pinching the milk from my doorstep,' she chuckled.

Martin and Jake looked at one another fondly, recalling the days they played 'knock door run' just to see Pat go totally mental when she realised her blue top was missing.

'And here you both are, decades later, living together like a couple of poofters.' Pat slapped them both gently on the cheek, and went inside to find Di.

Martin's face dropped, and he called after her, 'Hang on a minute, Pat, I'm just a lodger here. I've got me own house and a wife and…'

Jake shushed Martin; it was Christmas Day, and people thinking they were a couple was the least of either of their worries.

Janine had made a real effort to look like she'd not made any effort. She'd tried every single combination of clothing on that she owned and, when she couldn't quite nail the look, she'd emptied Michelle's wardrobe and tried on all her stuff too. Finally, she left the house wearing one of Michelle's tight-fitting polo necks and a pair of jeans she'd had to spray with Febreze as she'd not had chance to wash them. She rarely wore make-up – she didn't see the point – but that day she added some mascara and a touch of lip gloss.

Jake went in for a hug at the side of the van. It was a bit uncomfortable, as neither did physical affection naturally.

'You look great, Janine. Merry Christmas.' He kissed her on the cheek.

'Err, so do you,' she said awkwardly. 'Good beard and jeans and stuff.' They both laughed loudly, fully aware of their weirdness.

'That was some journey, by the way. Pat seems to be secretly working for Tinder.'

Jake was intrigued. 'What do you mean?'

'She asked me a ton of questions about my relationship status, my sexual preferences, and what I'm looking for in a partner – it was relentless.'

Jake glanced at the kitchen window, only to see Pat's blonde quiff and Di's grey bob duck down immediately.

'Diane Peterson, you meddling old witch,' Jake said under his breath.

Christmas lunch was a messy affair. Bert arrived and said nothing; he barely looked up from the floor, and he didn't acknowledge anybody. Martin had explained that, on the way over, Bert had repeatedly said, 'Take me back.'

'Why didn't you then?' Marnie asked. 'Now you've made him unhappy.'

'Let's just see if he picks up once he's around people, Marnie. Nobody should be alone at Christmas.'

Nevertheless, Bert insisted on eating his lunch in the lounge on his knee. He screamed 'TRAY!' into Martin's face just as he was supposed to sit down at the table. Alf shut his eyes – he couldn't stand to see it. He immediately plated his brother's food and carried the tray out of the kitchen.

'Just give him what he wants, it's his Christmas too,' he said as Di was about to insist they all stay together. Alf put the television on as loud as it would go, and placed the tray on Bert's lap. 'You shout if you need anything.'

Bert looked into Alf's eyes for a few seconds and then said, 'Thank you.'

Just before Bert began his soup, Marnie knelt down next to his armchair and held out a Christmas cracker. 'You can't eat your dinner without pulling this, can you?' she said softly.

Bert said nothing. He just stared into her huge eyes, trying to remember who she was. 'Do you know Amina?'

Marnie shook her head. She then opened the cracker carefully, removed a green paper hat and placed it onto Bert's head. 'Enjoy your soup, Uncle Bert.'

Pat Bayley's split pea soup happened to be very tasty, but she'd underestimated just how filling the soup actually was, and it seemed to expand once it hit the stomach.

'Is anyone else completely full?' Martin said as he scraped the last of the yellow mush into his mouth.

Janine nodded; she also felt incredibly bloated after her starter.

Pat put her spoon down. 'That'll be the Slim Fast – that's the base for the soup.'

'SlimFast?' Jake said, vaguely remembering Di living on something similar when he'd been younger.

'Yes, it's a powder you mix with water, and it keeps you full all day.'

The family looked at each other.

Alf frowned. 'Are you saying that this soup is a Slim Fast soup? I thought you said it was homemade.'

'It *is* homemade, Alf, thank you very much. Potatoes, onions, split peas obviously, and a large tub of vegetable SlimFast powder to thicken it up. You'll not need to eat again until next year.'

There were raised eyebrows at the table as the diners realised, they were only going to get fuller, and they still had the Jurassic turkey to get through.

'Is nobody going to have a glass of wine with their dinner?' Jake looked at the eight glasses of orange squash that did not lend themselves to a festive celebration at all.

'We don't need alcohol; we've got each other, and this wonderful spread,' Di said firmly.

'I've always preferred squash to beer anyway,' Martin said, as though he was reading from a script.

'I'm totally off it; it goes straight through me these days.' Pat rubbed her stomach and groaned for effect.

Janine grinned – all of this for Jake… he was a lucky man. She'd had Christmases with her family doing shots in the morning whilst they opened gifts, Martin being one of them. In fact, her own dad had handed her a Flaming Sambuca and said, 'Have a day off, Janine, for Christ's sake.' She had never experienced the sort of consideration that was being shown by Jake's family.

Although the turkey was insanely big, Di had still managed to overcook it, so much so that it was crumbly even by the bone. She'd put the thing in the oven the night before, because that's what her mother did, and hers before that. Jake hadn't tried to intervene, and he didn't say a word as he ploughed through meat that had the consistency of a cream cracker. He even ate his sprouts without any wincing – today he was just happy to be at home and not in rehab, prison or hospital.

Janine and Jake insisted on doing the washing up together whilst everybody else played 'Shithead' in the lounge.

'Fancy a walk after this?' Janine asked.

'I'm not allowed out, am I?' Jake said childishly.

'With my supervision, I think I can get you a pass.'

'So, you're going to stop me from hijacking a beer lorry, are you? I'm stronger than I look.'

'Just know that when you're with me, there will be no falling from wagons.'

'I would love to go for a walk with you and get some fresh air. I feel like I've been cooped up for weeks.'

'You get your coat, and I'll let the others know we'll be back in an hour.'

A strange phenomenon occurred that Christmas night on the streets of the village. The rooftops were white, the pavements slippy, and laughter could be heard from inside people's homes, along with the clinking of pots that were being washed by those who weren't sleeping off the banquet. The smell of turkey and the sound of drunken singing caused Jake and Janine to stop for a few minutes outside one particular cottage where spirits were high. Jake felt no urge to burst into a lounge and snatch the glass of port from a Twiglet-fingered aunty; Janine didn't feel even the slightest jealously when a woman doing the can-can waved through her window whilst holding a bottle of Heineken. For that hour, and they were under no illusion this was anything but temporary, both Jake and Janine felt completely content.

The hallway was a hub of activity when they returned to the house. Bert had his coat on back to front, and his shoes on the wrong feet. Di and Alf stood either side of him, shouting at each other and trying to rectify the mistake.

'Where's Martin?' Jake asked with concern. Martin was good at all of this.

Di hissed, 'He's upstairs, he's got some toilet trouble.'

Janine pinched her nose just in case. Pat shouted from the lounge, 'If it were my soup, we'd all be in bits before anyone starts blaming this on me – more likely the trifle. It was on the turn, I'm telling you.'

'Cream lasts for weeks, Pat, don't you blame this on me,' Di yelled, going red. She'd got the dessert at an incredibly low price, and she'd noticed it was a bit watery when she'd served it.

'He had two big bowls of that, absolute hog that he is,' Pat continued to shout from the other room.

'Well, is he alright, Mum?' Jake asked with genuine concern.

'He started sweating just after you left – next thing he was doubled up, off he went upstairs, and he's not been back since.' She tried to hide her guilt, wondering if a dodgy trifle could cause death.

'I got a text message,' Alf said, looking haunted. He pulled his old phone out of his top pocket and read it out loud. 'Got the tom tits, in a bad way, send up more bog roll.'

'Take me back,' Bert shouted aggressively. He had been standing in the middle of the hall with all of this going on around him.

'We will, but we need to sort this coat out and these shoes, Bert,' Di said, tugging on the sleeve, but Bert held the coat firmly in place.

'Just take him like that, Dad, it doesn't matter.'

'It looks like he's wearing a straitjacket, Jake. He looks mental.' Alf caught Bert's eye as he said that, and paused before saying, 'But who isn't mental, aye? We're all a bit cuckoo. Come on, let's get you home and into bed – I'll go and bring the car up to the door.'

Alf grabbed his car keys and marched off down the drive. Bert stood with his arms out in front of him, staring at Jake. Di had gone through to the lounge to continue her heated debate with Pat.

'Whose house is this, Moneybags?'

'It's mine, Uncle Bert, I live here.'

'Where's that nurse? I liked her.'

'You mean Marnie, don't you? She's not a nurse, she's my niece – Leanne's daughter.'

Bert screwed his face up – pictures of Marnie, Amina and Leanne flashed through his head. It was all so confusing, he did all he could to put it in some sort of order.

'Shame what happened to your Leanne, her whole life snatched away.'

Jake frowned – would he now witness the racist filth that Alf was still so furious about?

'Having a baby doesn't always ruin your life, Bert.'

Bert looked directly at Jake and said, 'Well, it does if you got raped.'

Cheese Toasties

On the thirtieth, Jake and Alf went for a coffee in the village. There was a tearoom of sorts, a little room attached to the village shop that was run by a couple of ladies from the church. It had been a quiet week – Jake and Janine had done a few more walks, and they'd been for a pub lunch successfully. Alf and Di were waiting at the door when they got back, worried the pair of them might stagger in covered in blood and sick, possibly carrying Lucy O's head in a carrier bag.

Marnie had been glued to her laptop most days, setting up files, downloading apps and FaceTiming Leanne on the big screen. Martin was working at the warehouse; he was getting the hours done so that he wouldn't have to scrimp when he took the boys to London.

Christmas week had been quite full-on and a little claustrophobic, so when Jake asked Alf to take a walk down into the village, he was glad of the fresh air, and an hour without Di chewing his ear off.

They settled into a corner of the café and ordered two cappuccinos and a cheese toastie each.

'Well, this is nice – your head looks better too, son, you're recovering well. That swelling has gone right down.'

'Yeah, I feel much better, Dad, and I'm sorry for putting you through all that. I really am.'

Alf nodded, blowing a hole through his coffee foam.

'I've brought you here to ask you something, Dad. I needed to do this away from the house.'

Alf felt his blood pressure rising. 'Good god, son, what is it this time? You're not going to ask me to get you a drink, are you?'

'No, of course not, it's about Marnie – it's about her father and who he is.'

Alf's hackles immediately went up. He coughed and sniffed and scratched his head. 'What about him?' he said defensively.

'Who is he? Is he a cab driver, a takeaway owner or what?' Jake had never really asked Leanne anything about this man – he'd just been told she was pregnant and that 'these things happen'.

'Not sure – it doesn't matter anyway. He doesn't even know she exists.' Alf looked behind him. 'Where's this food?'

But Jake pressed on. 'I thought his family wouldn't accept Leanne – some sort of culture problem, wasn't it?'

'Err yeah, that's right. They didn't want a British girl in their camp, you know what people can get like, especially round here.'

'So, it was her boyfriend. They were in a relationship?'

Alf became more flustered. 'I don't know, Jake, what's all this about? Why are we talking about this? Just leave it, son.'

'It's just something that Uncle Bert said, that's all – it's got me thinking.'

Alf knew deep down that with Bert's condition, it was entirely possible that he'd let something slip even though they'd vowed never to mention it again. He tried to bat Jake away one last time.

'Bert's away with the fairies, Jake; he asked me to thank Les Dawson on the way home the other night. He talks a lot of fluff. Where's those damn toasties? My blood sugar's dropping.' He spun around again, desperate for one of the church ladies to interrupt this excruciating conversation.

Jake could see Alf starting to panic – he could see in his eyes that he knew what was coming next. He wouldn't string this out any longer than he needed to, it wasn't fair. He changed tactics and laid it out on the table.

'So, it's true then? And you know exactly what Bert told me, don't you, Dad?'

The food arrived, giving Alf a moment to compose himself, to accept it was time to tell Jake the truth. Jake took a gulp of his drink and waited until Alf was ready.

'You were in London – you were working, and drinking, and there never seemed to be a right time to tell you, son.'

'I'm not sure there is a "right time" to tell me that my little sister had been attacked, Dad – I guess you just have to pick a moment.'

Alf stared at the toastie; his appetite had vanished.

'Were the police involved? Has he been caught?'

Alf shook his head. Jake felt sick to his stomach.

'It was never reported, and Leanne didn't tell us until after Marnie was born. We were told it was a one-night stand, and throughout the whole pregnancy, we believed it – you know our Leanne, she was always chasing after some lad!'

'So how did it come out? How did you and Mum discover the truth?'

Alf lowered his voice; the café was filling up, and he was still just as terrified that this would get out as he was back in 2007.

'She didn't really take to the baby. She was crying a lot, going missing at feed times and bath times. Your mum was furious with her, and demanded to know who the father was so we could ask for his help. And your mum was convinced there was another family out there that were missing out on this little girl.'

Jake just listened, horrified he hadn't been there for his family in any of this.

'Anyway, she told us that she'd been out one night and a guy had forced himself on her. She said she was ashamed and felt guilty that she'd put herself in that position and then, when she realised she was pregnant, she was too far gone to terminate.'

'She blamed herself?' Jake almost shouted. '*She* felt guilty?'

Alf nodded. 'I know it's madness, but even back then it would have been his word against hers – there was no way of proving it, especially after all that time. We decided as a family – and that included your Uncle Bert and Aunty Pam – that no good could come from saying anything.'

'So, you all keep quiet, and Leanne was okay with it?'

'Leanne never even wanted to tell us, Jake – it was only when your mum started going on about putting an ad in the paper and DNA tests that we got to know. Your uncle and aunty said Marnie should be put up for adoption, and that having a reminder of what happened was a bad idea. That's when we really fell out – no granddaughter of mine was being handed to strangers because of who her father was, or for the colour of her skin.'

'And Leanne, did she want to keep her?' Jake asked, already knowing the answer.

Alf looked away, saying quietly, 'She said it was up to me, so I made the call and took her under my wing.'

Jake put his head in his hands. 'I can't believe I didn't know this.'

'No offence, son, but you weren't on this planet – you were either drunk or sky high.'

'Okay, but I could have helped – paid for a solicitor, at least done something, Dad.'

Alf shook his head. 'There was nothing anyone could have done. Your mother concentrated on Leanne, trying to help her heal. That innocent baby lay there looking up at me from her cot night after night, and we developed a bond, Marnie and me. I didn't want the world to know how she came to be; I don't want her to think she's unwanted or worthless. I'd rather keep this secret buried and live a lie than ever hurt her like that.'

Jake swallowed hard – his family had really been through the mill.

'Right, now you know. Nothing needs to change, but perhaps you understand a bit more.'

The family dynamic that Jake had never really been able to put his finger on was now clear. Since Marnie was born, Di had never come down on Leanne for anything; she had never pulled her up for acting more like a sister than a mother to her daughter.

Alf's stand was that, no matter what, you're a parent and that comes first. You pull your socks up and you get on with it; he had taken on the role as chief protector when it came to Marnie, perhaps because he felt he'd let Leanne down, and he was making amends in the next generation. But Alf was getting old now, and he wouldn't be around forever; seeing his own brother with his coat on back to front was a stark reminder that perhaps not too far in the future, he wouldn't be able to protect Marnie.

And that's where Jake came in. The Petersons needed help; that help came in the form of an alcoholic son who had just spunked all his money up the wall, and crashed through the doors of Granada Studios – but he was family, and that's all that mattered.

'As the old saying goes, Jake, "it takes a village to raise a child",' Alf said as they walked back up to the house.

And at that moment, Jake knew what had to be done.

NYE

The New Year's Eve walk had been planned for two p.m. Peggy felt that if they split the day, it would stop people from getting drunk at lunchtime and give everyone the fighting chance to stay sober on that precarious night when most of the country would be hammered. Luckily, it was clear and fresh – the perfect environment for a stroll to say goodbye to the year.

'What time are you at the police station tomorrow, pal?' Martin asked as Jake put on his walking gear.

'Ten in the morning,' Jake laughed. 'What a way to start the year.'

'You'll be okay – sounds like you'll just get your knuckles rapped. I'll come with you.'

Martin was in high spirits. The boys had let it slip that, whilst they were away, Ste the snivelling gym wanker had dumped Michelle by text. 'He said that Mum eats too many carbs and that he wants someone completely ketogenic,' Tommy had told Martin, who immediately ate a jacket potato to celebrate.

'We'll all go with you, son,' Di said as she stirred her turkey soup. 'I'll be telling the police to lock that little runt Lucy up for good, too – she's the one that caused this whole mess.'

Jake groaned. 'We are not *all* going to the police station. I'll just get a cab and be back in no time. I'm meeting my solicitor there anyway.'

Alf's eyes widened. 'Solicitor! How much is that going to set you back? You've not got the money for legal representation, son. You paid your taxes, use legal aid like the rest of us.' Alf began to open all the cupboards and drawers in the kitchen. 'Where's the *Yellow Pages* in this house? I'll find you a brief.'

'Talking of Lucy O,' Marnie said, looking up from her shiny new device, 'Have you seen this, Uncle Jake?'

Jake stood behind Marnie, as did Di and then Alf, as Martin read a newspaper article from the screen. The headline alone was a shocker.

NO MORE NONSENSE NAN
 Coronation Street's Lucy O'Callaghan admitted to rehab after yet another drunk driving charge.
 But her nan says it's a waste of money, and that she's a waste of space.

'Blimey,' Jake sighed. 'Now *that's* a toxic family – what an absolute mess.'

Marnie scoffed. 'Her nan's done a whole story on her in the papers – pictures of her messy bedroom and everything. What sort of person lets a photographer take pictures of your unmade bed?'

Di was chuffed to bits. 'She should make her bed each morning – scruffy little cow, serves her right.'

Jake felt a huge sense of sadness for Lucy. Okay, she was spoiled and vacuous, and she was a liar. However, she genuinely had nobody in the world.

'She doesn't know any better, Mum – she was never parented and is completely alone.'

Di reddened slightly. 'Well, let's hope she gets some help, then.'

'Right, is this soup ready, Mum? People are starting to arrive.' Jake didn't want to think of negative things that day; he was determined to see the new year out serenely.

Alf carried a pan the size of a dustbin and placed it onto a trestle table they had set up at the front gate. Di had already put polystyrene cups and a platter of sliced bread and butter out for those who wanted it. The walkers would have something warm, comforting and filling as Di had secretly nicked Pat's clever idea and thickened it up with Slim Fast powder.

Tyler and Charlie were dropped off by Tyler's mum, who finally had some colour in her cheeks.

Peggy arrived in a cream snow suit complete with ridiculous snow boots, and wouldn't have looked out of place in a Bond movie. Jake noticed the curtain twitching as Alf tried to catch a glimpse.

'I'm afraid we have two fallers, Jake,' Peggy said sadly as she looked at her clipboard. This was a term Keith had used. Instead of 'relapsed', he would refer to those who had succumbed to temptation as 'fallers'. He felt it was more accurate, as these were unintentional accidents and addiction was often a slippery, unsteady path.

Jake looked around the group – they were all sipping soup and chatting away in anticipation of the walk. He presumed that when he didn't see Frank, a lonely Christmas had gotten the better of him, but when Frank popped up from tying one of his laces, Jake realised it was Dean who was missing.

'His ex-wife called me this morning,' Peggy said, shaking her head. 'He wandered off up the road to see his neighbour Claudia – remember the lady he brought to group last week?' Jake nodded. 'They both went missing on Boxing Day just after breakfast – he wasn't seen again until yesterday when he turned up wearing a hospital bracelet, claiming to have nipped to the shop for some piccalilli.'

'For fuck's sake, they went off drinking together then?' Jake was really annoyed.

'It would seem so – I'm not so sure she was ready to stop, she hadn't hit her rock bottom.' But Peggy remained positive. 'Look, this is very common at this time of year – at least he's alive, and his husband is looking after him. We've just got to hope we'll see him next week. Now come on, let's enjoy the day.'

Jake was genuinely shaken by Dean's absence. It was strange, really, as he'd relapsed himself two weeks before, so he struggled to understand why he felt this way. This was the nature of recovery – some people fell and got back up, this was the way it was. There was just something about Dean that gave Jake a sense of security. He had taken for granted the tremendous support he was surrounded with, presuming that it would keep him safe. However, there would always be little reminders that the devil sat on each of their shoulders, waiting for an opportunity to pounce.

As they walked, the group all told their stories of how they had got through Christmas. Jake told them about the dry turkey and Martin's diarrhoea. He said that the best part of the day was giving Marnie a laptop, even though he was constantly reminded that he couldn't afford it.

Peggy's Christmas Day was spent in bed. She had a tuna niçoise for her Christmas lunch and watched *Schindler's List* in the dark. 'It's the most un-Christmassy thing I could think of, and I needed to block out the festivities. That's how I dealt with it, and I'm glad it's over,' she admitted.

'I took the plunge and went to my daughter's,' Frank said proudly. 'Normally I refuse her invite – I prefer to stay at home brooding about my dead wife and the fact I'm not at the pub.'

Tyler put his arm around Frank. 'Well done. Did you have a good time?'

'No, I did not,' Frank said. 'First of all, she lives in Doncaster – have you ever been there? It's hell to get to, and hell when you get there. And secondly, she's a vegan. Not even a drop of milk in the house, never mind a bleeding turkey.'

The group laughed. 'At least you didn't drink, Frank,' Jake said, pointing out the positive.

'There is that,' Frank grumbled.

Tyler's mum had surprised her whole family by not cooking. She'd been in some therapy of her own, and something she'd learned in her last session was to step out of her comfort zone and use the 'let them' theory. On Christmas Eve, the online shop had arrived and she'd sent a group text to her family to say that she'd bought the food, but it was up to them to cook it. She then booked herself in for a mani/pedi and met a friend for dinner in town. After blank faces, confusion and a genuine suggestion to order a Domino's for two p.m. on the twenty-fifth, Tyler, his two sisters, Uncle Charlie and a wheelchair-bound grandfather set to work and somehow, using Jamie Oliver's website, produced a half-decent Christmas lunch.

'Wow, well done, kid.' Frank was impressed. 'See, I knew if you lost the eyeliner and the jewellery, you could achieve anything.'

'And I'm still clean,' Charlie said proudly. 'The first Christmas in twenty years that I've managed to stay sober.' Frank whooped. Surely whooping was allowed if you were outside. 'I might even consider trying to get my job back in the new year – I'm suspended at the moment, you see.'

'What is it you do, darling?' Peggy asked.

'I work for the Royal Mail. I'm a postman.'

'Ah,' said Jake with a smile as the penny dropped. 'Of course you do.'

It was almost dark when they got back to the house. Jake hoped and prayed that none of them would hit the pub that night. Peggy had suggested that they all put themselves to bed before ten o'clock and watch a wholesome film.

'Like what?' Janine asked. She didn't do wholesome, and preferred stuff about the Mafia and wise guys.

'Why don't we all watch *The Princess Bride*?' Peggy said. 'It's old as hell, but I think you'd all love it. Give it a go – we can talk about it at the next meeting. Go on, write it down.'

People put that into their phone notes and went on their way, hoping to wake up to a new year safe and sober.

'Oi Jake, do you fancy doing something tomorrow after your police interview?' Janine asked, smirking as she got into her van.

Jake walked over and leaned on the door. 'I can't, I'm taking the family somewhere – sorry, Janine.'

Janine's smile dropped slightly. 'Oh, okay – well, what about the second? We could go to a reclamation yard and look for cheap house stuff.'

Jake looked at Janine and shook his head; she immediately knew. 'What did I do?' she asked.

'Nothing,' Jake said seriously.

'Don't tell me – it's not me, it's you.'

Jake grabbed her hand and squeezed it. 'I'm not able to be with someone I like as much as you. I'm too new, and we're both too fragile for this. We could break each other, Janine. I can't allow that to happen.'

Janine squeezed his hand back.

Jake knew that a healthy relationship had to be built on a solid foundation; he'd listened to Janine sharing in the meeting, and realised that she was still clinging on by her fingernails. Along with his own relapse, and the fact he had to become a constant in Marnie's life, this was not the time to embark on a romantic connection with anybody.

That night, as Di served up a turkey casserole – which was basically the soup but with potatoes in it – Jake made an announcement.

'Right, you lot, I have a belated Christmas gift for you.'

'Is it a dog? I want a black Labrador,' Marnie said randomly.

'No, why would you think that?' Jake shook the thought off. 'I'm taking you all somewhere tomorrow at six p.m.'

'I hope it's not London – I hate London,' Di said with horror.

'It's not London, Mum, calm down.'

'Oh, it's not the cinema, is it?' Alf said gruffly. 'The prices they charge these days for the tickets, then you've got the pick 'n' mix – a few handfuls of jellybeans cost me eight bleeding quid last time I took Marnie. At least Robin Hood wore a mask.' Alf shook his fist at the brass neck of Cineworld Blackburn.

'No! Just listen, will you? We're flying to Spain just for a few days to spend some time with our Leanne! It's all arranged and don't worry, we'll be back before school starts.'

'All of us, going on holiday?' Marnie shouted.

'Yes, go pack,' Jake said, smiling.

'Can I take the laptop?'

'Of course.'

Marnie threw down her fork, thrilled to be going away with her three favourite people, but also to have got away with not having to finish her turkey mush.

Jake's parents immediately began their tirade of questions, panicking about a last-minute trip.

'That's very generous of you, son – I mean, can you afford this? We'll reimburse you for the flights, obviously. What's the weight allowance? Are we flying Ryanair? 'Cause Pat Bayley flew with them and they dented her suitcase – it was brand new, and they never said sorry. What's the temperature out there? I'll take my new big coat because they say it gets cool in the evenings. We'll need to ring the bank and warn them that we're leaving the country. Do we need to do a COVID test, or is all that stopped now? I'll be wearing a mask, I'm not getting taken down by flu again. And go get the toenail clippers out, Alf, your toes look like an eagle's claws...'

Jake just sat and listened.

About the author

NJ Miller is a sharp-eyed chronicler of northern grit, life choices and middle-aged mayhem. Miller mixes crime, comedy and chaos with an unflinching affection for the ordinary disasters of British life.

After years of collecting stories, playground gossip and the kind of overheard conversations that would make a priest blush, NJ Miller finally began to shove it all between two covers and make it her thing. The result? Darkly funny novels where crooks, drunks and dreamers collide in towns that never quite make the tourist brochures.

A Lancashire native with an ear for daft dialogue, Miller spins stories where humour and heartbreak sit at the same table.

When not writing, NJ can be found crying in her utility room.